LORD STANHOPE'S CONFESSION

"Calista is a very unusual name."

"My father chose it. Mama used to say he was in a Greek phase when I was born."

"Do you know Greek?" Stanhope asked with interest.

She nodded. "And Latin."

"Then you know it means 'most beautiful.' Suits you." His eyes were unreadable, almost black in the dim light, and his voice had taken on a husky note.

"I am hardly 'most beautiful,' my lord," she replied, reminding herself that the thing that separates a mere flirt from an extraordinarily successful flirt is the ability to make one believe the flummery is sincere. "Although it is kind of you to say so."

"I take leave to disagree, Miss Ashton." He reached across and, somehow unable to stop himself, took her hand in his and began to gently stroke the backs of her fingers. She looked down at her hand, small in both of his large ones, and tried to will it to move. But it seemed curiously unattached to her body, except for the little tingling trails of fire that shot up it every time he moved the ball of his thumb. She shivered with the sensation, feeling as if every nerve in her body was suddenly centered in her hand. "In fact"—his voice was almost a whisper—"it is the damnedest thing, but the more I am in your company, the lovelier you seem to become. . . ."

CELEBRATE THE NEW YEAR WITH ZEBRA
REGENCY ROMANCE AND THESE TALENTED
NEW AUTHORS

December 1999
LORD ST. CLAIRE'S ANGEL by Donna Simpson

January 2000
LORD CARLTON'S COURTSHIP by Debbie Raleigh

February 2000
AFFECTIONATELY YOURS by Kathryn June

March 2000
LORD STANHOPE'S PROPOSAL by Jessica Benson

April 2000
LORD LANGDON'S KISS by Elena Greene

LORD STANHOPE'S PROPOSAL

Jessica Benson

Zebra Books
Kensington Publishing Corp.
http://www.zebrabooks.com

ZEBRA BOOKS are published by

Kensington Publishing Corp.
850 Third Avenue
New York, NY 10022

First Printing: March, 2000
10 9 8 7 6 5 4 3 2 1

Printed in the United States of America

This book is dedicated to

My parents, for owning the two resources most valuable to a Regency author: the collected works of Georgette Heyer and the OED. And to my agent Laura Langlie, who was willing to debate such thrilling topics as British versus American spellings, and who never once suggested that I ditch the prologue.

And to

Andrea, Francisca, Lynne, Alicia, and Evelyn, our parade of indispensable and much loved baby-sitters.

And last, but not least, to

My husband, who believed so strongly that he made me believe too, that with the help of the above, I could do something interesting with my two minutes a week of free time.

Prologue

Thursday, April the third, dawned over London with fair skies. As fashionable London slumbered, a breeze came up, blowing away all traces of the acrid yellow fog that so often choked the city.

In Deepdene, Sussex—the other town with which we are concerned, where the day had also dawned fair, and where the villagers as a matter of course rose earlier than their London counterparts—the day was already well under way for our cast of characters.

At the vicarage, Miss Calista Ashton, clad in a shapeless gray wool gown nearly indistinguishable from the nine other shapeless gray wool gowns in her clothing press, was in the morning room. She was attempting to simultaneously tackle the huge pile of linens needing mending while reading *Considerations on Religion and Public Education, with Remarks on the Speech of M. Dupont, Delivered in the National Convention of France, Together with an Address to the Ladies, &c. of Great Britain and Ireland* by the notorious Hannah More. Calista was poised to hide the book should she hear the slightest hint of approaching footsteps. Her efforts at both reading and mending were somewhat hindered, as she was unable to lean back due to the fact that the vicarage had recently been redecorated by her sister-in-law, Hermione Ashton, to feature only backless sofas in the fashionable Egyptian style.

Miss Ashton's brother, the Very Reverend Adolphus Ashton—who due to the family's less than fortunate financial circumstances had been forced to take orders and who had had the living at Deepdene these past eleven years—considered Calista's reading tastes to be nothing short of heretical, and was sure to read her a crashingly dull and extremely lengthy scold should she be discovered.

Searching out Calista, however, was the last thing on the Reverend Ashton's mind. Having breakfasted early, he was now closeted in his study, ostensibly writing tomorrow's sermon (tentative title: "Parishioners! Give Thanks to the Merciful Almighty for Giving You the Opportunity to Serve Your Titled Betters"), but was in actuality reading a most unimproving work on hunting, while eating at a prodigious rate the sugarplums confiscated from Master Billy Trent at Bible study.

His wife, Hermione, having rung for her morning chocolate, reclined on her pillows and debated whether the day should bring a megrim or a much more energy-consuming spasm. In the end she decided against succumbing to a spasm, which would in all likelihood keep her confined to her bed, ruining the chances for a comfortable cose with her bosom bow, Lady Gladys Lyttworth.

Lady Lyttworth, who prided herself on keeping town hours (*"One* in my *position,"* she was fond of saying, "must strive to maintain some *modicum* of civilization even here in this"—here a delicate shudder would traverse her ramrod-straight spine— *"backwater"),* was abroad at such early an hour only because she was eager to inspect the new addition to her art collection. It was a portrait she had recently commissioned from Hethering. Lady Lyttworth's painting was not precisely a Hethering original but, rather, an Elizabethan-era portrait that Mr. Hethering had less than happily but as instructed amended to bear the charming nose of the daughter of the house, Miss Sofie Lyttworth (who was, incidentally, still abed with a concoction of mashed cucumber on her porcelain complexion).

The Baron Lyttworth was in the library snoring behind the *Morning Post* from a sennight ago Tuesday. That the news was woefully out of date was of little consequence, as its main purpose was to keep him from being disturbed during his habitual post-breakfast, pre-lunch, late-midafternoon, and early-evening naps. Lady Lyttworth insisted that she had long since given up relying on the *Post* for the latest gossip. Her *dearest* London friends, she said, corresponded quite frequently enough to keep her apprised of all the latest *on-dits*. If any of her acquaintances privately thought Lady Lyttworth's news not much fresher than that contained in their own out-of-date *Posts,* they were much too polite to mention the fact.

The Lyttworths' nearest neighbour, Squire Everard Greystock, sat alone in his breakfast room, his seven children having been banished to the nursery in order that he be able to enjoy his morning meal in peace. It had been his late wife's idea to have so many children, which was exactly, he thought, the type of rackety hen-witted caper that was to be expected from the weaker sex. Despite the fact that he had not been particularly fond of his wife, her demise some eighteen months previous had discommoded him sadly. A few crumbs fell from thick lips as he polished off the remains of a rack of toast. Despite employing a veritable gaggle of nannies, nursemaids, and governesses, the squire was constantly being plagued by his offspring.

As he attacked the last morsel of creamed kidney, the idea that what his children really needed was a stepmama crossed his mind. If he must needs marry again, rot the luck, he thought, it would have to be someone who would be grateful for his offer. Someone past her last prayers. Someone who would set a fine table, not insist that he bathe, or interfere with his passions— riding to the hounds and drinking port. Someone, in fact, not unlike Calista Ashton. Bit of a favour to his crony Adolphus, actually. Lord knew, the gel *needed* a man's influence to set her to rights—going to end up dashed potty, she was, if left to her own devices. And come to think of it, she might make a nice armful come a cold winter night—he'd wager that hidden under all those frumpy clothes there were some curves to tempt a man.

Suddenly feeling at charity with the world, he belched and rang for a second platter of sliced ham.

Back in London, in a small but by no means modest house in Belgrave Square, Tristan Richard Rutherford-Hayes, sixth

Earl Stanhope, came reluctantly awake only to find that he had a devil of a headache. Too much claret. Too late a night. Gingerly prying open his left eyelid, he raised a straight, dark brow at the ornate and exceedingly improper frescoed ceiling that met his gaze. All that gold leaf had no doubt cost him a king's ransom. He settled back against the lily-scented pillows and wished his head would cease its throbbing.

It was a summons delivered the previous day that bore responsibility for the fact that he was arising at this shockingly unfashionable hour. The missive had begged that he in his position as head of the family attend his dear aunt, Lady Earla Cravanndish, Dowager Viscountess of Elston, at her house in Upper Brook Street at nine of the clock to assist her in her moment of dire unhappiness and great need. The sad occasion, the letter had gone on to lament, being a crisis with her scapegrace second son, the Hon. Oswald Cravanndish.

Unlooked for though the summons was, it did at least offer a not altogether unwelcome opportunity to crawl out of bed without having to endure the tedium of listening to Amanda—a not insignificant bonus. He stretched and very carefully, so as not to wake Amanda, rose.

Meanwhile, at Grillon's Hotel, Elmo Lyttworth, who had yesterday journeyed to London from his hometown of Deepdene, and who will shortly unite our characters, remained happily abed. On his own in the metropolis for the first time, he sighed and rolled over, dreaming of the bang-up bit of blood he planned to purchase at Tattersall's that afternoon—plans that surely would have come as a surprise to his father, the Baron Lyttworth, who had dispatched his son to London with the express purpose of purchasing a gentle mount suitable for his horse-shy sister, Sofie.

One

Some time later, Stanhope suppressed a sigh. Only the first of many, he guessed as he sat perched uncomfortably on a spindly, gilded chair, in his aunt's second-floor drawing room. Opposite him, the Lady Earla had disposed herself on the most comfortable sofa in the room with her vinaigrette to hand, a pose that in itself boded ill of the interview to come.

Stanhope struggled to offer every appearance of listening attentively as the dowager droned on, alternating between sobbing and cataloguing the faults of the wayward Oswald. His head hurt more with each sobbed syllable. *Anywhere,* he could not help thinking, would be preferable to being here. Well, anywhere except, perhaps, listening to a recitation of Amanda's poetry.

"And one can hardly be surprised that he is late to attend his own mama," his aunt sobbed, the appointed hour for the interview having passed by one minute.

In response to which Stanhope offered as close to a sympathetic and yet noncommittal noise as he was able. Perhaps he had been hasty, after all, in judging that this would be less painful than conversing with Amanda, he decided.

His aunt paused in her tirade and took a deep sniff from her vinaigrette and then gave vent to a hideous cross between a hiccough, a sob, and a coughing fit.

He was just on the verge of deciding that perhaps Amanda's poetry was actually underrated, when Griggs, the Lady Earla's extraordinarily starched-up butler, ushered in his cousin Oswald. Catching sight of Ossie's expression, Stanhope knew a wild flash of envy of the dreaded Napoleon Bonaparte. Sunny exile on Elba sounded downright inviting.

His cousin was all too clearly not pleased. A pout had stolen across his face at the tableau that greeted him, and Stanhope could hardly blame him. "Mother," he acknowledged with a slight bow toward Lady Earla. "You here too, Cousin?" he asked uncivilly. "Come to help m'mama call me on the carpet, I suppose?"

Not bloody willingly, thought Stanhope, but all he said, as pleasantly as he could, was, "And a good morning to you too, Ossie." He studied his cousin, whose lateness, he concluded, was undoubtedly due to how many tries it must have taken his valet to manage that cravat. Finished, it was a work of art, its snowy folds arranged in the intricate cascade of a waterfall. Oswald's shirt points rose high enough that they offered him no peripheral vision whatsoever, and his waistcoat was a highly embroidered affair of turquoise and primrose, setting off to perfection the bottle-green pantaloons that encased his plump thighs. Curl papers had rendered his hair a stunning cascade of gleaming gold ringlets. If his figure leaned toward heaviness and his chin toward recession, it truly could be of no account next to such sartorial splendour, Stanhope thought.

Oswald, still petulant, returned his cousin's regard. Stanhope had been thrown in his face as a paragon of perfection for as long as he could remember. Known as "the Nonesuch" due to his excellence at all sporting pursuits, he was rich as Croesus, had excelled when he read classics at Oxford, and, as the dowager was wont to point out at every conceivable opportunity, as if the blame for this circumstance could be laid directly at Ossie's door, was an *earl,* no less. If only, Ossie reflected with no small amount of envy, his mama were privy to the intelligence he was about his cousin's amorous adventures. She could hardly have held him in such high esteem then!

Despite all that, Ossie was forced to admit liking the fellow. Hell, everyone liked him. Known almost as well for the perfection of his address as for that of his phiz, Stanhope was not the least bit toplofty and unlike many of the Corinthian set, Ossie conceded, knew how to have a laugh—not, mind you, that he was one for cutting capers like his own cronies Squibby and Nev!

But how the fellow had come to be considered, albeit unwillingly, an arbiter of fashion was beyond comprehension! He *was* handsome, to be fair, tall and athletically built with dark hair, eyes that were almost unnervingly green, and a mobile mouth that left the ladies sighing. Year after year he was considered the prime catch on the marriage mart. And year after year he eluded the hopefuls. Ossie, though, could only deplore Stanhope's lack of sartorial taste. Eschewing bright colours, he habitually sported deucedly dull, almost spartan rig-outs. Today, for example, he wore buff-coloured trousers and a plain coat of navy superfine. His cravat was a simple mathematical, and he wore no jewelry or fobs—not even a quizzing glass!—his only ornamentation being a plain gold signet ring. His cousin was almost as bad for English fashion as the Brummell fellow! There was not a doubt about it though; the coat was Weston and the enviably blacked boots Hoby. The broad shoulders were unpadded, as were his legs, and nary a curl paper had touched the straight dark hair cut short in the back and falling slightly over his forehead in front. It had not been a particularly fashionable style until he cut it that way. Now it seemed every other buck on the street aped it—or at least those unfortunates without curls, Ossie thought as he patted his own.

Tiring of being kept waiting, his mama rose from the sofa and began to pace the floor. A small, brick-shaped woman with large hands and a red face and a mammoth shelflike bosom, the dowager favoured clothing combinations not unlike those beloved by her son. Today she was attired in a lime-green morning gown with a delicate magenta stripe and a matching magenta turban. Her hem trailed behind her as she walked, making a swishing noise against the fine Turkey carpet. "I do hope you realize, Oswald," she began without preamble, "that we are ruined!"

"Surely not," gasped Ossie. His quizzing glass, which he had been in the process of raising, fell from his fingers and hung dangling on its ribbon.

Holding up a hand for silence, the dowager walked to the

Adam mantel and stood with her back to the company. "Sit down on the hassock, Oswald," she commanded.

Subsiding, Sir Oswald did as he was bid.

"As I was saying, we, Oswald, are *ruined*. As though that were not enough, I am persuaded that I am utterly to blame." After which baffling pronouncement the dowager paused for a moment, beginning to sob as she affected a dramatic turn to face her son once again. Her voice rose to a shriek. "For I was used to believe that I had raised two fine sons. And now, after over *six hundred* years of honourable service to England the ancient and revered name of Cravanndish along with the House of Elston are disgraced," she choked out as Sir Oswald opened and shut his mouth in a decidedly fishlike manner. "The entire family is utterly brought down. It will be no thanks to you and your runabout ways if we are spared the further disgrace of having to crawl off to the *Continent* in the dark of night. And think of poor dear Priscilla, in her *condition*. I hardly dare hope the strain is not too much." Here she paused to give vent to a particularly large sob before subsiding once more to her cream and gold spindle-legged sofa, fumbling for her vinaigrette.

Catching sight of Ossie's astonished expression, Stanhope, who, despite his distaste for the task, had barely been able to suppress a smile at his aunt's antics, realized that it had fallen to him to fill the poor fellow in. He took a deep breath. "I believe what my aunt refers to, Oswald, is the small, er, incident, at Sally Jersey's rout. It would appear that word has reached her that there was a slight contretemps with the . . . punch bowl, I believe it was?"

At his words there was a renewed burst of sobs from the sofa as Lady Earla, apparently having made contact with her vinaigrette, revived. "How could you?" she wailed. "We might even have to go to *America.*"

"What sneaking screw prattlebox ran to you with that tale?" Sir Oswald demanded.

A screech from his mother brought his words to a halt. "It is outside of enough, Oswald, that a son of mine should bring shame and disgrace on the entire family by attempting to dive— *dive*—into a punch fountain! But it is a true mark of how far you have fallen that you could use *cant* in your own mother's drawing room. I vow, I simply cannot bear it," the dowager sniffled. "Although I have never been of a nervous disposition, it is something of a wonder under the circumstances that I have managed to avoid succumbing to a distempered freak. It is clear that I shall never hold my head up in polite society again."

At this, Stanhope decided it was time to bring a small measure of sanity to the proceedings. "I think, Aunt, that the situation might not be as, ah, dire as it appears at first glance." He got up and strolled to the bow window overlooking the rigidly ordered garden behind the town house, thinking how much more pleasing it would look if the flowers were allowed to escape the confines of their perfect beds. "Admittedly, it was rather foolish of Oswald to attempt to start a romp by diving into the punch fountain." He turned away from the window and folded his arms across his chest, and Ossie saw a light come into the clear green eyes. "And having tried the abominable stuff myself, I must confess that why one would desire even a cupful let alone a bath in it escapes me. However"—he fixed his aunt with a gaze that most effectively closed her opening mouth—"I am without doubt that no excessive harm has been wrought upon the family name. Elston House surely is lined with portraits of ancestors who may lay claim to deeds far worse—the fourth viscount and his unfortunate championage of the Stewarts in 1714 comes to mind as presenting infinitely greater possibility of social ruin—yet the family has managed to remain good *ton*. Were Sally Jersey not such a prattlebox, I doubt anyone would have remarked it at all. And had her gown not been ruined—"

"Her gown?" Ossie interjected with considerable heat. "What about my gold and puce waistcoat? Jensen was aghast. He went quite pale, as I recall, and found it necessary to lie down a spell when he saw it! It dried stiff as a board. I may never wear it again!"

"As it is," Stanhope continued, ignoring both the interruption and the possibility that his cousin was about to join his mother in a bout of sobbing, "even with her bandying the tale about every drawing room in town, it will hardly provide more than a nine days' wonder."

"I find myself excessively relieved by your assessment of the situation, Cousin," snapped Sir Oswald, pushed beyond endurance by the memory of the ruined waistcoat. "But I scarce see what this is to do with you."

Now truly impatient for escape from this family drama and a good head-clearing gallop in Hyde Park, Stanhope looked levelly at Ossie. "It seems that as your brother has removed himself to the country"—exceeding wise man, he added to himself—"and your mama has expressly requested my assistance in this matter, I am to bear the not altogether welcome responsibility of calling you to account for your foolish behaviour."

"Of all the crackbrained notions," retorted Ossie, going quite red in the face. "You're barely three years older than I, Tris."

"Quite so," Stanhope replied, giving up his post by the window and sinking onto a hassock directly facing his cousin. Despite the fact that they were seated evenly, Ossie retained unhappily the impression of being much the shorter of the two. "Which makes you two and thirty—more than old enough to conduct yourself with decorum. But the fact remains that disinclined though I am to embroil myself in your affairs, your mama has called on me, and it would seem my duty to assist."

"What is it to be, then, Tris? Am I being sent down? Is my allowance to be cut off?"

"Touché." Stanhope allowed himself a brief smile before recalling himself at the dowager's continued sniffling. Hastily, he returned to the business at hand. "The thing of it is, Ossie," he began, "that it appears that your mama's fondest wish is to see you, ah . . . settled."

"Not *leg shackled!*" Sir Ossie squeaked, jumping off the hassock as if bitten.

"Sit down, Oswald!" thundered his mama in dangerous accents before commencing once again to sniffle into her lace-edged handkerchief.

Sinking down again as bid, Ossie plowed ahead. "You must be gammoning me, Tris. *You!* Of all people! You are notorious for avoiding the parson's mousetrap! The matchmaking mamas

have been throwing their daughters at your head these ten years
and more, and I ain't seen you getting spliced. Why, you've had
more high flyers than a Covent Garden abbess! Dashed if Harry
Ottomly didn't tell me not yesterday that you have *two* in keeping now. Which bed did you come from this morning—" At the
sound of a horrible moan from the direction of the sofa, he
recalled himself and pulled up short.

Stanhope's drawl was level, but the green eyes were suddenly
hard. "Agog though I am to hear your further assessment of
my . . . *character,* shall we say, Cousin, I am obligated to remind
you that your mama is present."

Ossie, aware that he had gone too far, looked down at his
boots in silence.

Stanhope continued quietly. "Let us be reasonable. I have
avoided embroiling myself in your affairs, Ossie, despite your
mama's repeated pleas for my intervention, because, honestly,
I've no taste for playing nursemaid." He gulped the rest of his
coffee, wishing heartily that it was brandy, and set the cup back
on the tray. "But the fact remains, deucedly unfair as it may
seem, that you must remain in your mama's good graces until
you pass into control of your own income. And all levity aside,
I have only just managed to dissuade her from cutting you off
altogether on the condition that your behaviour come up to
snuff."

"I suppose the two of you have picked some green debutante
for the honour." Ossie pushed his plump lower lip forward.
"Who's the gel, then? Is it to be Lady Carrington's bacon-faced
wet goose of a daughter?"

His mama's sobs came to a sudden halt as she gasped in
outrage, her face now matching her turban.

"Or the carbuncled Harrison brat?" Ossie's voice rose as he
thought of a far worse possibility. "Or Georgiana Warwick's
girl. Does she not wear *spectacles?* What would Squibby and
Nev say an' they heard I was to be leg shackled to a chit with
spectacles?" he squeaked.

"Oswald," thundered his mother, apparently recovering. "I
have never, and I do mean never—"

Stanhope knew he had to insert himself between them if he

ever wished to end this tedious interlude. "Come. Let us talk
some sense," he said, effectively cutting off his aunt mid-
harangue. He walked over to the sideboard and poured coffee
into a gold-edged Limoges cup. He stood for a moment, eyeing
the combatants who were eyeing each other—Ossie, wearing a
sulk, and his aunt, openmouthed and apoplectic. Silently, but
in a manner that brooked no disagreement, he handed Ossie the
cup. "If you would listen a moment, Ossie, you would realize
that I said that your mama wanted to see you *settled*. She feels
it is time you came up to scratch in your behaviour as is befitting
a Cravanndish embarked upon his fourth decade. Her dearest
wish, of course, is to see you wed, but as I have a dislike of
seeing anyone enter that state against their will, I have prevailed
upon her good nature to offer you some choice in the matter."
Stanhope was acutely aware of how stuffy he sounded but could
think of no alternative, caught as he was between his harridan
of an aunt and scapegrace of a cousin.

"And what might that be? If I may be so bold as to inquire
what future has been decreed for me?" Ossie asked, glaring at
his mother's purpled face and wishing he had the bottom to
survey her through his quizzing glass.

She glared back. "You may visit your aunt Ottile in Bath—"

"Leave town? Now?" Ossie yelped before his mama could
finish. "But the season is barely begun!"

"Or you may, of course, go to your brother in Leicestershire,"
she continued as though he had not spoken.

"Hah! Not likely. I should *die* of boredom."

"Or you may remove to a destination of your own choosing—"

"Where? Besides, I've several new rig-outs on order—"

"Where you may find a suitable young woman to court. And
note I said *suitable,* Oswald—"

"And a bet on the books at White's that old Skeffingham
don't bathe before August! I can't rusticate now—"

"If after a period of one month I have deemed your behaviour
to be unexceptionable, *and* acceptable progress to have been
made in fixing the affections of an exemplary young woman,
you will be permitted to return to society."

Really, this was altogether too much, thought Sir Ossie, pushing his lower lip farther forward. It was as if he were not even present! But before he was able to give voice to this thought, his mother swept to the door.

"I thank you for your support in my moment of need and distress, Stanhope. It is comforting to know that at least *one* member of this family may be relied upon at the lowest point in one's life," she said. "And now, if you gentlemen will excuse me, I find I am far too distraught to continue further in company. I pray you will understand if I have Griggs escort you to the door. I take it I have made myself clear, Oswald?"

At his reluctant nod, the dowager pulled the bell and, fully dry-eyed now, exited the room.

"I will show you gentlemen to the door." Griggs had appeared as if from the shadows.

"If you don't mind, Griggs, I should prefer to sit for a while," pleaded Ossie, who had sunk back on the hassock and was attempting to recover from the shock so recently dealt him.

Griggs's tone was as unyielding as his face. "As I said, Sir, I should be happy to show you to the door."

"Thank you, Griggs," Stanhope interrupted, "but there's no need to tax yourself. We will show ourselves out momentarily."

"Very well," Griggs replied, and unbent enough to say, "Do visit again soon, my lord, as Cook is most disappointed that it is too early in the day for jam tarts."

Stanhope bent a smile on the butler. "I shall stop and tell Cook myself that I am devastated to have missed such a rare treat."

How *did* the fellow do it? Ossie wondered, as Griggs bowed and retreated. Stanhope had directly contradicted his mama's orders, and the notoriously stiff-rumped butler had not only accepted it but had been cozened into offering him jam tarts!

Stanhope crossed to the Sheraton cabinet and poured two healthy shots of brandy from the decanter that sat there. "It's a bit early, I realize," he said, holding one out to his cousin with a grin, "but somehow an interview with your estimable mama leaves me in need of a little courage."

Ossie, who was once again sunk in sullen contemplation of his boots, roused himself to take the proffered glass. "Know what you mean," he replied gloomily.

"To courage then." Stanhope lifted his glass. "Better?" he asked when they had both drunk.

Ossie nodded silently, so Stanhope replaced the glasses on the tray and sat down, looking once again completely at his ease. Somehow Ossie doubted he had been as shaken by the interview as he made out. "Now, let us talk reasonably, man to man, Oswald," Stanhope began. "You know there are a thousand places I'd much prefer to be than having this conversation—"

"I'll wager there are," interrupted Ossie, not bothering to repress a smirk. "Is it true then, Tris, that you actually have *two* fancy pieces at the moment?"

"Regrettably, Ossie, I seem to have made a brief foray from my better judgment. It is nothing I am particularly proud of, however, and rest assured I am putting an end to that situation."

"Bit much even for you, Tris?"

"Not if they don't attempt conversation," Stanhope replied, his expression almost dour. "But the point is," he continued, his voice once again its customary light drawl, and his face so severe that Ossie wondered if he had imagined the bleakness, "that while I'm in no position to pass judgment on your morals—"

"Damme but *that's* true!"

"I do want to point out that what a man does in private and what a man does in public are different things. Or can be. All you need to do to keep your mama out of your hair—and, blessedly, out of mine—is to introduce the smallest speck of decorum to your public behaviour. Court some nice young woman—"

"Doubt any would have me, not ones that m'mama would approve of anyway," confessed Ossie in gloomy tones. "Look dowdy next to me," he explained, "and no female likes that!"

"Rusticate for a month, then. It's hardly the end of the world.

Go stay with your brother and do the proper with the local debutantes. And by the time you get back, the whole thing here will have blown over and the season'll still be in full tilt."

"I can't like it."

"I know," Stanhope replied with something approaching sympathy now that the whole sorry episode was nearly behind him. "But try to bear up."

And with that, satisfied that he had done his duty, he made his hasty—and extremely relieved—escape.

Two

"Rusticate? Now? Ain't possible," Mr. Squibby Stoneham gasped when Lord Oswald found him at Tattersall's, where he was engaged in looking into the mouth of a fine chestnut. "Everyone's in town. Look devilish queer to go haring off with no explanation."

" 'Morning, gentlemen. Nice waistcoat, that, Ossie," commented Lord Neville Ffolkes as he strolled over. "Not like the green watered silk you sported yesterday." He shuddered delicately, overcome by the distressing memory.

"Leave off, Nev," said Squibby. "Cravanndish's in a bumble bath and needs our assistance."

Neville raised a brow.

"Been ordered to rusticate," Ossie mumbled by way of explanation.

"Terribly *mauvais ton,* that, to go rushing out of town as the season is just begun. Ain't done," Neville said with an air of finality.

"Don't be such a dashed bufflehead, Neville," said Squibby with no little exasperation. " 'Course it ain't done. That is why we must contrive a way out of this."

"Deuced inconvenient, the country," agreed Neville. "Dirty. Rustic. Always avoid it myself whenever possible." He shuddered slightly and flicked some dust off his raspberry pantaloons.

" 'Pon rep, ain't that Elmo Lyttworth?" Squibby, changing the subject, squinted across the yard. "Capital fellow, don't you know? M'father's estate marches alongside his uncle's in Shropshire. Wonder what he's doing in town. Lyttworth!" he shouted, waving.

The young man, reed-thin and obviously aspiring to the Corinthian—his dirty-blond baby-fine hair was even cut in a "Stanhope crop"—straightened up from his perusal of the hoof of a flea-bitten white nag and raised a hand in greeting. "Stoneham! Good to see you, old man."

"What brings you to town from—Deepdene, is it?" Squibby asked.

"M'father dispatched me to buy some cattle," explained Elmo, stretching the truth a tad. "Fine beast, this, eh?"

"You are obviously an excellent judge of horseflesh, sir," said the clerk at his elbow. "The Earl of Stanhope expressed a most pointed interest in her not yesterday."

That Stanhope's pointed interest had consisted of the dryly muttered comment that such a knackered, flea-bitten nag surely deserved to spend her remaining days in a pasture rather than ferrying overweight bucks around town, and that the horse had failed to garner even a single bid in Tuesday's auction, were facts he neglected to elaborate upon.

"The Earl of Stanhope?" Elmo uttered in accents of wonder. "The Nonesuch? Why, he is the greatest whip in all of England! Interested in this horse, you say?" He turned to his three companions, his face lit with delight. "His lordship is rumoured, y'know, to have bested Hell Fire Dick in a curricle race on the London-Brighton road!"

"Brighton ain't half far enough," Squibby replied in grim tones.

"M'cousin," was Ossie's morose explanation to Elmo's puzzled expression. "He and m'mama cut up stiff over a lark," he elaborated, indignation taking over. "Been ordered to rusticate. *And* find myself a respectable female to pay court to!"

"Stanhope's *your* cousin?" asked Elmo, looking doubtfully at Ossie's rounded physique and many-hued rig-out. "You must be tickled to have such an out-and-outer in the family."

"Lamentable wardrobe. All black and white or sometimes navy!" Neville exclaimed, shaking his head.

"Handy with his fives, though," Elmo defended his idol. "They say he drew Jackson's cork, you must know!"

"Fellow don't own so much as one canary-coloured waist-coat!" retorted Neville, his disgust apparent.

"Ain't seemed to hurt him where females are concerned," countered Elmo.

"No. Talk of the town, in fact," Squibby interrupted, sighing with envy. "Got two prime articles in keeping. But all this jawing about Stanhope ain't helping extricate Ossie from his fix. And we must! Can't leave now, bets on the books and all."

"Waistcoats on order," chimed in Neville helpfully.

"Ain't about to get leg shackled, neither," added Ossie.

"Lord, no," agreed Elmo with feeling. "Even Stanhope ain't buckled, and he could have his pick of any number of diamonds! *Two* mistresses, did you say?"

The three nodded glumly.

The Tattersall's clerk, disliking the direction in which the conversation appeared headed, coughed discreetly. "As I was mentioning, the gentleman in question, who is reputed to be a fine, fine whip indeed, *did* express a most determined interest in this very horse."

Elmo's head swam with rosy visions of owning a horse coveted by Stanhope. "How much?" he queried.

"Two hundred guineas." The clerk prided himself that he could always spot one right for the plucking.

Elmo fixed him with his shrewdest look. "Don't be ridiculous, man. Not a penny over a hundred fifty."

"His lordship was prepared to offer one eighty—"

"One eighty-five," countered Elmo hastily.

"The earl will not like to be outbid."

"One ninety!"

"Sold!"

"Excellent! I will send a draft on my father's bank before the day is out."

"Well done, Lyttworth," said Squibby, casting a doubtful eye over the horse. "Perhaps a celebration at White's?"

In prime twig at being invited to such exalted premises—

Stanhope himself was known to be a member, after all—Elmo agreed with alacrity.

A short time later, seated in the depths of a comfortable chair at White's, an excellent nuncheon in his stomach and an even more excellent claret in his cup, Elmo, still flush with his victory at Tattersall's, turned his attention to Ossie. "Seems to me, Cravanndish, that what you need is an excuse that will enable you to leave town without sinking you below reproach in the eyes of polite society. Allow you to make yourself scarce for a month. Pay court to an eligible female, which will appease your mama. Return to town. Water under the bridge."

"Exactly so," agreed Squibby. "Told you Lyttworth was an excellent fellow. Fine head on his shoulders. Wise beyond his years, etcetera."

Elmo inclined his head graciously at such high praise. "It seems that all you lack is the excuse."

"A bet!" Squibby suggested. "We leave for a mill, or perhaps a cockfight."

"No. Doncha see that will put Ossie's mama further out of charity with him," Elmo said thoughtfully. "What he needs is a reason that smacks of propriety. A house party!" He looked up in his excitement. "All Cravanndish needs is to wangle an invitation to a house party! Bound to be ladies there."

"Wrong season, old man," Neville explained as Elmo's face fell. "*Tout le monde* is in London."

"Besides. Not sure we're quite the thing at house parties after that dustup at Blenheim when Ossie got cup shot and accidentally crawled into bed with old Lord Skeffingham, who thought at first he was the downstairs parlourmaid. Lord, I ain't laughed so hard since . . ." Squibby trailed off as he caught Ossie's eye. "Sorry. Go on, Lyttworth."

"M'mama!" Elmo's face lit up. "Would be over the moon to have you. Always prosing on about how lowering it is to be out of society. Come to Deepdene!"

"My good man!" Neville threw himself to his feet in alarm. "I loathe rusticity. Cows. Dust. Insects! Thank you very much, but no." He shuddered.

"Stubble it, Nev. Lyttworth's in the right of it. Perfect solution." Squibby's brow wrinkled. "Any eligible chits there?"

Elmo thought. "Hardly. Small town and all, y'know. M'sister, of course, coming out next year. Said to be devilish good-looking but subject to queer fits, if you ask me. Gel's afraid of horses," he confided darkly. "The Searle twins. Faces like goats but huge dowries. Emily Enright's too young. And there's Calista Ashton. Excellent sort of female but been on the shelf forever. Good birth but no blunt to speak of. Her brother's the vicar. Doubt she's in your style anyway." He threw a glance at Ossie's splendid outfit. "Bit plain and all," he explained.

Squibby frowned. "She just might be perfect for our purposes. Any suitors?"

"Shouldn't think so," Elmo said, shaking his head. "She's *old*—four and twenty at least. Bit of a bluestocking too."

"Perfect! Suitable enough that Ossie may set up a courtship to soothe his mama but unsuitable enough that it will not be taken seriously." Squibby's tone brooked no opposition. "We are honoured to accept your invitation, Elmo. Oswald! We will retire to the country to enjoy the hospitality so kindly offered by the Lyttworth family, and you will pay your addresses to Miss Calista Ashton for the period of one month, after which we shall return to town. And before we depart we'll place a few bets on the success of your efforts at wooing the lady. That way everyone who counts will think we're off on a lark! What could suffice better?" He called for more claret and the betting book. "Let us raise a toast, gentlemen, to Sir Oswald's rustication."

Three

"They went *where* to do *what?*" Stanhope asked. It was three days later, and he had made his way to White's in anticipation of nothing more taxing than a good meal, some congenial masculine conversation, and a decent bottle of claret. Instead, he had run into his friend Lord Peter Gresham, who had apprised him of the latest tittle-tattle regarding his cousin.

"He, Ffolkes, and Stoneham left for Sussex this morning," Gresham explained in a low voice. "It was remarked that between them, four carriages were required for their wardrobes alone."

Stanhope rubbed the bridge of his nose. "Do go on."

"You're certain you want to hear the rest?"

"No. But I'll not contrive to avoid it for long." Stanhope's tone was light. "Best it come from you and not some scandal-mongering dowager."

Gresham laughed. "Very well. It is rumoured that Cravanndish intends to court some vicar's sister. There are upward of twenty bets on the books as we speak. I believe they started out as to whether he could win the damsel's affections, but the ante has been raised to an engagement—the odds are running two to one in favour of the banns being read." He shook his head. "Hardly seems right, somehow, dragging down the name of some innocent ape-leading female. They say she is an elderly, bookish spinster with no blunt and no looks."

"Brandy, please. A *very* large decanter. And fast," Stanhope replied to Raggett's discreet inquiry as to whether my lord desired anything further. "You're telling me, Peter, that those three buffleheads have rushed pell-mell out of town, having cooked up some half-witted scheme without a care to this poor woman's reputation?"

"Sorry. Exactly what I've been trying to say. Should hardly come as a surprise though. Neville Ffolkes is an empty-headed fribble, to be sure." Peter shook his head. "Stoneham's not a bad chap though. Perhaps a bit gambling mad and one hates to mention it, but not exactly a bright bulb. As for Cravanndish, I know he's your cousin, Stanhope, but he's getting a bit on in years to be behaving like such a greenheaded fool at every opportunity."

"I couldn't agree more," Stanhope mumbled half to himself. "And perhaps more to the point, neither could his mother."

"Ah, the Dowager Viscountess of Elston." Peter looked uncomfortable.

Stanhope laughed, seeing his friend's expression. "Don't worry. Bit afraid of her myself, Peter. I just survived one interview with her, and believe me, I've no taste for another. And it just might be more than my life's worth to let Ossie fall into another scrape. If he does, well . . ." He shuddered. "It doesn't bear thinking about what she'll have to say. The question is how to extricate him without raising more of a breeze. Where did you say they went?"

"To Elmo Lyttworth's in Deepdene, if I collect properly."

"The Lyttworth puppy?" Stanhope said with surprise. "I didn't realize Oswald was acquainted with him. Some type of distant connexion of mine, actually, on the mother's side— rather toadying woman, as I recall; buys portraits, retouches them, and claims the subjects for ancestors." He broke off with a sigh. "The young man, I understand, fancies himself something of a whip, but seems to be a lamentable judge of horseflesh. Bought Beresford's nag at Tatt's."

"That white piper? He bought *her?*" Gresham demanded in incredulous tones.

"She's on her last legs, I should think. They offered her to me—a broken old horse like that deserves to live out her days in the country munching on buttercups—and when I went to collect her, he'd come in and dropped a hundred and ninety guineas."

Gresham gaped. "*A hundred and ninety guineas?!*"

Stanhope nodded.

"*On that horse?*" At Stanhope's nod, Gresham shook his head. "But what do you intend to do about your cousin? Many men would have washed their hands of him by now. Not as if he's your ward or anything."

"It's true, Peter. But his mother is my father's older sister, and I can't help feeling obligated. His father died young, brother's a country squire at heart, mother's a harridan, and I've given him precious little guidance," he said on a sigh. "I should have knocked some sense through that thick dandy skull years ago, but I didn't. And now I suppose my penalty is that I'll need to ride to Sussex, *ventre à terre,* to try to convince Lyttworth to sell me that piece of prime cattle." His lips twitched. "It goes without saying that now that I've seen such a sweet goer, I must have her." He grinned outright as he poured out the brandy. "It is not for nothing that I am a member in good standing of the Four-in-Hand Club, you know. With any luck I should be able to lay claim to the horse and bail out my cousin without creating any undue talk. Fancy a sojourn to Sussex to play knight errant?"

Lord Gresham shook his head. "No, thanks. I know the area though. My godparents—Gordon and Elleanor Stanley—live the next town over. I do visit them from time to time, and I must say, there's not much there. Which, come to think of it, might be a good thing. Shouldn't think there's much more trouble your cousin and his cronies can get into once they are safely planted there. No, all things considered, I think I'll pass."

"Somehow I thought you would. I'll give your regards to the Stanleys anyway."

"Truth to tell, I hadn't thought to see you taking this so well. Especially so near the start of the season."

"I've been on the town too many years to harbour any anticipation in that direction," Stanhope replied in an offhand manner. "Not that I'm a-twitter with excitement at the prospect

of a stay in Deepdene, mind you. But I can't say that the thought
of leaving London for a spell leaves me overly blue-deviled."

Gresham looked surprised. "Not like you, Tris."

Stanhope waved away his alarm. "No cause for concern, I
assure you. It might be prudent for me to make myself scarce
for a week or so anyway."

Lord Gresham leaned back in his seat and grinned. "So that's
the way of it, is it? The charms of beautiful Amanda are wearing
thin? Or is it those of the equally fair Rosamunde that are pal-
ling?" he quizzed.

"Actually"—Stanhope's voice dropped as he leaned closer
to his friend—"it appears I'm in the suds with both of them.
Bit of a set-to the other night at Vauxhall. I was escorting Rosamunde—not particularly happily, mind you—and as it turned
out, Amanda was in attendance also."

"Well, well." Lord Gresham was clearly enjoying himself. "I
never thought to see the peerless Beau Stanhope turn tail and
flee London because his two *chères amies* were milling over
him. Serves you right for being so greedy, Tris. Gentlemen all
over town, you realize, are bereft of female companionship
while you monopolize *two* stunning creatures."

"Laugh if you wish, Peter, but it was terrifying, I assure you,"
Stanhope returned good-naturedly. "The two of them threatening each other with grievous bodily harm, Amanda all in blank
verse of course, and Mrs. Drummond-Burrell positively cran-
ing her neck around backward, hoping for a bit of scandal."

"Shouldn't think you'd need to run away from scandal, Tris.
It's amazing what excesses of behaviour even Mrs. Drummond-
Burrell can overlook when they are coming from such a very
eligible earl with a vast fortune."

Stanhope grinned over the edge of his glass. "I'd almost forgotten how easily a fellow can develop a swelled head around
you, Peter. And here I thought I was such a favourite of the
patronesses for my excellent manners and witty conversation."

Lord Gresham laughed easily. "Sorry, old man. You've bid
both ladies adieu with exorbitant baubles, I trust?"

"Bracelet for Amanda and ear-bobs for Rosamunde, actually
purchased *before* the scene, and not a moment too soon. But

it's not only that I seem to be turning chickenhearted in my dotage, Peter. It's that suddenly the prospect of another season of Almack's and breakfasts, and balls and routs and musicales, and paying enough attention to all those insipid milk and water debutantes—but not so much as to raise their hopes—and fighting off their mamas, and sidestepping the question of when I plan to settle down and provide an heir, leaves me longing for escape. I just don't feel like doing the proper this year."

Gresham looked surprised. Whatever he did in private, Stanhope *always* did the proper in public. "The season will grind to a halt! The hopeful mamas will go into mourning! Why, I should not be at all surprised if there is a rash of debutantes throwing themselves into the Serpentine when word of your desertion gets about."

Stanhope's sudden dazzling grin reminded his friend of just why the man was so sought after. "Doing it too brown, Peter. Besides, I've another confession."

Gresham raised a brow. "You're unusually forthcoming this evening, Tris."

"I know," Stanhope replied, still grinning. "It's the disaster in the midst of which I'm no doubt about to land myself, or possibly it's the moon."

"Waning crescent last I saw, so no explanation there. Tell."

"I was bored to tears, Peter. I learned that juggling two vacuous women is exactly twice as tedious as having one. Nothing more, nothing less."

"Good Lord!"

"Exactly."

"Perhaps you do need a sojourn, then. Just remember what Samuel Johnson said—"

"And well I do, my friend, but sometimes it seems to me a man is just tired of London after all. Come, let us raise a glass to Sir Oswald's rustication. And then I will retreat home to pen a letter expressing my eagerness to be reunited with that flea-ridden collection of bad points Lyttworth carried off."

Four

Stanhope's missive, delivered as it was by liveried messenger, caused a great flutter in Deepdene. Lady Lyttworth, who had already been in a twitter over preparations for the upcoming house party, was sent shrieking down the stairs.

"Mr. Lyttworth! Mr. Lyttworth! Wake up," she demanded in uncharacteristically unmodulated tones. When her spouse did nothing of the kind, she resorted to shaking him. "Do wake up. The most famous news has arrived."

"Hrmph wazzit?" her life partner replied.

"It is the Earl of Stanhope. He has written!"

"Written what?" asked the baron, feeling distinctly fuzzy-headed. He resolved to ask that vegetables, which he was certain disposed him to sleepiness, no longer be served at nuncheon "Not one of those dreadful novels like *Glenarvon* I trust."

"A letter," returned Lady Lyttworth breathlessly, clasping the document in question to her chest. "He has written a letter! Oh, and it is the most *famous* thing. He is coming! For our Sofie!"

The baron reached for the letter. "Stanhope? Here? Sofie? Don't sound possible. Chit ain't even out yet." With that pronouncement he took the proffered paper. "Says here he is coming about the filly, that she is more and more in his thoughts, and he is sorry he let her slip through his fingers. What filly?" He looked at his wife for clarification.

"Don't you see, George? He refers to the time Sofie and I visited London to attend the *modiste*. As our carriage turned down Bond Street on our way to Madame le Rotille's establishment—I recall the day clearly as we had just purchased Sofie the most *cunning* Kutusoff mantle in peach, when Stanhope strolled down the street on foot, on his way to his club, I imagine, and most distinctly raised his hat to us. He must have been unable to erase her from his mind this past year!"

"But he says 'the filly.' There is no mention of Sofie," her spouse pointed out reasonably.

"Honestly, George. What on earth else would that refer to?" his wife asked crossly. "He is horse mad, just as Elmo is. That is the way all the young bucks about town talk! Everything is couched in terms of the stable."

"Seems deuced odd to me." The baron remained skeptical, but his London-born wife did know the ways of the *ton* better than he did, so he shrugged at her assurances. "Stanhope'd be quite a catch though."

"Quite a catch? He is only *the most* eligible man in England!" his wife said severely. "And we must impress upon him that we are up to snuff. Come to think of it, though, it is not all that odd that he would look to Sofie for his bride! We're plump enough in the pocket and we *are*—thanks to my connexions—family after all. His *dear, dear* mama is my grandfather's sister's husband's niece. He and I are accounted to be possessed of the same chin, you know." She turned profile so he could observe this phenomenon for himself.

"If you say so, m'dear." Her spouse, having declined to ponder the genetic impossibility of this claim, was already resettling the paper across his face. "Mind you, I ain't having Sofie entered in any races. Won't stand for that." From behind the paper he guffawed at his own witticism.

His wife gave a delicate snort of disgust. "It is time you tried to learn the ways of the polite world, George. It would not do to appear a bumpkin in front of your future son-in-law! I shall send a message posthaste, telling him to come. And then I really must start planning a ball suitable for the announcement of such an important betrothal! Stanhope, of course, will want his mama to fête Sofie accordingly in London, but we still must throw together a modest little country celebration here. I shall need to call on Hermione—she will be beside herself with envy. She is at her wit's end over Calista, you know—and, oh, just imagine! Our Sofie, a *countess!* I do hope there is time to do something about her complexion. I thought yesterday that I spied an incipient *freckle.*" Primed to do battle with this impending disfigurement, Lady Lyttworth rushed from the room.

Her bemused spouse grumbled to himself, "Don't care what she says. Dashed rackety way to behave, referring to gels as horses, if you ask me," before lapsing back into slumber.

Some time later, satisfied that Sofie was on her bed with a compress of Roman balsam on the offending blemish and orders not to stir until supper, the baroness made her way over to the vicarage. Having filled Hermione Ashton in on the wondrous news, she relaxed with a cup of tea as they discussed the ball.

"I'm not sure that a punch fountain would be the thing," she replied to her friend's suggestion. "According to Elmo's letter, one of the gentlemen that accompanies him, the Hon. Oswald Cravanndish, I believe, had some type of altercation with one at *dear* Sally Jersey's house. Perhaps an ice sculpture of the earl," she mused. "So tasteful, and yet it would provide no opportunity for high jinks. Oh, I do so wish Elmo and his cronies had not decided to stop off for a prizefight in Little Swindale on their way," she wailed. "I would be able to ask him whether he deems one safe."

"They *are* all the crack," agreed Hermione, who knew nothing of such things. "Of a certainty the earl can hardly fail to be impressed. But what of the expense? Whatever will George say?"

"Pish!" The baroness waved her concern away. "He is about to become father-in-law to one of the wealthiest men in England. What can the trifling expense of an ice sculpture signify? And beeswax candles! We must have hundreds of them in the ballroom. I shall have to send out the cards immediately! Oh, and the flowers . . ."

An hour later, in agreement that they had made gratifying progress in their plans, Hermione Ashton rang for fresh tea.

"Has there been any headway with Calista?" Lady Lyttworth

inquired in a confiding tone as her friend poured out her second cup.

"None," sighed Hermione. "No matter what I do or say, she will persist in cluttering her mind with the works of those . . . *heretics* Sydney Smith and Robert Owen—no, I do not think that is coming it too strong, Gladys! Did you know that they advocate *educating* the great unwashed? And Mr. Smith even asserts that women would still be fit to care for children even were they to be educated in Greek and mathematics! I am certain it is all that mumbo jumbo about women being the equals of men—"

"I know that I for one am glad to enjoy the ignorance of the fairer sex," her friend put in.

"Which is as nature intended," Hermione replied. "But I am certain that is why Calista refused dear Everard's suit. All this scandalous talk has addled her poor brain, I fear. She pays endless visits to the parishioners, even to that disgusting Whitston family. Why, their cottage positively *reeks!* When I taxed her with it, she said it is our duty simply because Adolphus is vicar! Imagine! My goodness, with all her traipsing around, tending the sick, it is something of a wonder we haven't all been carried away by some dreadful illness. My constitution is quite delicate, as you know." She paused in her conversation to consume a large tea cake in a single bite.

"You poor dear," Lady Lyttworth said, leaning forward to pat her friend's hand sympathetically, if not a little smugly, from her new position as mama-in-law to an earl.

Hermione swallowed. "Why, I was even forced to take it up with Adolphus. 'Adolphus,' I said, 'surely I know my Christian duty as well as anyone, and surely,' I said, 'last time I checked, cleanliness was still next to godliness!' "

"And does she still refuse to reconsider Everard's offer?" asked Lady Lyttworth as she popped another ginger biscuit into her mouth.

"Yes," sighed Hermione around a mouthful of cake. "As if she will ever get another offer. I told her, I did. I said, 'Calista, if you will forgive my engaging in a bit of plain speaking, you are past your last prayers. If you hope ever to have an establishment of your own, this is likely your only chance.' "

Lady Lyttworth nodded her approval. "And what did she say to *that?*"

Hermione sighed her exasperation. "She said he was fat, smelled of the stable, and had no teeth. As if any of that signified, Gladys! She said that she would sooner die unwed and that, come to think of it, would suit her just fine! She has some ridiculous notion of setting up her own establishment in Rose Cottage, you know, when she comes into her inheritance. I've never heard such fustian!" Hermione stopped, her chest heaving with indignation.

Lady Lyttworth's brows went up. "I had quite forgotten that she had an inheritance. From her maternal grandmother, is it not?"

"More of a competence, really. Not anywhere near enough to keep her in the style she could command as the squire's wife."

"When does she receive it?"

"On her twenty-fifth birthday. In eight months."

"I daresay, I cannot credit any female of her age behaving like such a goosecap! And Everard, I daresay, offered you a handsome settlement?" Lady Lyttworth inquired as she daintily drained her cup.

"Very generous," confirmed Hermione. "He is, as you know, quite well to grass despite his nipfarthing ways."

"Hmm, I will take a little more tea, if you will, my dear," said Lady Lyttworth slowly. "It seems to me that you must needs contrive a way to do the deed with or without her cooperation. To that end, Sofie's engagement ball might be just the occasion."

Hermione's brow wrinkled. "I fail to see—"

"My dear, if it were to be presented to the world as a *fait accompli—*"

"Surely you can't mean announce her betrothal without her acquiescence?" gasped Hermione.

Lady Lyttworth nodded firmly. "It would be for her own good—don't you see? Once the engagement is made public, it's as good as accomplished. And something must be done to save the poor misguided girl—well, hardly a girl, after all—from this frightening tendency toward independent thinking and radicalism before she harms herself. You said yourself that she is addled enough as it is! When matters have been made sure of for her, Calista is bound to see where her duty lies. Even *she* must realize that to cry off then would spell ruin. Besides," she added in a bracing tone, "if you wish to see any of the squire's blunt, this is the only way. Once the ungrateful girl controls her own money, you shan't see a farthing of it, mark my words."

"You are in the right of it, Gladys," Hermione replied thoughtfully. "I will take the matter up in all haste with Adolphus. With some luck we will contrive to see Calista settled with Everard. For her own good, mind you."

"Trust me, she will thank you for it in the end," Lady Lyttworth said comfortingly.

Five

By happy coincidence, the day after the one bringing news of the impending arrival of the Nonesuch was the second Tuesday of the month—the customary meeting day of the Deepdene Ladies' Sewing Circle. It need hardly bear mention that in this instance, the ladies did not lack for conversation.

"Calista, you are the first to arrive, prompt as usual!" said Lady Enright, who, standing on little ceremony, opened the door herself. "Far too brisk out for April, is it not? Come into my sitting room, my dear, where there is a fire lit." She led the way, and in no time Calista was settled before the crackling applewood fire, pulling her knitting from a straw basket. "I'm afraid we shall be rather a small group today, as Gladys is far too busy readying the household and has issued a decree forbidding Sofie from handling a needle for fear her hands might be marred in a way not befitting a future countess." Lady Enright's tone was carefully neutral, but Calista, who could well imagine her hostess's true thoughts on the subject, dropped her head over her work to hide a smile.

Emily Enright, a small brunette of young but promising beauty, her face spoilt only by her sulky expression, appeared through the door in time to hear her mother's words. "It is vastly unfair," she cried, her lip trembling. "Why should I be here, when Sofie is not?"

"Because there is much to be done before the spring fête, and you embroider so beautifully, my love," her mother replied in an unruffled tone.

"If Sofie doesn't have to—"

"Hush, Emily." Lady Enright shot a speaking glance toward Calista. "Don't mind her. She's been in the sullens ever since she heard Sofie's news," she explained.

Whatever Emily might have replied was forestalled by the entrance of Mrs. Elleanor Stanley. "Good morning," said the new arrival, slightly breathless. "Oh, good, a fire. Just the thing this morning. She shook out the altar cloth on which she was working as she settled her plump form on a chaise. Sighing with pleasure, she declared herself ready for a good gossip. "I know we are only the neighbouring town, but I vow, Redingcote is positively abuzz with talk of the impending visit! And one must admit it *is* most romantical," she said, clutching her work to her ample chest. "According to Gladys, he caught one glimpse of her through a carriage window in London and has been positively unable to put her from his mind since!"

"I told you that we should have gone to a London *modiste* instead of frequenting that provincial local," Emily burst out. "Perhaps if we had, it would have been me instead of Sofie!"

"My love," began Lady Enright, "it would be much more becoming if we were to rejoice in Sofie's good fortune—"

"But it is vastly unfair!" cried Emily, tears threatening. "Why should Sofie have the brilliant match while I rot here simply because my parents are too cheeseparing to take me to a *proper modiste!*"

"I shouldn't think your parents can be entirely to blame, Emily," said Calista in a soothing tone. "And only consider, a man of his years . . ." She allowed her words to trail off thoughtfully.

"He is old?" Emily managed to ask through her sniffling.

"Hadn't you heard?" Calista replied with gravity. "According to Elmo, the man is five and thirty. At least."

"Over thirty?"

Calista nodded as she untangled a skein of yarn. "Indeed. And just think what a shame it would be were you to become engaged now. You would miss all the excitement and gaiety of a coming-out season."

"I suppose you are right," Emily said, drying her eyes. "I *am* looking forward above all things to being presented at court. And I *should* dislike being saddled with a very elderly husband. Is he arthritic?" she asked hopefully.

"Quite possibly. Tell me, have you engaged a house in London yet?"

"Oh, yes. On Curzon Street!" replied Emily, diverted for the moment. "Tell Calista about it, Mama."

"Well, it—" began Lady Enright, her eyes meeting Calista's gratefully over her daughter's head, but before she could continue she was interrupted by the arrival of the Searle twins, Rose and Ivy, and their mama.

"Oh, it will be *famous!*" exclaimed Rose.

"Mama says there will be entertainments day and night once *he* has arrived," chimed in Ivy, leaving no one in doubt as to what Rose had referred.

"There will?" asked Emily, looking much more cheerful.

"Oh, yes," said Rose. "Balls and picnics and musical evenings. Deepdene will never have seen anything like it before."

"I suppose it *does* sound diverting," ventured Emily.

"And we are to have new dresses!" exclaimed Rose, her face alight.

"Mama, may I have new dresses also?" Emily appeared to have quite forgotten her distaste for the provincial seamstress.

"Of course, my dear," her fond mama replied, grateful that the storm had been averted. "And, Calista," she added, fixing her with a sharp eye, "I do not expect to see you, your hair put up under caps, sitting with the chaperones."

Calista did not look up from her needles. "Actually I had not planned to attend these entertainments, Roberta."

"Not planned to attend!" Lady Enright cried.

"But surely you must, my dear." Where Lady Enright's tone had been indignant, Mrs. Stanley's was mild but insistent. "Everyone will."

"I am quite busy, as you know," Calista replied, sounding imperturbable. "And I do not suppose that the notorious earl will remark my absence. Besides, it is past time, as you are all well aware, that I put on those caps for good."

"Nonsense!" retorted Lady Enright roundly. "You are a

lovely young woman, and I will not hear of you shutting yourself away. Your dear mama, rest her soul, would never have allowed it, and I won't either!"

Calista smiled. "You are kind, Roberta, but surely my mama would have accepted the inevitable by now. I am a bookish spinster of advancing age, no particular looks, and very little fortune. I am content with my lot, and"—she held up her hand to forestall Lady Enright's reply—"I have no intention of toadying at the feet of the Earl of Stanhope. As I said, I have little time to spare from my work."

"It is certainly thanks to you, and not to that brother of yours," Lady Enright said darkly, "that the villagers' lives have improved so drastically. You should be proud of yourself, my dear, that they have dry cottages and medical care, and that so many are literate now. But is that truly enough for a young woman such as yourself?"

"It is more than enough."

"If you would forgive my impertinence," said Mrs. Searle in a timid voice, "it would seem a terrible shame were you to have no babies of your own, Calista. You are such a wonder with children."

"I thank you for your concern, Alice." Calista smiled as she picked up a dropped stitch. "But I am quite resigned, you know, to a life of spinsterhood, and I do not for a moment subscribe to the notion that the state rules out a fulfilling life. In fact, Mary Wollstonecraft said—"

"Please, my dear, do not start quoting the Wollstonecraft woman," Lady Enright interrupted hurriedly. "Once you are begun, there will be no stopping you." At Calista's good-natured laugh, she continued. "But please don't rule out attending at least a few of the entertainments. It would do my old heart good to see you out and about and enjoying yourself."

"But, Calista, are you not in the least bit curious to meet this paragon?" queried Ivy.

"Not particularly." Calista's tone was dry.

"I confess I am all agog to see him," Rose replied.

"In my experience, very sporting gentlemen are wont to be a collection of sad rattles. It does not do, you know, to harbour too many romantic illusions. Most often they smell of the stables and strong spirits and boast of their exploits on the hunting field at extremely tedious length."

"Well I for one am convinced he is bound to be fascinating," pronounced Rose.

"Elmo says he is accounted the handsomest man in England!" chimed in Ivy, very much as if that settled the matter.

"Indeed." Calista was unmoved. "I hope he is, but I am not at all certain that Elmo is to be relied on for an accurate assessment of his idol," she reminded them dryly.

"He must be handsome," pronounced Emily triumphantly. "He is, you know, a famous rake. Ooh, this is so exciting! To think, a rake in our little village."

"Emily!" chided her mother.

"Rakes are not always handsome," Calista pointed out. "All that is required for raking is a lack of morals. In fact"—she surveyed the three eager young faces before her—"dissipation is rarely kind to the face or figure. Most of the rakes of my acquaintance have been running to fat. It's quite sad, really. Why, look at Prinny!" She busied herself looking for a new ball of yarn to hide her smile at their groans of dismay.

"Well, this one is bound to be a veritable Adonis," Emily assured them, rallying. "And at the very least he will liven up this dull town. Mama, may we be excused?"

"Yes, girls, you may go to Emily's bedchamber to giggle to your hearts' content."

"D'you suppose there will be *waltzing?*" they heard Emily ask as the three girls departed amidst a buzz of excited chatter.

Lady Enright turned to Calista, raising a brow. "I had not realized you were quite so well versed in the ways of rakes, Calista Ashton."

"Hardly indeed, ma'am," Calista admitted with a laugh. "But I do know that it will not do at all to have those three romanticize him else they will all be abovestairs, trying to hatch schemes to lure him away from Sofie and on to Gretna Green. Surely waltzing, as we all know, is but the first step in that direction."

"My godson, Peter Gresham, was at Christ Church with the earl, you know," said Mrs. Stanley when the laughter that had greeted Calista's comment died down, "and has always spoken most highly of him. And *he,* unlike Elmo, is quite a good judge of character."

"I must confess, I'm all curiosity to meet him," Lady Enright admitted. "I well remember his father, who left more than a few broken hearts in his own wake before settling down."

"Honestly, Roberta, anyone would think you were a green girl of Emily's stamp instead of a happily married matron, with the way you are sighing over rakes," scolded Calista, her eyes brimming with merriment.

"It might do *you* a bit of good to sigh over a handsome face for a change, my girl," retorted Lady Enright.

"I am not much for sighing, Roberta. But *if* I were going to, I would hope I would be sensible enough to choose a gentleman with a pleasing substance of mind and a principled outlook. Not some flashy rake with reprehensible morals and well-shined boots!"

"You are becoming quite narrow in your thinking, Calista, if you think that poorly shined boots are indicative of high moral caliber," Lady Enright shot back.

"You know what I mean, Roberta."

"I do. But remember that experienced men can be very interesting, my dear. They always say that there is no husband like a reformed rake."

"Not being in the market for either a husband or a rake, reformed or otherwise, this surely is of no concern to me," Calista replied.

"Be that as it may, there is no reason you cannot attend a few social events. Consider yourself warned, my dear, that if you insist on shunning society during the visit, I shall not hesitate to take any steps I deem necessary to keep you from isolating yourself."

"Heaven forbid!" Calista looked up, laughing. "I'd not thought you a blackmailer, Roberta." She stood and began to gather her things. "I'd best be on my way, as I promised Hermione I would be back before nuncheon."

"Bear in mind, my dear," advised Lady Enright, rising to give her a fond kiss on the cheek, "that I *never* make idle threats."

When she had returned from seeing Calista to the door, she turned to the other two women. "I could throttle that rackety brother of hers, not to mention his dim-witted wife!"

"Roberta!" chided Elleanor Stanley in shocked tones. "That is hardly charitable."

"I don't care, Elleanor. It's a positive disgrace the way they use that child. She practically runs the parish while Adolphus drinks and hunts himself into insensibility and Hermione lounges around and has megrims and spasms!"

"It *is* true that neither of them does a whit more than is absolutely necessary," agreed Mrs. Searle.

"One must admit," said Mrs. Stanley, biting off a thread, "Calista does run things a sight better than any of the vicars we've had hereabouts for the last thirty years."

"But she's old before her time! And far too serious," said Lady Enright. "Those awful dresses. She should be dancing and laughing and allowing the bucks to steal kisses at the Redingcote Assemblies. And to try to sell her off to that disgusting old lecher, Everard Greystock, for their own gain!" She was so overcome with anger that she stopped and fanned herself with her handiwork. "Thank goodness the girl had the good sense to nip that in the bud!"

"But a life of spinsterhood," clucked Mrs. Stanley. "It seems such a shame."

"Well I for one have no intention of allowing either to come to pass," said Lady Enright in a tone that would have caused Calista to shake had she been privy to it. "Even should it require resorting to nefarious means."

Six

It was three days later that the Earl of Stanhope, bareheaded and in his shirtsleeves, finally tooled his phaeton at an unremarkable pace into Deepdene. Seeking some solitude, he had set out a day in advance of the carriage containing his valet and most of his luggage, and so arrived quietly, with none of the fanfare that ordinarily accompanied a traveling earl.

Stopping to ask the Lyttworths' direction of the first person he chanced upon, he found himself looking down at a young woman. That she was gently bred was immediately clear to him despite the fact that she was wearing a brown wool morning dress so atrocious that your average London scullery maid would have refused to venture abroad in it. Not by any means a beauty in the current mode, he nevertheless found himself thinking that she was very fresh and appealing—a thought he immediately attributed to the country air, as he personally preferred a much more polished, voluptuous type. She was possessed of a clean-scrubbed heart-shaped face with a small, straight nose, and large hazel eyes fringed by dark lashes. Her auburn curls threatened escape from the ribbon intended to hold them back, and her mouth, he mused, feeling suddenly fanciful, was made to laugh.

Unfortunately, it was primmed up with disapproval at the moment. "The Lyttworths?" she replied to his query. "You will find Moreford Park just down this road a half-mile or so. It would seem unlikely that you will find much in the way of a cordial reception, however," she went on in such disgusted accents that Stanhope thought for a delighted moment that she would actually snort in disgust. To his disappointment, she restrained herself and continued. ". . . As they—and the rest of the county, to be disgracefully fair—can think of nothing but the imminent arrival of the Somewhich."

"The what?" Stanhope asked, momentarily diverted.

"The Somewhich," she replied in tones that left no doubt as to her feelings regarding such personage. "A regular out-and-outer, very high in the instep, who, if Elmo Lyttworth's raptures are to be countenanced, will no doubt arrive in a driving coat sporting no fewer than fifteen capes, behind four of the finest horses in a red high perch—" She trailed off, eyeing his red conveyance as if noticing it for the first time, a hint of pink washing over her face.

And very becomingly too, Stanhope thought, reflecting that he might just enjoy the country more than he had expected. "I must plead guilty," he said as he executed a slight bow. "But it is the Nonesuch."

"I beg your pardon?" She looked full at his face and realized with a little shock that he was without a doubt the handsomest man she had ever seen. He was tall and broad of shoulder without being heavy in any way. Even seated atop his ridiculously high sprung curricle, his lithe, athletic grace was apparent. He was possessed of thick, dark hair that was lifting slightly in the breeze. His green eyes held a gleam of wicked-looking amusement, but his finely chiseled lips were turned up in a warm smile, and to her own chagrin, Calista felt an unasked-for flutter of response.

"It is the Nonesuch, not the Somewhich. It is not, however, a sobriquet of which I am overfond, so do not trouble yourself in the least." He jumped down lightly from the vehicle. "Please accept my apologies. I am devastated to disappoint you, but a tragic circumstance has delayed the arrival of my valet with said driving coat—with any luck it should be among us in but a day, and I promise to sport it often. And apparently that font of wisdom, Mr. Lyttworth, mistakes himself, as it needs only two cattle to pull this conveyance." He made a graceful bow. "Tristan Rutherford-Hayes. Your servant, ma'am."

"Otherwise known as the Earl of Stanhope." It was a statement, not a question, and although her blush deepened, her tone
warned him that his title was as little asset in her eyes as his
sporting reputation appeared to be. "I should have realized.
Even a miserable judge of horses such as myself can see that
those two are bang up to the mark."

"Just so," he said gravely. "If it would but appease your
image of me, I might see my way to having my teeth filed to
points during my stay here."

"There is no need to bamm me, sir," she said severely, but
Stanhope thought he had almost realized his goal of seeing her
smile. "You had best continue on to Moreford Park, as word of
your arrival has surely taken the village by storm. There has
been talk of little else these three days past, and Lady Lyttworth
is certain to be close to a swoon should you fail to make an
appearance soon."

"Well, I should dislike above all things to be responsible for
Lady Lyttworth's discomposure," he replied, thinking that really
he'd much prefer to tarry in the lane and try to entice a smile.
"I don't suppose you have seen the horse?" he inquired, half
hoping to hear that the exhausted old hack had the good fortune
to have expired en route.

"Horse, my lord?" Calista queried, thinking that he might be
almost unbearably gorgeous, but it was exactly as she had expected: The man was quite unable to converse for more than
thirty seconds without introducing sporting pursuits.

Surely in such a small town everyone would know why he
was come—an earl's arrival was hardly an everyday occurrence,
as she herself had pointed out, Stanhope thought with perhaps
a touch of arrogance. Perhaps the poor girl was not altogether
there, which seemed a shame, but went a long way toward explaining her absolute lack of interest in his arrival. "The-horse-
I-am-come-to-purchase." He spoke slowly to give her a chance
to understand.

Did the blasted man think she was simple? Calista wondered
as Stanhope continued in patient tones. "Master Elmo
Lyttworth purchased her at Tattersall's," he explained, and then
remembered to add, in case she was becoming confused, "A

horse purveyor in London. I would like to buy her. I wrote expressing my intent. You said yourself that I was expected. I assumed—"

The girl's laugh that greeted his words was as pleasing as he had first guessed it would be, and the expression of shrewd amusement in her eyes put a stop to any idea of her being simple. That laugh, in fact, was doing something odd to his breathing. Country air was much overrated, he decided. Goodness knows, he had never had difficulty breathing in the London smog. "I have amused you, Miss . . . ?" he inquired in silky tones.

"I am ever so sorry," she gasped, wishing heartily that she could be there when the true reason for his visit was discovered. "Please accept my apologies for my rag manners." She paused to recover as another giggle overtook her. "Calista Ashton, sir," she said without offering the customary curtsy.

Stanhope tried to swallow his gulp of astonishment. *"Hardly* an elderly dried-up spinster!" he exclaimed before he could stop himself.

"Why, thank you, sir," she said tartly. "Small wonder you are known the country over for your polished address." He felt himself flush like a schoolboy as she continued. "It is no bad thing that your reputation as a shocking flirt precedes you, else I might let your flummery swell my head."

"Please, Miss Ashton, do accept my apologies," Stanhope begged, bowing again, feeling at a loss for words for perhaps the first time in his life. "I can only plead great fatigue from the journey. I did not mean—"

"I am sure you did not," Calista replied as crisply as she was able, as her stomach seemed to have resumed the flip-flopping that it had started the first time she looked him full in the face. Clear broth for supper tonight, she decided, as I am obviously coming down with something.

"No, I—"

She waved aside his apologies. "Think nothing of it." She tilted her head to one side and surveyed him appraisingly. She was actually thinking that Emily and company could hardly be disappointed—the man *was* an absolute Adonis. Stanhope in his discomposure felt that she was taking his measure and finding him lacking. Not a sensation he was used to. But all she said was, "So you are the famous Nonesuch."

"Hardly famous," he supplied hastily.

"I am most cast down, I must say, that you do not even make use of a quizzing glass."

He smiled evenly, and Calista became aware of that odd, fluttering sensation in her chest again. "Alas, it is also with my valet. Once again I find myself in the position of begging your pardon for having offended your sensibilities. I do try to reserve that item, however, for setting down toadies and mushrooms and would, in any case, be loath to unleash such a fearsome weapon on a defenseless young lady on a quiet country road."

"Hardly defenseless, sir."

He smiled, his eyes meeting hers with unspoken understanding, and she felt her heart thud. "Touché, Miss Ashton. Please, allow me to make amends for my abominably rude behaviour by offering you a ride to your destination?"

"Thank you, but that won't be necessary, as I am going only down the lane to the next cottage."

"Then, please, let us start again," he begged, somehow wanting to feel that all was right before they parted.

"Certainly," she replied, smiling up at him, and he noted with surprise that she had dimples.

"Tristan Rutherford-Hayes at your disposal, ma'am," he said with a proper bow, as if they were being presented to each other at Almack's.

"Miss Calista Ashton, my lord," she replied equally properly, offering her hand.

"It has been a pleasure to make your acquaintance, Miss Ashton," he said, surprising them both by raising her hand to his lips in a brief salute.

So brief that Calista wondered if she had imagined it. But no, if I had, then it is doubtful that my heart would be pounding so hard, he can probably hear it from where he stands, she thought. "Well, now that we are dispensed with the formalities, I really must be on my way," she said hastily, suddenly eager to be out of his unnerving presence.

As she made to walk away, Stanhope noted that a hideous, large gray knitted item was snaking out of her basket and dragging in the dirt. "Miss Ashton?" he called in mild tones, feeling that he had once again gained some control over the situation.

She turned to look at him. "Yes, my lord?"

His lips twitched, and he could not resist teasing her. "You appear to be dragging something. An, er, a deceased animal? Perhaps?"

With a look of outrage she snapped, "I will have you know, sir, these are stockings that I knit for the village children who are in need and can ill afford to purchase them on Oxford Street." She stopped, directing a penetrating glance at the expensive Blücher boots he wore. "You and those of your stamp, I am sure, have no such concerns. And now, as I am late to help Billy Trent with learning his letters, I will not detain you longer."

"The expected parting line, Miss Ashton, would be that it has been a pleasure to make my acquaintance."

"Would it indeed?" she replied, but to his amusement refrained from uttering the words, saying, instead, as she stuffed the knitted monstrosity firmly into her basket, "I trust you will enjoy your stay in Deepdene, sir."

"I'm beginning to think I just might, Miss Ashton," he replied.

"And by the way, my lord"—she paused, laughter coming again, knowing that what she was about to do was absolutely wretched—"about the horse—"

"Yes?" he queried.

"I do think that you will be so *very* surprised when you see her!"

"Why—" he began, but she had already turned and was marching down the road, away from him, her sturdy jean half boots kicking dust all over the back hem of her deplorable dress. She was greatly relieved, she told herself firmly, to be out of his company.

"Alas, it appears the pleasure was all mine, then, Miss Ashton," Stanhope called out to her retreating figure as he sprang back up behind his restive horses.

And it was, he reflected. In fact, he couldn't remember the last time he had been so well entertained. And unless he missed his guess, the lady was not going to take kindly to the news that she was the current topic of interest in fashionable London's most exalted betting parlours.

Seven

Miss Ashton, it seemed, had spoken no less than the truth. Moreford Park was indeed in a high state of readiness for his arrival, Stanhope realized with a touch of unease. The reception accorded him there was more in line with a visit from the Regent himself than someone coming to purchase a knackered horse. After driving up the long, poplar-lined road that constituted the entrance to the park, he brought his team to a stop in the semicircular drive. The house itself was a nicely proportioned Palladian-style structure of mellow honey-gold stone, boasting six impressive pillars at the front. Immediately upon jumping down, he was met by a groom of the chambers, who tossed the reins to a footman with instructions to see to the horses. With dispatch he handed his lordship's case to another footman and bade it conveyed to the Royal Chamber. "If you would follow me, my lord," he said, bowing, "I will announce that you are arrived."

Before Stanhope could object that he had every intention of putting up at the Horse and Castle in town (which was generally accounted to be a first-rate inn), he found himself efficiently swept inside. The simplicity of the exterior of the house had offered little preparation for the gilded rococo splendours of the interior. He had barely assimilated the grandly appointed entry hall in black and white marble with gold leaf covering every available surface, when Lady Lyttworth accosted him in greeting. "Welcome, welcome to our humble home, my lord," she cried, sweeping down the gracefully curving, Turkey-carpeted stairs. "You are come at long last to claim your filly."

"Lady Lyttworth," Stanhope replied, making his bows. "It is charming to once again make your acquaintance."

"Silly boy." She tapped him coyly, having arrived at the landing. "There can surely be no need to stand on points. *Do* call me Cousin Gladys. We are, after all, family—some say possessed of the same chin!—and it has been far too long since we have had a chance to catch up. Now, come, let Enders show you to your chamber. I'm sure you don't need a rest, as you young bucks never seem to feel the fatigue, but I will have some tea sent up—or would you prefer something stronger?—and you must desire to rid yourself of your travel dirt."

He would indeed welcome an opportunity to wash and change his dusty clothing, and tea would be just the thing, Stanhope agreed before beginning his protestations that he intended to put up in town.

"Nonsense." Lady Lyttworth waved his objections aside. "You will stop with us. And I shan't hear a word of cavil! I have such *marvelous* entertainments planned, you will hardly know you are out of the metropolis! You will be pleasantly surprised, I think, at what a congenial little society we are here—although I must warn you, a trifle more democratic than one could wish, but there is naught to be done about that!"

"That sounds all things delightful," Stanhope forced himself to say. "I promise, however, not to trespass on your hospitality a moment longer than is necessary to complete the transaction."

"Nonsense!" Lady Lyttworth waved away his concerns. "I refuse to treat this as a matter of business. You shall quite be one of the family, you know, so we will expect you to stay at least a month! Now, will a half hour suffice before your interview with the baron? A mere formality, of course," she hastened to assure him.

"That should be plenty, my la—er, Cousin Gladys," Stanhope replied, his heart sinking at the mere thought of a month's stay. "I am given to understand that my cousin, Oswald Cravanndish, and two of his friends are also imposing themselves upon your kind hospitality. Do I find them in?"

"Alas, they have not arrived as yet, as they stopped to attend a mill in Little Swindale on the way. I can well sympathize with your desire to have *dear* Ossie—goodness, I feel quite as if he is family already—present at this happy occasion. I am certain he will be entirely cast down to have missed it."

Stanhope tried not to allow his complete incomprehension of Lady Lyttworth's conversation show.

"But have no fear! The *filly* is here!" Lady Lyttworth continued, tapping him playfully. "This is all that is splendid! We will, of course, have champagne afterward to celebrate, and then perhaps I can contrive to have you spend a few moments alone," she giggled.

Wondering just how attached the Lyttworth family had become to the blasted horse—especially considering that she could not have been in Deepdene above a day—Stanhope allowed himself to be borne up the stairs to the Royal Chamber.

Thirty minutes hence, attired in beige doeskin trousers, a fresh white lawn shirt with a crisply starched cravat and a navy coat, he was ushered into the library. The baron was for once awake.

"Stanhope, old man. Welcome. Welcome," said the portly man striding over and pumping his hand. "Sit, do." He indicated a grouping of chairs in front of a crackling grate. "I trust you have been made comfortable, my ord?"

"Exceedingly comfortable, thank you," replied Stanhope, choosing a thickly upholstered red velvet and gilt chair.

"M'wife's in alt, naturally. Brandy? Make your question a little easier, eh?" his host asked jovially, missing Stanhope's puzzled look.

Stanford accepted the proffered glass.

"So, you're come about the *filly*," prompted the baron with what Stanhope could have sworn was a wink. He was not accustomed to thinking of himself as unusually dense, but there was no question that from the first he had been missing something here.

"Er, yes. I would like to come to terms and take her back to

London as soon as possible," he replied, trying to force a suitable enthusiasm into his words.

"I understand your impatience, son. Believe me I do," replied the baron. "I was young and looking to *purchase a horse* once myself, after all."

"Well, I—"

"M'wife would have my head if she knew I was saying this to you, but take my advice. Don't rush your *fences*. Court her awhile. She can be a bit tricky, this, er, filly. Needs the right *rider*, one who will *hold the reins* tight. Ha!" chortled the baron, thinking this horse-talk thing was easier than he had imagined. "If you rub along, we'll have our men of business settle the specifics. No need for us to sully our hands with the details."

His host could not possibly be speaking of the half-dead mare he had seen at Tatt's. "Right. Well, perhaps I could just see her teeth once again," Stanhope said, trying to contain his puzzlement.

"Of course. Of course," said the baron. "Understand perfectly, my boy. Have to keep breeding in mind, after all."

"I, er, actually, I'd not planned on breeding her, sir," Stanhope replied thinking that such a thing would, in all likelihood, prove an impossibility.

The Baron's moonish face registered surprise. "Really! Well, I confess I assumed you would want to. Seems a bit of a waste, fine bloodlines and all, but, er, up to you and all that." He shrugged. "Anyway, I will desire the *filly* be sent in. You can enjoy a few moments alone together, and then we'll raise a toast, aye?"

"In here?"

"Of course in here. Didn't think to find you so old-fashioned, lad. Not with all I'd heard about you." The baron clapped him heartily on the shoulder.

Stanhope decided it was definitely not his imagination. The baron *was* winking at him. Concluding it was none of his affair if the Lyttworths wanted to allow a horse in their library, he settled back with his brandy to wait.

Eight

Several moments passed before the library door opened and a stunning creature, blond ringlets artlessly arranged à la Venus, tripped in. The vision, resplendent in a peach muslin morning dress, sank into a deep curtsy as Stanhope stood and made a bow.

"Miss Sofie Lyttworth, my lord," she smiled charmingly up at him, dimples flashing, aquamarine eyes sparkling. "But of course you know that already. Welcome."

At that very moment a newly returned Elmo was in the front hall shaking the dust of travel from his shoes. "The Earl of Stanhope? Here you say?" he asked with delight as he divested himself of his multicaped driving coat. He dropped his gloves absently on a piecrust table and adopted a world-weary air. "I rather expected that, you know. He has come for the horse, I suppose. He cannot bear it that I stole a march on him!"

"Horse? What horse?" commanded his mother—who had met him at the door with the wondrous news of His Grace's arrival—in urgent accents.

"Why the bang-up-to-the-mark piece of horseflesh I purchased for Sofie at Tatt's," Elmo explained smugly. "A prime goer. Being stabled right now. Stanhope had his eye on her, y'know. But I stole her out from under his nose for a paltry hundred and ninety guineas— What is it, Mama? Is something amiss?" he asked at her expression.

Lady Lyttworth did not reply, as she had sunk onto a Grecian stool and was holding her head in her hands while the baron looked accusingly at her. "Well, how was I to know, George? I thought—"

"Thought what?" Elmo asked suspiciously. "Look, the other chaps will be in any moment."

"Your mother thought that his lordship was here to offer for your sister—"

"What! Stanhope shackled? To Sofie? Not likely after escaping the nets of some of the most beautiful women in London. Ho! That's rich," Elmo crowed. "Where is he anyway?"

"In the library with Sof—oh, my Lord! We must stop her, George, before she makes a cake of herself!" shrieked Lady Lyttworth as she rushed down the hall with the baron puffing behind her.

"Never say you left the Nonesuch alone with Sofie!" Elmo called after them. "He will take a disgust of us. Chit's afraid of horses! Whatever will he think?"

"This is indeed a pleasure, Miss Lyttworth." Stanhope vaguely recollected that the Lyttworths had a daughter in addition to the horse-mad Elmo. Gallantly, he raised her hand to his lips. "I have often been told of the beauty of Moreford Park, but I had not dreamed that it could boast such a stunning adornment."

She giggled happily. "La! You flatter me, my lord. Pray be seated. It would not do to make yourself uneasy on my account." Still smiling, she took the seat the baron had recently vacated, and swinging her delicately peach-slippered foot back and forth, waited expectantly. It was true that she was not sure what to expect, never having been proposed to before. To be sure, she was a tad disappointed that the earl did not appear particularly loverlike. She had hoped that he might throw himself onto the floor in front of her and beg for her hand while rhapsodizing about her face and figure. But her mama had assured her that the best *ton* marriages were arrangements and not to expect this one to be any different.

He was by far the most handsome gentleman she had ever laid eyes upon, and he had, after all, been swept away by her beauty. Sofie, generally admired as the diamond of her admittedly small social circle, patted her blonde curls complacently as she took in the fine figure her suitor presented. Her head swam with visions of her new life: shopping on Oxford Street, ices at Gunther's, trips to Hatchard's, carriage rides in Hyde Park at the fashionable hour, balls in the great houses of London, a box at the opera. And all of it to be accomplished on the muscular arm of this paragon of masculine beauty. Why, his eyelashes were even longer than her own and needed no blacking! she noted, sneaking a discreet look. She was roused from her rosy visions of the Earl and Countess of Stanhope as the toast of London society by the realization that he had not spoken further and, indeed, seemed to be waiting for her to do so.

"I trust your journey was accomplished without mishap, my lord?"

"It was a delightful journey. I have had far too little opportunity to spend time in this part of the country," Stanhope responded politely. "I look forward to getting to know the area better."

"I am pleased that you are enjoying our local colour," Sofie replied a mite stiffly. This conversation was not at all what she had in mind! He did not appear in the least worried or uncomfortable, noted Sofie with a hint of pique. Indeed, rather than trying to curry her favour, he seemed well content to converse as though he had nothing at all of moment on his mind. She continued. "It is the *most* diverting thing, my lord, we have so many entertainments planned for your visit. Why dull old Deepdene will be positively *lively.*"

"How edifying," he said dryly, giving no hint of the alarm he felt at the length of stay that was expected of him. *A month, at least,* Lady Lyttworth had said.

"Oh, yes. In fact, we are twelve to dinner this very night. Lady Enright is planning a dinner and musical evening. The Stanleys will host a Venetian breakfast. Mama has planned an alfresco nuncheon expedition for tomorrow. And, of course, there is *the ball.*"

"Of course," he responded with a smile, since that seemed to be the expected reply.

A crease marred Sofie's ivory brow as she wondered when he would get down to the business at hand and then kiss her. She was quite looking forward to the kiss. Judging by the practiced ease with which he had kissed her hand, it was an undertaking at which he promised to prove quite adept. His lips had been nicely dry and feathery, and the kiss had been not at all like the wet smacking Robert Enright subjected her to at every possible opportunity.

"Tomorrow's expedition should be quite droll," she said for lack of anything better. "Or it would be if not for the horses."

"Horses?"

"Yes. We are to *ride* out onto the Downs. And I," she confided artlessly, "am simply terrified of horses, beastly creatures."

"I can well understand, then, why you would prefer a different type of excursion."

"Ordinarily, yes, of course I would. But with a sportsman of your reputation to watch over me, I know I can rest easy."

"Nothing could give me more pleasure, indeed, Miss Lyttworth, than to be the one entrusted with the delightful task of watching out for your safety," he replied gallantly, and Sofie preened.

"None of the others will be half so safe," she assured him.

"You flatter me, Miss Lyttworth."

"Of course, everyone else rides like the wind. At least Elmo *thinks* he does. The Searle twins get on excellently with horses on account of looking so much like them," she confided with a ladylike titter before resuming her steady stream of narrative, "and the Squire Greystock and his fiancée (well, soon-to-be fiancée) Calista Ashton are both bruising riders. They are to be the chaperons. Mama enlisted them, and Mama brooks no refusals, you can be sure! But mostly the outing is meant for young people."

"Ah, in that case we will doubtless find it difficult to keep up," replied Stanhope gravely, wondering exactly what kind of antique he must appear to Sofie's dewy eyes. "Perhaps we could arrange some stops along the way so the elderly among us could rest their weary bones," he suggested, repressing a smile.

"You don't seem at all old," she reassured him kindly, "and Calista and Everard are, as I said, bruising riders despite their years, so it should not be a problem. We must only hope that the squire is not foxed, because in that instance he does fall off on occasion, and that Calista does not go all prosy on us."

Stanhope nodded with the distinct feeling that if he were to spend any more time in Miss Lyttworth's company he would know everything there was to know about the citizens of Deepdene. "I shall certainly hope for that, then."

Sofie nodded. "It can be most tedious when she begins discussing the need for equality—as she calls it—in society and literacy among the lower classes. Mama is convinced she is becoming addled. She does not care a whit about fashion and does not go in company overmuch, preferring her books and her good works," she explained in a tone that left little doubt as to her view on this.

So Miss Ashton was a prosy do-gooder. He might have guessed from the knitting. She would no doubt on closer acquaintance turn out to be a censorious bore and an avid supporter of the Society for the Suppression of Vice, Stanhope thought with disappointment, having known her type before.

Sofie, trying to repress her frustration with the way things were going thus far, looked up at him from under her long lashes as she had practiced in front of the glass.

The move was wasted on Stanhope who, despite his misgivings, was deeply conscious of a stab of disappointment at the news that Calista Ashton was spoken for. Not that he had any reason to care, as he had no interest at all in setting up country spinsters as flirts, he reminded himself. But she had seemed so refreshingly different from the women he was used to. And there was something about her that had stayed with him.

Sofie prattled on about tomorrow's excursion, and he let his mind wander back to his brief meeting with Miss Ashton. It was novel to meet a female who did not flirt or simper, one who seemed genuinely disinterested in—disapproving even of—his title and reputation. He had been distinctly amused by her pointed omission of a curtsy when he had introduced himself. And there was definitely a sense of humour under her prickly exterior. He couldn't shake the idea that she would be delightful to tease into blushing and smiling again. He hoped very much that she would indeed join them on the morrow.

Sofie, growing impatient with Stanhope's wool-gathering, began to tap her foot, almost forgetting to flirt. She decided to take matters into her own hands. This was taking eons, after all, and she had so wanted to appear at dinner a future countess. "I am told, my lord"—here she leaned forward and tapped him on the arm with her fan—"that you wished to see my teeth." She simpered up at him archly.

"Er, yes. Of course." Stanhope was startled out of his contemplation of Calista Ashton's smile. "Matched pearls. Each one more precious than any for sale at Rundell and Bridge," he replied automatically, trying to repress a grin at this outrageous piece of flummery. But Sofie was rapt, leaning forward for more. "In fact"—he looked at her consideringly—"you should never wear pearls, as your teeth, I am convinced, would quite cast them in the shade," he said, deciding as he did that it would be far safer for Miss Ashton if she did not join their expedition as he was sorely tempted to kill her. What a dirty trick to have served him!

"La, sir," Sofie giggled. "I am flattered, and it is true, my teeth are considered quite fine. Is there not, however—"

"Oh, Sofie dear, *there* you are. I vow I have searched high and low," Lady Lyttworth trilled as she burst into the library, her husband in her wake. Ignoring her daughter's puzzled glare, she rushed on. "I see you have met our most distinguished guest!"

"Yes, Mama," she replied, wondering what odd start her mother had suffered. "You told me—"

"I only hope you have not talked his ear off, naughty girl!" Lady Lyttworth paused for a nervous giggle. Turning toward Sofie, she said brightly, "Sofie, his lordship is amongst us for a few days to try to steal away your lovely new horse!"

"My what?"

"New horse, m'dear," her father said. "The one Elmo purchased in London."

"Just wait until you see her! You will be in raptures, my love. Our Sofie, you must know, loves horses beyond anything," Lady Lyttworth confided to a decidedly amused-looking Stanhope.

"Who's afraid of horses?" Squibby asked, coming in the front door on the heels of Lady Lyttworth's departure.

"M'sister. Already told you that," Elmo, still in transports over the Nonesuch's arrival, answered shortly.

"Well, ours are all settled. Capital pair already out there. Regular set of high flyers," Squibby said. "Truth to tell, old fellow, the new one don't seem to have undertaken the journey too well."

"Probably don't like the country either," sighed Neville as he followed Squibby in and sank gracefully down on the Grecian stool recently vacated by Lady Lyttworth. "Say"—he straightened up, and, pulling the quizzing glass from his pocket, gazed at a portrait on the wall—"ain't that Edmund Hartford's father? Didn't remember his nose quite that way though, not so sharp and ferrety-looking. What the deuce is his portrait— oof . . ." He trailed off as Squibby, aware of Lady Lyttworth's proclivity for lining her walls with amended portraits of illustrious ancestors she did not possess, elbowed him in the ribs.

But Elmo took no offense. "He's here," he said dreamily.

"Who's here?" Squibby asked, thinking that since their arrival in Deepdene, Lyttworth didn't seem quite right in the head.

"The Nonesuch!"

"Stanhope is here?" Neville goggled.

Squibby frowned. "What on earth is *he* doing *here?*"

Elmo looked wounded. "Came about the nag, of course," he replied. "Wants to take her off me!"

"Ossie ain't going to like this above half," Neville put in. "Perhaps he is just passing through on his way to some . . . *sporting event.*" He gave a little shudder, recalling his own inferior accommodations and the rough company he had recently been forced to endure in Little Swindale.

"We must warn Ossie!" said Squibby as he started for the door.

"Of what?" Ossie asked, entering with his valet, who was staggering under the weight of a waistcoat-laden portmanteau.

"Stanhope's here," said Squibby grimly.

"Where? *Here?* At Moreford Park?"

They nodded.

"Well, if that don't beat all!" Ossie coloured with fury. "How d'you like that! Conceited, puffed-up fellow don't even trust me to rusticate properly! Damme, if I don't have a word or two to say about that! Where is he?" he demanded

"Library," Elmo said shortly, pointing the direction. "With—"

But Ossie, deafened by rage, had already followed the direction of his finger. He strode to the library door and threw it open, only to behold his blasted cousin in conversation with perhaps the most enchanting creature he had ever had the good fortune to gaze upon.

"Oswald, how nice to see you again! What a coincidence that we should both descend on the Lyttworths' kind hospitality at the very same moment." Stanhope, apparently in fine twig, stood and said pointedly, "I trust you have made yourself known to our most gracious hosts."

Ossie, momentarily forgetting to simmer over his feelings of ill usage, made his bows to the Lyttworths. He cursed the necessity of his corset, which prevented his bow being as low as he felt this nonpareil deserved. Just then the remainder of the group burst in, and under the general babble of introductions Ossie felt a firm hand on his shoulder. He reluctantly tore his eyes from Sofie and found himself in a corner, *tête-à-tête* with Stanhope. His rage of a moment ago gone, he decided nonetheless to brazen it out. "What a shabby trick to have played, Tris," he said in reproachful accents. "Tracking me down here! Dashed maggotty piece of work!"

"Don't talk to me of shabby tricks, Ossie," returned his cousin, "when you are the one who bears responsibility for dragging a stranger's name through the mud. The unfortunate Miss Ashton is all over the betting books at White's! All you had to do was rusticate quietly for *four weeks*. I was under the sorry misapprehension that even such a clothhead as you could manage that without disaster. But no! And now, no thanks to you, I've been obliged to make this trip under the guise of desiring to purchase that blasted horse on which young Master Lyttworth foolishly threw away his blunt at Tatt's—and mind you, I only refer to her as a horse for lack of a better word. I don't suppose she stuck her spoon in the wall on the journey?" he asked hopefully.

A rueful smile escaped Ossie. "No, but damned close. I'll lay odds she don't see May."

"And now it appears I'm expected to purchase the Lyttworths' daughter also, who, I assure you, I desire even less than the horse," Stanhope muttered.

"Beg pardon?" Ossie stared at him.

Stanhope lowered his voice further. "In the name of an excuse that would allow me to extricate you from this muddle before you irreparably damaged this Miss Ashton's reputation, not to mention your own, I wrote ahead declaring my intentions of buying that flea hotel you brought back. But through some misunderstanding that I shudder to imagine, they appear to think I mean to propose marriage to the lovely Sofie. I've been cooped up in this library, fobbing them off by playing the nickninny this past hour."

"Marry her?" Ossie gasped. "She's exquisite. A prime article!"

"Try for once not to be such a sapskull, Ossie," Stanhope snapped, as close to outright anger as Ossie had ever seen him. "I'll tolerate the horse. I'll even throw away a ridiculous amount of blunt to do so. I don't want the girl. If I'd wanted a beautiful peagoose, I'd have plucked one off the floor at Almack's this age. Need I point out that this is not the type of scrape in which I am accustomed to finding myself, Oswald."

Ossie's corset suddenly felt as though it had grown even tighter. "I shall contrive a solution to your problem, Cousin, never fear!" he all but yelped.

Stanhope crossed his arms. "Somehow considering your record in the past, your assurances fail to fill me with confidence."

"Leave things to me." Ossie's tone was considerably airier than his feelings. "And as to Miss Lyttworth," he said hopefully,

"I will divert her attention from you! It would be a pleasure, as I for one can think of no fate more delightful than to be wed to such a diamond of the first water."

"You will not take offense, I trust, if I point out that not a week ago, Oswald, you were decrying the married state as a fate lower than visiting your aunt Ottile," Stanhope replied somewhat snappishly.

"That was before I laid eyes on *her,"* sighed Ossie gustily.

"And what of Miss Ashton? How do you intend to extricate her from this devil's own mess?" Stanhope asked in a pointed way that made Ossie reflect that the fellow really did not need a quizzing glass to make one feel like an insect. "I've half a mind to make you marry her, but she can hardly deserve such ill usage."

Ossie waved the thought away. "What can a few bets signify to an elderly countrified spinster? Not exactly likely to turn up in town! Ho? No need to get yourself in an uproar, y'know."

Fortunately for Ossie, before Stanhope could reply, Lady Lyttworth stood and clapped her hands.

"I don't know where the time has gone," she cried. "But we must all change for dinner. Let us reconvene in the Red Salon at eight of the clock. No country hours here! But remember, please"—her voice took on an arch, teasing note—"we *do* live *simply* here. Simple food and simple friends, so do not let us overdo the London finery, gentlemen, or you will quite cast us *poor* country mice into the shade." She smiled to show that she fully understood the impossibility of anyone eclipsing Sofie's radiance. "Come, love"—she turned to her daughter—"let us make ourselves ready."

"But, Mama—" cried Sofie, who had hoped to have in her possession a large betrothal ring with which to dazzle the dinner guests.

"No buts, my love," Lady Lyttworth said sternly. "Do let us depart." With that she swept out, leading her puzzled daughter.

Nine

A quarter of an hour later, Stanhope, the only person at Moreford Park to have completed his toilette, strolled the grounds. Darkness had fallen, and he could see his breath in the rapidly cooling air. This was well and truly the biggest disaster of his life. He could, he reflected, have happily boxed Ossie's foolish, plump ears and called it a day were it not for Miss Ashton's unwitting involvement. As a gentleman he had to stay long enough to at least help extricate her. Not, to be perfectly honest, that he had any idea how to accomplish that.

And something told him that the lady was not going to take kindly to the role of damsel in distress. He grinned, albeit reluctantly, as he thought again of the trick she had served him— really, it was unconscionable that she had let him plow headlong into this disaster. Wretched female. He wished her fiancé luck. The man would certainly need it! His smile turned to a groan. Whatever would this Squire Greystock say when he learned, as he inevitably would, of the scandal to his future wife's name? I hope he is not a hotheaded fellow, at least, reflected Stanhope, who didn't much care for the idea of meeting some country sportsman at dawn.

And truth to tell, he was perhaps just a bit piqued that he had come all this way to learn that by rights, defending the lady's honour should fall to another. Not that she was his type, of course, he reminded himself again—a country spinster of eccentric tendencies and no looks to speak of could hardly be of interest to a jaded sort like himself. The most reasonable course of action, he decided as he walked toward the ornamental trout-stocked stream, was to speak with the Greystock fellow man to man, hope he would be understanding, and depart for London at the soonest possible opportunity. Having decided on such a levelheaded solution, he decided to at least allow himself the thoroughly unreasonable luxury of resolving to dislike Miss Ashton's no doubt eminently eligible country squire.

From an upstairs window Lady Lyttworth watched the earl's exemplary broad-shouldered back as he walked toward the stream. Behind her, the sounds of her daughter's sobbing echoed, strengthening her conviction that Sofie must in this instance not be treated with kid gloves.

"You must stop this caterwauling on the instant," she said with resolve. "Flying into a passion will serve no purpose, and it simply will not do to greet our dinner guests with puffy eyes."

At this, Sofie, her eyes remarkably unscathed by her bout of hysterics, sat upright. "You cannot mean for me to attend the dinner, Mama!" she cried. "I can never face Stanhope again!"

"Nonsense, my dear." Lady Lyttworth gently tilted her daughter's chin up. "I am certain he thinks you a charming girl!"

"But I bade him look at my teeth!" cried Sofie, sounding decidedly watery again. "He must think me the veriest widgeon!"

"I am sure that his lordship did not even remark it," Lady Lyttworth assured her bracingly. "Town beaus are accustomed to all sorts of odd starts, after all."

"I did *so* want to be a countess," Sofie wailed.

"And now that you have met his lordship? Do you still feel the same way?"

"Oh, yes! He is so very handsome." Sofie sighed. "A fine figure of a man, indeed. One has only to look to see there are no false calves or buckram padding on him!"

"Don't be vulgar, Sofie," her mother admonished. "It is of much more importance that he is exceedingly plump in the pocket."

Sofie joined her mama, who was once again at the window. "I have never met a gentleman with such address! Or such *speaking* eyes. And I *do* think he was somewhat smitten by me. Truly I do."

"We are decided, then," Lady Lyttworth said approvingly. "It will be no difficult matter for you to charm him into proposing. After all, regardless of his purpose in coming here, he can hardly spend time in your company and remain unaffected, my love!"

"I suppose that is true," Sofie replied slowly, beginning to smooth her curls into place.

"Of course it is! I will ring for Trudy to help make your toilette and then I will go wake your father, who has no doubt decided that the most prudent course of action to undertake in this mess is to go to sleep."

In the East Wing, the rest of the gentlemen were also making themselves ready for the evening's festivities. The baron, blissfully unaware of the campaign to be mounted, was indeed catching a quick predinner snooze in his dressing room. Elmo was on his ninth unsuccessful attempt to form his cravat into the simple style that Stanhope had sported that afternoon.

And Ossie was trying very hard *not* to think of Stanhope as his man brushed out his curls. Truth to tell, he was just a little afraid of the fellow. Not that his cousin had ever treated him with violence, of course, but one was never certain exactly what lurked beneath that polished surface. And he *did* seem awfully cut up over this! I shall simply have to contrive a solution, thought Ossie. That, he reflected, with a long-suffering sigh, was the price of being the clever one in the family!

Ten

In the event that the guests finally found themselves assembled in the front parlour, Stanhope had no difficulty honouring his resolve to dislike Miss Ashton's country squire.

The party consisted of himself, the three London dandies, the Lyttworth family, Squire Greystock, and the Reverend and Mrs. Ashton—who explained to their hosts that Miss Ashton did not attend because she was visiting a sick parishioner.

"The gel has ever been subject to the oddest fits," the Reverend Ashton complained with a shrug. "Not as if the fellow won't still be sick in the morning, eh?" And the assembled company nodded their agreement.

No sooner had sherry been poured than Stanhope found himself cornered by none other than Everard Greystock, which gentleman immediately launched into a lengthy discourse on his own exploits on the hunting field. Listening with half an ear, Stanhope was aware of Elmo standing on the periphery of the squire's monologue, attempting to screw up his courage to the sticking point and actually approach his idol.

". . . and so I took the fence regardless, horse pecked a bit on the landing—I'd no idea there was nothing but rocks there, how could I? And I always bring a few extra mounts to a hunt in case a few go down—and Assheton Smith said, and I quote, 'Never seen anything quite like that before!' Heh-heh." The squire paused, chuckling with amusement at his own derring-do.

Stanhope forced a polite smile as he examined the man's

slovenly physique and food-stained clothing. He had nothing but disgust for any man who would risk a horse in the field. Surely Miss Ashton could not entertain warm feelings toward this gentleman? If she did, he had indeed misjudged her. Perhaps he was one of her do-good projects. Like the knitting. "Ah, Master Lyttworth," he said, acknowledging the lurking Elmo. "Come, join us. Mr. Greystock is telling me of his adventures with the hunt."

"I am to ride with the Quorn next season," Elmo, elated at such condescension from one so lofty, ventured. "I hear you sometimes ride out with them, sir," he added.

"I do," Stanhope replied. "And I hope you will see your way clear to stopping with me for a few days once the season is begun."

"I wasn't fishing for—honest, sir, my lord, I didn't mean—"

"It would be my pleasure to have you as my guest," Stanhope assured the stammering Elmo, who was overcome with gratification.

"Excellent pack, the Quorn. Enjoy riding out with them m'self," interjected Greystock, angling for a similar invitation. When none came, he continued in a confiding tone. "Cooped up here part of the season last year, y'know. Wife stuck her spoon in the wall. Saddled with seven children." He waved away Stanhope's murmured condolence, saying heartily, "No matter. Another season starting soon, hey? Plan to have a new wife this year to oversee the brats, er, family."

"Then it would seem that congratulations are in order," Stanhope replied coolly.

"Aye. My friend the reverend's sister." The squire laughed. "Bit of a queer bird, mind you, but she'll make a nice armful those cold winter nights." He winked leeringly, and blind to the quick look of revulsion that crossed Stanhope's face at the mere thought, continued. "Ain't been announced yet. Plan to make it official soon though. Looking forward to sampling the goods a little in the meantime." He rubbed his plump hands together. "Heh-heh. Man-about-town such as yourself understands these things, of course."

Stanhope forced a stiff smile but did not reply as he moved

aside to allow the Reverend Ashton himself to join their little circle. What could the vicar be about to allow this match? Stanhope wondered before deciding in the next instant that it was none of his business, and the best course of action was to force Oswald to explain all to the squire and make his apologies to Miss Ashton and then buy the horse and leave as quickly as possible.

Hermione Ashton, a tall, thin woman in a ruffled Clarence blue dress that showed off a good deal too much sallow shoulder, was in whispered conversation with Lady Lyttworth. "All here is not as it should be," Gladys Lyttworth hissed. Lowering her voice confidentially, she took Hermione's arm. As she strolled her around the perimeter of the room, explaining the change in circumstances, she noted that Sofie had chosen to strike an attitude—Venus in Thought—and looked quite becoming. Sneaking a glance at Stanhope, she was gratified to note that he also was gazing at Sofie, an unfathomable look in his green eyes.

"Never say he is actually interested in purchasing a *horse!* I can hardly credit such a thing," Hermione Ashton gasped.

"Indeed," Lady Lyttworth replied *sotto voce*. "Sofie, however, is most firm in her resolve that this little problem shall not be her undoing—you may depend on it. She is quite determined that he *will* propose," she said with a trace of self-satisfaction.

"Then, he will, of course. Of that there can be no doubt," her friend replied with gratifying alacrity. "Surely all that is necessary is that she set herself to charming him. With her beauty the rest must be a snap."

As the highest-ranking gentleman present, Stanhope was seated to the left of Lady Lyttworth at table. And since it was a simple country house party, that lady had decreed that Sofie might sit to his left despite the fact that she was not yet out. It transpired, therefore, that Stanhope was subjected to a lengthy discourse on the objects of natural beauty that they would see on their expedition on the morrow which Sofie had immortalized in watercolour. And thus, by the end of the meal, was even more firmly decided that boredom with London or no, he would return there at the earliest opportunity.

Eventually, the covers were removed, and the ladies retired. As the gentlemen sipped their port, the squire's forthcoming engagement was the main topic of discussion.

"Should think it would be a relief to have someone there to nurse you during your attacks of the gout. And since we never expected to get rid of her, she's coming at quite a bargain," Adolphus Ashton said, confirming Stanhope's black opinion of his character.

He was refining on this thought, when he suddenly became aware that Ossie seemed to have developed a facial tik. He looked again and realized that in fact it was a wink. And it was aimed in his own direction. Despite the wild panic that rose in his chest—no! no more winking—he carefully controlled his cool facade. *Whatever can the idiot be about now?* he wondered fearfully.

"Aye," the squire agreed, lighting up a cheroot and helping himself to another handful of nuts and the remaining half of a peach tart, which he topped off with a wedge of Stilton. "And you'll no doubt be relieved to know, my friend, that I've a mind to keep her too busy for some of her queer starts," he said with a lascivious chuckle.

Stanhope tried to contain his queasy disgust at this sally and the large amount of ribald laughter that followed and concentrated, in vain, as it turned out, on catching Oswald's eye to warn him off of continuing with whatever crackbrained notion had engendered the wink. His cousin, however, seemed to have developed an excessive interest in his plate, and Stanhope knew with a certainty he could feel through his entire being that the foolish fop was going to do something corkbrained.

"I've been thinking that a few babies'll put an end to those radical notions," Greystock chortled. "And what's a few more signify to me? I'll hardly notice 'em!"

"Cheers to that. And a toast to your being shot of Calista at last, Adolphus! I never thought I'd see the day that my good friend Everard would marry a radical bluestocking," proposed their host as glasses were once again merrily raised.

Stanhope was trying to decide just exactly from whom Calista needed rescuing more—his cousin or her own intended husband—when he realized with a sinking heart that Oswald himself was entering the conversation. "As long as we're toasting, might as well raise one to Stanhope," he said.

"No, Oswald—"

" 'Bout to get shackled himself, y'know!" Ossie continued by way of explanation in response to the curious looks that greeted this pronouncement.

I will kill him with my bare hands, thought Stanhope. I will. But he managed only "I am not—" before Oswald again cut him off.

"Now, Coz," Ossie said, "no need to be so circumspect in present company. Surely! Among friends and all that."

The others were staring at them with undisguised interest. As well they might be, since they are most likely about to witness a murder, Stanhope reflected. "Well, no, except, of course, that I am *not*— " he tried again.

"You sly dog!" Ossie replied, trying for a lightly teasing tone but achieving instead a begging sort of wheedle. "D'you mean to say you've neglected to mention that your affections are engaged?"

Fine, thought Stanhope, contenting himself with giving his cousin a long look that he trusted conveyed to that gentleman that he had much to fear, I will play it your way for the moment. But you will suffer the consequences. "I must have," he said, tilting his chair back with his long legs, an odd expression on his face.

Ossie beamed around the table at the assembled company. "Betrothed to Amanda Prescott. The playwright."

Stanhope, who thought he was prepared for any lengths of stupidity, had been in the process of raising his glass nonchalantly. But he had been wrong. This was beyond anything he might have imagined. And the port apparently went down the wrong way, judging by the choking noise that came from him.

The London gentlemen, who knew that Amanda Prescott had been his mistress, stared at him, mouths agape. Seeing his expression as he lowered his glass, Ossie hastily amended, "Well, not betrothed exactly. More of an *understanding,* really, but as good as engaged. Expect an announcement any day now!"

"Poet," said Stanhope in silky tones that he trusted disguised his desire to do enormous violence in the Lyttworths' dining room.

"Pardon?"

"She's a poet, Oswald. Not a playwright."

"Right. Close enough."

"Er, congratulations, then, Stanhope. Congratulations," said the Baron Lyttworth, whose drunkenness could not quite conceal his shock. "Played it close to the chest on this one. Never would have guessed. Wish you happy all the same."

Stanhope acknowledged the congratulations as coolly as he could, wondering all the while how the deuce he could ever hope to extricate himself from this dismal mess, which grew ever deeper by the moment. He couldn't exactly denounce his own cousin as a liar and a simpleton.

Not only had his attempts to rescue Miss Ashton been in vain, but he was about to end up leg shackled to someone he didn't even want to take tea with. "Didn't know myself until, er, quite recently, actually," he said, shooting Ossie a look that would have quailed a more sensitive man. Why, oh, why, had he been foolish enough to place himself in Oswald's hands? This news would be all the way to London by sunset tomorrow, unless he missed his guess.

Shortly thereafter, their host suggested they join the ladies. Oswald, however, found himself detained in the dining room by a firm hand.

"Be careful, Tris. You are mangling my cravat," he said pettishly.

In response to which complaint, Stanhope's grip only tightened. "I won't ask you what you were about, because I do not think I care to sully my head with what passes for thought in your tiny little brain," he said quietly with a glitter in his eyes. "If, however, you have not extricated me from this mess by the time I rise tomorrow—and I, unlike you, Oswald, rise early—I shall not only mangle you, but I will ensure that your mother hears every last bit of this night's work. And I hardly need remind you, I *never* make idle threats."

"Please, Tris," Ossie began to beg. Stanhope inclined his head almost imperceptibly in the direction of the footmen clearing the table, and Ossie, taking the hint, dropped his voice. "Please, just give me a chance," he implored almost in a whisper.

"A chance for what? To completely destroy *my* life along with Miss Ashton's?" Stanhope inquired softly.

" 'Course not." Ossie could not quite conceal an exasperated look at his cousin's lack of understanding of how to work a proper scheme. "I just wanted time, you see. Time to figure out how to, er, extricate Miss Ashton," he explained. "And, of course, to spare you from what in your opinion can only be the odious lures of Miss Lyttworth."

"Unless I miss my guess, neither of those are easily done."

"Exactly!" cried Oswald before recalling the servants and again lowering his voice. "But that is the beauty of this scheme!"

Stanhope raised a brow in silent inquiry.

"Well, doncha see?" Ossie rushed on. *"They* think you're engaged. Amanda don't travel in these circles, so *she'll* never have to know of the tiny little deception. Sofie will leave you alone and *I* shall win her!"

"And Miss Ashton?"

"I need some time on that one. But I'll put it right. Just give me a chance."

"See that you do," Stanhope said softly. "It defies reason that any of this can possibly come about, Ossie, but very well. As my only choices are going along with this ridiculous charade or exposing you for a fool and a liar, I shall go along—although I am clearly run mad. But only for a few days," he warned.

"A month. I'll need a month."

"I'd strongly suggest that you wind this farce up in considerably less than a month," Stanhope advised. "I am not the most patient of men. And now I'd recommend that you slope off to bed and begin your cogitation. I shall make your excuses."

"Thank you, Tris. You won't regret this," Ossie gasped.

"Yes, I will," Stanhope replied, turning tail and leaving.

In fact, I already do, he thought within five minutes of entering the drawing room. Lady Lyttworth insisted that she must have word of the latest London fashions and the *on-dits* on all her acquaintances, in both of which quests Neville was only too happy to aid her. So the evening passed interminably, and Stanhope was greatly relieved when at last he was able to make his way to the Royal Chamber, snuff out the candles, and crawl between the quilts.

Sleep, however, eluded him. I wonder why that would be, he thought wryly as he tossed and turned, thinking of tortures to inflict on his cousin. He had just ended a particularly satisfying fantasy in which he had consigned, one by one, Ossie's entire waistcoat collection into the fire, when, oddly, Calista Ashton's face came to mind. Whatever would she have to say, he wondered, about a merrily widowed, second—no make that third—rate poetess with good breeding, loose morals, and not one whit of common sense? Something tart, if he didn't miss his guess. I may be a good candidate for Bedlam, but at least things won't be dull, he decided.

"Engaged?" screeched Lady Lyttworth as she sat at her dressing table, allowing Trudy to brush out her hair. "Are you sure you've got this straight, George?" She squinted in the mirror at her spouse, who stood behind her. "Just how many glasses of wine had you partaken?"

Her long-suffering husband decided not to defend his sobriety—wisely, as he had consumed at least twelve glasses during dinner alone—in the interest of sticking to the matter at hand. "Well, more of an *understanding,* really. And I even know the gel's name."

"Leave us," his wife said curtly to Trudy. "Who is she?" she demanded immediately after the maid had quit the room.

"Name's Amanda Prescott," said the baron, savouring the feeling of possessing knowledge his wife did not.

"Amanda Prescott?" Lady Lyttworth's voice rose again. "It can't be."

"You know her?"

"Of course I know her, George! She's Drusilla Littlefield's eldest girl," she replied. "Amanda always was an ungrateful, foolish, headstrong girl. Came into some money—I have said time and time again that it is a great mistake to give a woman control over her own finances!—when Mr. Prescott passed away. He was much older, and she surely would have made him most unhappy had he lived more than six months after the wedding, which fortunately for him, he did not. It is rumoured that she is"—her distaste became apparent—"somewhat *loose* in her ways. Fancies herself an Original—you know the type. Taking lovers. Writing poetry. Holding salons, and all that. But the thing of it is"—she waved a dismissive hand—"that after the life she has chosen for herself, how she could even be considered fit to be Stanhope's countess is beyond comprehension."

"Perhaps he's in love with her."

Lady Lyttworth turned on her husband in a fury. "Don't be ridiculous, George! That is so . . . *gauche.* So"—she paused to search for a properly scathing adjective—*"rural!* So lower class! The *ton* don't marry for love, and mark my words: Stanhope is no exception! He needs a wife to preside over his many establishments and bear his children. Surely any fool—even you!—can see that Sofie is far better suited than one of Amanda Prescott's ilk."

The Baron Lyttworth either chose to ignore this slur on his intelligence or failed to hear it. "Well, whatever the reason, m'dear," he replied in infuriatingly calm accents, "it would seem that he is spoken for."

The baron's reasonable words served only to put the baroness into a further taking. She stomped her foot. "Do not talk fustian, George. Until the announcement has been placed in the *Post,* this means nothing. Nothing! All that needs to be done is for Stanhope to be brought to see that Sofie is far more suited to be a countess than that dreadful . . . *poetess.* In fact," she said in a thoughtful way that made her husband groan, "now that I think upon it, all that should be necessary is for him to have an opportunity to compare the two of them. . . ."

"No, Gladys." The baron sounded unusually firm. "I will not have you undertaking any schemes."

Her laugh tinkled through the room. "Schemes? Don't be silly, Mr. Lyttworth. I am simply about to pen a letter to my *dear* friend Drusilla's daughter, inviting her to round out our little party. I vow it's been an age since I've seen the girl!"

"But—"

"Oh, hush, George, do. Go to sleep. I've a letter to write." For lack of a better alternative, her husband obeyed.

Eleven

The next morning's ride out on the Downs and alfresco nuncheon expedition got off to a somewhat later start than had been anticipated. First, there was a messenger bearing the news that a vastly disappointed Emily Enright and the Searle twins were all down with spring colds and therefore unable to join them. Then Squibby, Elmo, Ossie, and Stanhope found themselves cooling their heels in the front hallway as they awaited the appearances of Neville and Sofie.

The first of the latecomers to arrive was Neville, who, at half past nine, joined the company to await the completion of Sofie's toilette.

When she did at long last appear some thirty minutes later, looking absolutely dashing in a pink frogged habit with military epaulets and a poke bonnet sporting a sweeping pink plume perched on her spun gold ringlets, Stanhope was momentarily concerned that the London blades might swoon with admiration. Sofie, however, after pausing briefly at the top of the stairs to bask in their collective gasp of admiration, had eyes only for the earl.

"Do not say that I am late!" she cried prettily as she twinkled up at him. "I do so hope I have not made you wait, my lord. I well know that gentlemen despise that beyond all things."

"Stubble it, Sofie," recommended her brother. "You ain't been on time above twice in your life! Spend far too much time making sheep's eyes in the mirror."

When Stanhope diplomatically replied that no wait was overlong if it resulted in such a vision, she giggled and took his arm. "La, you are too kind, my lord. Surely the belles of London society must cast me quite into the shade!"

"Ha! The crabfaced ones do that," Elmo crowed, which sentiment promptly resulted in him being the butt of lowering glares from the three London blades and having his arm snatched up by his mother, who bore him away for a whispered conference.

" 'Tis obvious you have spent little time in London, Miss Lyttworth, or you would know that no one there could compare with the bloom of such a perfect country rose," Stanhope assured her lightly.

"I told Mama that you would forgive us females our little vanities, my lord," she said with a glowing smile. "And do you know, Robert Enright *did* compose a sonnet comparing me to a rose!"

"Ah, very properly done, I'm sure," he responded.

"I do not recall it in its entirety, of course, but I believe it began: 'Oh, Sofie,' " she recited, " 'I do think/Is a vision/In her dress of pink/Her glowing bloom/Is enough to brighten any gloom.' " She lifted a shining face.

"I was not aware there was such a skilled poet in our midst," said Stanhope with a wry smile. "I've a friend I rather think he should meet."

"It was only Robert." She waved dismissively. "I've known him all my life. He is at Cambridge now. Of course," she prattled on, "since then, I have dressed only in shades of pink and peach!"

Stanhope expressed dismay that he was not to meet this literary genius as well as admiration for her considered wardrobe choices. And then, impatient to at least be on horseback, he tucked her gloved hand into his arm and led her outside.

There was then a further delay as Sofie, quite unable to overcome her terror of horses despite her mama's repeated admonitions that Stanhope's bride must prove her mettle in that arena, balked at actually getting *on* the beast. After much coaxing she finally agreed, albeit with deep reservations, to be handed up onto her new horse—who she had decreed would go from this day forward by the improbable name of Angel Fire. She reached to Stanhope for assistance in mounting, but he was very nearly elbowed aside and Sofie pushed into the dust as Ossie, Neville, and Squibby jostled to assist her.

Stanhope, who was not enjoying the feeling he was destined to play governess on a schoolroom outing, finally coaxed Sofie into mounting her horse, which had apparently dozed off.

After what seemed like days, the party had ambled snaillike out of the gates of Moreford Park and were no more than a few moments on their way, when Elmo, who had been completely engrossed in commenting in hushed but awed tones on everything from the excellence of the head on Stanhope's bay to the prime nature of his kerseymere tailcoat, cried out with something approaching distress, "Never say that we have forgotten Calista and the squire! They were to chaperon!"

Stanhope, who had been fully engaged trying to persuade Miss Lyttworth that she would in fact be safer with her eyes open, and who had assumed that the two had wisely decided against accompanying them, turned toward Elmo. "Where are they?"

"We were to stop by the vicarage and collect them above an hour ago," Elmo said before once again lapsing into rapt contemplation of the lightness of the Nonesuch's hands on the reins.

"Which way?" asked Stanhope shortly.

"Oh. Beg pardon." Elmo brought himself up and pointed down the road.

The party's progress was slowed considerably by the fact that Miss Lyttworth steadfastly refused to be urged to travel faster than a sedate walk. "I am sure that his lordship would have a disgust of seeing me injured should I be thrown from this *beast!*" she replied complacently to her brother's urgings that she hurry.

"As if the Nonesuch cares a rush for whether you fall, Sofie!" Elmo snapped, forgetting his mother's adjurations. "He is a goer among all goers! He wants to give the horses their heads. Not tend to a sniveling brat!"

The party was then forced to halt altogether as the dandies competed to offer Sofie a handkerchief with which to mop up the tears that threatened to spill out of her beauteous eyes at such monstrous unkind words. She was sufficiently restored, however, by Stanhope's patient assurances that many gently bred females of his acquaintance expressed a most natural trepidation toward horses to call Elmo "a prime clunch."

Seemingly against all odds, the little party eventually ambled into the vicarage yard. Stanhope had anticipated another lengthy wait while Miss Ashton made ready, but once again the lady surprised him. She was seated on the grass under a tree, reading a book, while a placid-looking gray hack nuzzled her ear. She was rigged out in a habit of a dreadful mud-coloured kerseymere, at least two sizes too large, topped off by an even more atrocious straw bonnet that looked as though she had plucked it from a scarecrow. Before she became aware of their approach, she turned her face up and nuzzled the horse back, and the sound of her carefree laughter gave Stanhope that constricted feeling in his chest again. She should have looked appalling next to Sofie Lyttworth, he thought, but for some reason her appearance was like a glass of cool water after overindulging in sweet sherry.

She caught sight of them and tucked her book away. "Good morning. Mr. Greystock has desired me to relay the message that he has ridden instead over to Little Elm to sample a new shipment that Lord Enright has just had delivered."

The gentlemen dismounted so Elmo could present them. Stanhope, who had decided that the best thing might be to avoid mentioning their previous encounter, smiled pleasantly. "Very nice to meet you, Miss Ashton," he said.

Why, she wondered, trying to repress a frown, was he not acknowledging their earlier meeting? "Nice to make your acquaintance, sir," she said, extending her hand.

As he bowed properly over it, Stanhope was all too aware of the scrutiny she was being awarded by the three dandies, jaws dropped, as they took in her attire.

Neville, his quizzing glass raised to better study her, muttered wonderingly, "Good Lord! It looks like something that would be used to drown kittens in!" Apparently overcome with horror, he mopped his perspiring forehead delicately with a fine lawn handkerchief and was heard to whisper before being silenced by Stanhope's glare, "You can't court her, Oswald! What if word of that habit was to get out? You would be destroyed!"

After greetings were exchanged all around, the party once again set off. Miss Lyttworth declared extremely prettily that she could not possibly feel the least ease upon the back of such a brute unless she was allowed to set the pace and as noted a horseman as Stanhope remained close by her side. To this Stanhope replied, as he joined her at the head of the party, that of course her comfort must be his first concern. Bringing up the rear with Elmo, Calista chided herself for the unasked-for stab of longing that went through her as she watched the earl pull his horse closer to the beauty in a solicitous manner.

Between rode Ossie, Squibby, and Neville, three abreast, arguing in hushed tones.

" 'Course I can't court her!" snapped Ossie. "I ain't such a flat as that!"

"No choice," Squibby hissed. "Already in the books at White's. Honest wagers have been placed!"

"That surely is of no account when one has seen that *habit,*" said Neville, rising to Ossie's defense. "Got a reputation to uphold, etcetera."

"Gentleman's reputation is only as good as his word," Squibby reminded him peevishly.

"But what of a fellow's sensibilities?" snapped Neville. "Anyone with eyes can only be cast into hysterics by that getup."

"Anyway, got half a mind to court Miss Lyttworth instead," said Ossie airily.

"Half a mind is exactly what you have!" Squibby glared. *"You,"* he said stubbornly, "are here to win the heart of Miss Ashton—which from the looks of her should not be beyond even your miserable capabilities!—so all the fellows in town will think you're off on a lark, trying to win a wager, instead of rusticating because your mama controls your purse strings, if you recall. And anyway, *I* am planning to court Miss Lyttworth!"

Neville intervened, checking Ossie's angry rejoinder. "Surely you cannot be deluded that Miss Lyttworth could want either of you! It is plain that she desires, no, *needs,* a gentleman of greater refinement! Such as, well, *myself.*" He cast a fastidious eye over their red faces. "Both of you possess a coarseness of manners and a lack of delicacy that can only cause such a lovely creature consternation." On that note he spurred his horse elegantly forward to overtake the riders ahead of them.

"Gudgeon!" said Squibby.

"Muttonhead," agreed Ossie as they urged their horses forward to catch up with him.

Stanhope gladly allowed himself to be displaced in the jostling for position that resulted and reined in to fall toward the rear of the party.

Meanwhile, Elmo was waxing enthusiastic. "He is not only an excellent sportsman, you know! He is a great gun!" he exclaimed.

"The gentleman seems a paragon, to be sure," Calista replied.

"And completely without pretension! He has ridden with the Four-in-Hand Club, after all!"

"Imagine! An out-and-outer like that riding out with the likes of *us,"* Calista responded dryly.

Irony, however, was lost on Elmo. *"And* he has invited *me* to hunt with him!"

Before Calista could formulate a suitably ecstatic reply, the object of Elmo's raptures himself fell into stride beside them with the rather prosaic announcement that Sofie was desirous of a word with Elmo about the arrangements for nuncheon.

"In all the years I have had the pleasure of Sofie Lyttworth's acquaintance, she has not once cluttered her beautiful head with such mundane thoughts as arrangements for nuncheon," Calista said far more coolly than she felt as Elmo spurred his mount ahead. "Why did you want to rid us of Elmo's company?"

"As it happens, I desired a word with you," he said, giving her a severe look. "Alone. Also, I am tiring of the tedium of surreptitiously jabbing Angel Fire to keep her awake—"

"Angel Fire?"

He grinned wickedly, and Calista's breath caught in her throat. "Yes. Newly christened. But if I may continue?"

She nodded, and he went on. "—all the while having pointed out to me every piece of shrubbery and natural beauty that Miss Lyttworth has reproduced in watercolour to the apparent raptures of her governess."

"And very lovely they are. You must ask to see them sometime."

"Somehow I doubt such a request will prove necessary," he replied, turning a speculative look on her. "And you, Miss Ashton," he queried, "do you watercolour?"

"Abominably."

"With more or less skill than you knit?"

"Oh, much, much less. My efforts were always more likely to send poor Miss Pratt, my governess, into hysterics than raptures. Her opinion was later soundly backed by the drawing mistress at Truffam's Select Academy for Young Women of Quality. Why do you ask?" She sneaked a look at him out of the corner of her eye to see if he was making sport of her, but he was watching the path ahead, his glorious face giving nothing away.

He changed the subject. "Do you always bring reading material on excursions?"

"Sofie has also never once been punctual. And I dislike to waste time."

"And you are always on time?" he quizzed.

"Assiduously."

"And what were you reading, if I may be so bold?"

"Vindication of the Rights of Woman."

If shocking him with her choice of reading material had been her goal, she failed. He nodded, saying equably, "Ah, the estimable Mary Wollstonecraft. You are reading her for the first time?"

"No. Rereading."

"Do you find you are getting more out of it each time?" he asked in what appeared to be all seriousness.

"You *read?*" she asked rudely to cover her surprise.

"I am generally accounted able and have even been known to do so when not overly preoccupied with the shine on my boots or shaving seconds off my Bath Road time," he replied.

"I am sorry. That was rude," she started to say, but broke off on seeing the laughter in his green eyes.

"No Miss Radcliffe for you, I suppose," he quizzed, and was further amused by the telltale blush that gave her away. "On occasion, perhaps?" he asked, lifting a brow.

"On occasion."

"You surprise me, Miss Ashton. I'd have thought you above that."

"Would you?" she asked without apparent interest, and then continued, before he could respond. "You still have not told me why you sent Elmo on a wild-goose chase. Surely not so that you could take a catalogue of my womanly accomplishments and my tastes in literature? I can assure you, I have few of the first and my choices in the second are eclectic. I am known in these parts as being a shocking bluestocking."

"Not to mention for harbouring radical ideas?"

"Indeed." She sounded impatient with the direction of the conversation. "Why did you wish to have words with me, sir?"

"I desired to converse alone, Miss Ashton, so that I could tell you privately what a complete wretch I think you!"

She opened her eyes wide, and he admired for a moment their unusual colour. "How unkind you are, sir," she said in dulcet tones.

"You well knew what awaited me at Moreford Park. Why did you not forewarn me that I was in the basket?"

"I'm afraid I misunderstand you, sir."

"No, you don't." The sidelong glance he sent her was so conspiratorial that she flushed with sudden physical awareness of him. Was he actually *flirting* with her? "Not for a moment."

She gurgled with laughter, thinking that she had best leave unexamined the reason for her instant lightening of spirit. "I am sorry. I could not resist. Do you not think she is lovely?"

"She *is* lovely. Her complexion is porcelain. Her eyes are aquamarines—or possibly sapphires. Her teeth—"

"Her teeth?"

"Yes. As I was forced to discuss at length yesterday, they are like so many matchless pearls." At his expression, Calista laughed again. "She is without question exquisite," he went on. "The dandies will no doubt come to fisticuffs over her shortly."

"And yourself?"

"*I* am here to purchase a horse," he replied stiffly.

"Really?"

"I am wounded that you would doubt me. The very horse, in fact, that Miss Lyttworth rides to such advantage, as we speak."

She cast a quick eye over Sofie's mount. "I should hardly have thought that horse in your style, my lord."

"My style might surprise you, Miss Ashton," he replied softly, wondering as he did why he was flirting with this woman.

"I doubt that," she retorted, the acid in her tone unmistakable.

"Perhaps I am developing more elevated interests."

"And I am Sydney Smith, sir."

He emitted a crack of laughter, and she admired the way his eyes creased and his mouth opened to reveal very even white teeth. "You have a sharpness of mind that may not be altogether becoming, Miss Ashton."

"So I have been told, my lord."

"And very lovely eyes," he said softly, his words for some reason causing Calista to shiver a little. "Which is why I have decided not to wring your neck," he added, his voice suddenly brisk again. "But honestly. Referring to prospective brides as fillies? I feel I have been done a grave injustice!"

"It seemed odd to be sure, but then, who am I to question the ways of gentleman of your stamp, or for that matter, Lady Lyttworth's word?"

He contented himself with giving her a black look. "And just what, may I inquire, is my stamp?"

She went a fiery red.

He lifted a brow. "You are not above listening to gossip, then, Miss Ashton?"

"One hears things, my lord," she replied stiffly.

"I suppose it was you who told Emily Enright who, I've had it on excellent authority, then told Rose Searle, who told Sofie, that I would be dissipated by drink, high living, and old age? Not to mention likely crippled by arthritis?"

She is so easy to read, he thought, enjoying the way her emo-

tions played across her expressive face, not at all like the so-
phisticates he was used to. But he suddenly, unaccountably, felt
sorry that he had embarrassed her. "You may rest easy, however," he hastened to assure her. "Sofie is certain that I am not
in the least like Prinny!"

"I can well imagine your relief, sir!"

"Indeed. It knows no bounds. But I've yet another bone to
pick with you, Miss Ashton."

"Another? And to think, we've only just met."

He grinned at her. "I think I was gulled into believing you
an indifferent rider, when you clearly are not." At her blank
look, he continued. "You told me yesterday that you were a
lamentable judge of horseflesh, yet you sit admirably. And you
assessed Angel Fire's worthiness in a single glance. You certainly deserve much better than that hack." He cast an eye over
her elderly mount.

"I am very fond of Tasket. And in any case, the vicarage
stables do not offer the variety I am sure you can command at
a snap of your fingers, my lord. I did not mean to imply that I
was ham-handed. I said *judge*, and that much is true. I am ever
being taken in by a pretty exterior."

"I doubt that," he said, and she knew they weren't talking of
horses. "And there is no need to get on your high ropes. I meant
to say only that I would very much like a chance to put you up
on one of my horses during my stay, Miss Ashton," he said in
that soft tone of voice that for some reason brought a blush
back to her cheeks.

"You are kind, sir, but I am quite content with what I have."

"Does that apply to your squire too?" he asked, still softly.

Calista drew up straight in the saddle, taking herself firmly in
hand. She had been perilously close to losing herself in those
laughing eyes and that flirtatious manner. The man had clearly
come by his reputation as a rake *par excellence* honestly. "I cannot see what he is to do with anything," she said in frosty accents.
"And he is hardly 'my squire.' Now, if you will excuse me, I
must ride ahead to meet the coach with the servants and see to
nuncheon, as it was I who arranged it for Lady Lyttworth."

Just then the little party that had made up the head of the

expedition fell back, Elmo clamouring to hear about the time Stanhope had felled Gentleman Jackson himself and Sofie pleading that he cease such indelicate talk as her nerves were already overset from trying to control the brute beneath her. By the time he had satisfied Elmo's curiosity—that he had, in fact, planted that gentleman a facer, not actually felled him—and teased Sofie out of her hysterics, Calista was long gone.

Following a substantial picnic of ham, cold beef, game pies, cheese, tarts, cakes, hothouse oranges and grapes, and iced champagne and lemonade, all served by uniformed servants, the party agreed to take a stroll before setting out again for home.

As they began their walk, Sofie stumbled on a rock. When Stanhope gallantly offered her an arm, she took it and clung to it resolutely for the rest of the outing. Which Calista, who had ridden away from Stanhope with substantial resolve to avoid that gentleman's company, found unaccountably disappointing.

On the journey home, Sir Oswald brought his horse into stride next to her own and rode the rest of the way by her side, rattling on at length about a comment that Miss Amelia Farham had made to him at the Sandringham's musicale about his mane of curls. "Why, to think," she had apparently whispered, "that Byron himself could even *hope* to hold a candle to you in that regard!"

Since the only conversational contribution required of Calista was to nod enthusiastically, she was able to refine on the completely inappropriate attraction she appeared to be developing to the Earl of Stanhope. Really it was ridiculous what the man seemed to have done to her with a few smiles and that husky, intimate voice. *I have no interest in gentlemen of his ilk,* she reminded herself, which thought lacked consolation somehow.

"And to think! I accomplish the thing without spouting any of that frippery poetry nonsense the fool Byron chap is so full of," Sir Oswald said, interrupting her musings as they neared the vicarage. Apparently taking something in her expression as agreement, he covertly reached out and took her hand, giving it a damp squeeze in his own, and assured her somewhat mysteriously that *he,* unlike some others he *could* name, did *not* subscribe to the old adage that it was not possible to make a silk purse out of a sow's ear.

Now completely nonplussed, she bid farewell to the rest of the party and turned up the vicarage drive. What she needed was clearly more work to take her mind off this silliness. She would prepare tomorrow's lessons, make up some calf's-foot jelly to bring to poor Mrs. Firth, who was down with a putrid throat, deliver some stockings she had just finished, do the flowers for the church, and by all means steer clear of further socializing with the house party from Moreford Park!

Twelve

Despite her admirable resolve, it was not with characteristic serenity that Calista reentered the vicarage. So the news that her sister-in-law was awaiting her in the drawing room caused her something approaching irritation. She thanked Annie, who had been her family's housekeeper since Calista was a babe, for delivering the summons, and turned toward the mirror in the hall. Removing her bonnet with a sigh, Calista set it on the hall table. Looking in the glass, she saw that she looked hot and dusty. Taking a deep breath, she steeled herself for another set-to over her refusal to accept Squire Greystock's suit, although, admittedly, over the last few days that topic had gone unmentioned. She stopped in her tracks. How on earth had the Earl of Stanhope known about *that?* she wondered.

To her surprise, Hermione waved to the tea tray and bid her to join her without so much as a word on her hoydenish appearance.

"The outing, I trust, went well," Hermione began.

"Very nicely, indeed," Calista responded, taking a seat across from her sister-in-law. "It was a lovely day for a ride."

"And the London gentlemen? How did you find them?"

"They were all that is amiable." And one, she thought, has the most devastating smile imaginable.

"I am agog to hear whether the earl's courtship of Sofie has begun!"

"It is difficult to say," replied Calista slowly. "He is all that

he should be. He seems very attentive and his manners are unexceptionable, certainly."

"Gladys is certain that she had detected a marked interest in
his manner—and she is in an excellent position to judge. They
have the same chin, you know! But," Hermione said, leaning
forward confidingly, "he *actually* came to purchase a horse!
Imagine!"

"Imagine!" Calista echoed, biting back a grin.

"But Sofie, plucky gel that she is, has set herself to winning
him regardless. So it can only be a matter of time!"

Calista did not respond but busied herself adding milk to her
rapidly cooling tea.

"Of course," continued Hermione, "there is the slight problem of his already being affianced—"

"His already being *what?*" Calista's hand shook as she wiped
up the milk she had spilled.

"Affianced. Do try not to be so clumsy, Calista! But Gladys
is convinced that will amount to nothing more than a slight
bother." Hermione waved away the notion it could be anything
more.

Calista hoped she sounded considerably more disinterested
than she felt. "How did you hear of this?"

"His cousin apparently announced it last night. More of an
understanding, really."

"But to whom is he *understood?*"

"I don't know. That is hardly the point—some poetess named
Amanda Prescott, I collect. But our Sofie is bound to put her
quite in the shade, you can be sure!"

"I suppose we will never know," said Calista in her most
repressive tone.

"But we will! *That* is what I have been *trying* to tell you. If
you would but listen for a change. Gladys has invited her here
to make up one of the house party, and I am all that is certain
she is en route as we speak! But enough about that. And Everard?" Hermione queried with an arch look. "Did he enjoy the
ride?"

Calista ignored the sinking feeling Hermione's confidences
had left in their wake. "The squire," she said tartly, "became

bored waiting for Sofie to complete her toilette. After his attempts to squeeze my knee met with the end of my riding crop, he recollected a prior engagement to sample a new shipment of port that was delivered to Little Elm."

Hermione frowned. "Oh, dear! I hope you did not give him a disgust of you, Calista," she fretted. "Adolphus also headed over to Little Elm, but *he* said something about discussing scriptures with Lord Enright. I only hope he will not return bosky and sleep through church again on the morrow. There was such a dust-up last time! I know the villagers expect some type of service, but every Sunday? Honestly! He *is* only one man. Well, I suppose that can be of no account." Hermione waved a languid hand. "I wished to have words with you, Calista, because as you know, not having been blessed with children ourselves, Adolphus and I consider you a daughter. And I fear so for your future," she went on. "Which is why I beg that you will reconsider Everard's offer."

"I have already given that all the consideration due it, Hermione, and I am well convinced that we should not suit."

"But what else can lie ahead for you? A post as a companion?"

Calista forced herself to remain calm. "We've been over this far too many times. You are well aware that I will inherit a small but entirely sufficient income upon my twenty-fifth birthday. I plan, as I always have, to remove to Rose Cottage and continue my work from there," replied Calista, thinking uncharitably that her sister-in-law's sudden solicitousness stemmed no doubt from fear of missing out on the fat settlement the squire had offered.

"But what kind of a life is that for a young woman?" demanded Hermione. "Just think of Sofie and the exciting life she will be leading as she assumes her rightful place in society! Do you not wish to do the same?"

"Assuredly not!" replied Calista as, unbidden, a picture of green eyes in a handsome face made her catch her breath. "And most especially if my rightful place in society is downwind of Squire Greystock!"

"Calista!" gasped her sister-in-law. "Such improper talk! He is all that is eligible! He has a lovely home and already has his heir, goodness knows! And he is frequently away hunting, so I am sure he will make no excessive . . . *demands* on you. The only thing he asks in return is that you give up that absurd reading and those preposterous 'progressive' notions of yours!"

"Even one *demand* would be excessive as far as the squire is concerned," retorted Calista, ignoring Hermione's shocked expression. "Let us speak of this no more. My mind is set."

"Very well, then," said Hermione, surprising Calista with her easy capitulation. "I confess I *am* looking forward to watching Sofie best this London poetess! Are you not? What a coup it will be for our little town, and, I daresay, Stanhope is likely already halfway to smitten!"

Having finally made her escape from Hermione's prattle, Calista sat disconsolately at the little escritoire in her room and picked up Thomas Broadhurst's *Advice to Young Ladies on the Improvement of the Mind*. Her mind, try as she might to improve it, kept drifting back to the picture Stanhope had made as he rode beside Sofie. What man, she reflected, could remain impassive to such beauty for long? *And* he had a fiancée he had not seen fit to mention! Not that there was any reason he should have, she admitted. So why, then, did his omission feel like a betrayal? Hermione was right though: Sofie would doubtless eclipse her rival and shortly be headed to take her rightful place in society. And I, she thought, am less than a year away from beginning the life I have so carefully planned. The devil of it was that the years of good works that stretched out before her that had always seemed so worthy and appealing now seemed suddenly and unaccountably lusterless.

What on earth can be the matter with me? Calista wondered, putting aside her reading and crossing the room restlessly. She spied her knitting basket and picked up a new skein of dun-coloured wool. She had just begun to wind it into balls, albeit without her usual zeal, when there came a tap on the door.

"Come in," she called, relieved at having her thoughts interrupted.

"Oh, Miss Calista," said Annie, her ample chest heaving with the effort of climbing the stairs as she stuck her head around the doorframe. "There is a footman here from Moreford Park with a letter for you. He says he has been instructed to await a reply."

"Lady Lyttworth no doubt, wanting assistance with preparations for yet another entertainment," Calista told her as she put down the yarn and swiftly crossed the room to take the missive. "Every available hand in the village has been enlisted for some task. I made no doubt I was next."

"Is it true that there is to be a life-sized ice sculpture in the shape of a man on a stallion in honour of the Earl of Stanhope at Sofie's ball?" asked Annie. Without awaiting a reply, she rushed on. "They are saying in the village that he is the most handsome man in England! Is it true?"

Calista laughed at Annie's avid expression as she broke the seal without looking at it. "To the first question, Annie, I had not heard that, although I confess no amount of excess would surprise me. And as to the second, I cannot say, the vast majority of my experience having been confined to Deepdene and its immediate environs. His countenance is pleasing, but surely you know it is beauty of spirit not of face that—oh!"

"What is it, Miss Calista?" Annie was positively alight with curiosity at the expression on Calista's usually imperturbable face.

"Nothing of moment, Annie. It is just that the earl asks if I would care to join him for what he terms a 'real' ride tomorrow after nuncheon." Calista hoped her brisk tone hid her wistfulness. "Of course I shall send regrets."

Annie, however, was not so easily fooled. "If I may be so bold as to ask why?" she queried with the impertinence of a servant who had known her charge all of her life.

" 'Tis apparent that I have more than enough to do here. There will be guests for nuncheon after church—assuming there is church," she added, remembering her brother's current whereabouts.

"If I may indulge in some plain speaking, Miss Calista?"

Since the question was purely rhetorical, Annie ignored the

trace of sarcasm in Calista's muttered "I would expect nothing less."

"Might do you a bit of good were you to enjoy yourself. Maybe even bring the roses back to your cheeks!" Annie crossed her arms over her substantial chest, which Calista recognized as a sign she was settling in for battle. "Why not let your wastrel brother and his good-for-nothing wife shoulder their own responsibilities for a change?"

"Annie!" Calista gasped.

"Just calling it as I see it, miss."

"I know. Plain speaking."

"Fact is, Miss Calista, it would not do to become a bore."

Calista's surprise registered on her face. "A bore, Annie? Eccentric, perhaps. Blue. Most definitely. I can accept that. But a bore!" She stopped at Annie's expression. "So that's the way of it, is it?" said Calista wonderingly after a second. "Well, goodness, we can't have that. So is it your deeply held belief that only a ride with the Earl of Stanhope can save me from that fate, Annie?" She raised a brow.

If Annie caught any sarcasm this time, she once again staunchly ignored it. "Yes," she replied, straightfaced.

"Well, then, by all means, reply to the effect that I would be pleased to ride out with his lordship tomorrow."

"Excellent. And about your knitting!" Annie seldom let an opportunity slip past.

"Enough plain speaking, Annie." Calista held up her hand. "Even I can take only so much in one day."

Annie left calling over her shoulder, "And, Miss Calista?"

"Yes, Annie?"

"You might want to consider wearing a different habit."

After the maid's departure, Calista stood staring at the closed door for a moment before striding over to her clothes press and yanking open the doors. "Oh, I might, might I?" she murmured to herself as she surveyed the garments within. To say that it was filled with lovely things would be an exaggeration, but as Hermione gifted her with her own castoffs, which Annie then altered to fit Calista's slighter frame, there was at least an abundance of respectable ensembles. She actually went so far as to remove a bottle-green wool habit with a smart matching hat before collecting herself. With effort she replaced the habit. Then she flung herself onto her bed in despair. She had been in Stanhope's company only twice, and already moral decay was setting in!

Thirteen

The next afternoon, at exactly two of the clock, Stanhope, on a splendid black horse, trailed by a groom mounted on a well-ribbed-up bay, rode at a smart clip into the vicarage yard. "Out in a tick," he called to the groom as he dismounted and threw him his reins. Which prognostication, as it turned out, was overly optimistic, as he had failed to reckon with the force of the elder Ashtons. A fluttery Hermione and a decidedly bosky Reverend Ashton were equally insistent that he stop and take refreshment.

"I feel sure that my teeth are floating," he confessed to Calista as they exited. "I take leave to doubt I have consumed as much tea in my lifetime as I have since my arrival in Deepdene."

Calista, who despite her firm resolve not to be corrupted by vanity was feeling dowdy next to Stanhope's splendidly fitting, obviously expensive tailoring, responded in her most damping accents that she supposed a life of roistering and raking left little time for civil occupations such as taking tea, and then immediately wondered what about this man brought out her most priggish, repressive side.

Stanhope fixed her with an odd look. "It might surprise you, Miss Ashton, to know that a fellow can work up a prodigious thirst roistering and raking, as you so succinctly put it."

She was preparing what she hoped would be a blistering set-down, when they rounded the corner and she caught sight of the horses. "Oh," she breathed, forgetting her retort and quickening her pace, "they're lovely."

"Thank you." Stanhope dismissed the groom, wondering why he should feel so flattered that Calista Ashton approved of his horses. What was wrong with him, in fact, that ever since she had ridden away from him on her high ropes yesterday, he had been unable to get her out of his mind? "This is Aurelius," he said, gesturing toward the bay, whose silky nose she was rubbing as she murmured nonsense to him. The vague suspicion that he was jealous of the horse nudged at him. Look at me with that besotted expression, he wanted to say. Stroke my head and whisper to me! Blinking to clear his head of that very odd notion, he continued. "He's one of my favourites. Spirited but not overly high-strung. I think you'll find him an excellent goer. And this," he said, patting his enormous black gelding, "is Raleigh."

"They're perfect. Utterly perfect," she said with a conviction Stanhope found gratifying. He helped her mount and noted that she sat as well as anyone he had ever seen. But when he complimented her, she waved it away. "I am country born and bred, my lord. I could ride practically before I could walk. My father was used to keep an excellent stable."

As they ambled side by side down a leafy green lane flanked by tall, shady beech trees, he was gratified to see that his hunch was correct: Aurelius responded to her excellent horsemanship as if he had been broken just for her. When she spoke of her father's stables, Stanhope heard what he instantly pegged as an uncharacteristic wistfulness in her voice. "Your father taught you?" he asked, truly wanting to know more.

"Yes. He did not believe in entrusting lessons so important to his grooms."

"Sensible man," Stanhope approved. "But who bears responsibility for the knitting lessons?"

She fixed him with a severe look. "I have been taxed quite enough on the subject of my knitting of late, sir!"

He bowed as much as his position on horseback would allow. "It seems I am forever finding myself begging your forgiveness, Miss Ashton," he said meekly, and then ruined the effect by adding, "What brave soul took it upon themselves to abuse your stocking project? I should like to offer them my sincerest admiration."

"Do you know, my lord, when you hold yourself in that very way—no, do not move!—just the way you are now, you bear a most striking resemblance to Lady Lyttworth! Especially around the chin. Has anyone ever mentioned that?"

"Baggage!" he laughed. "I should know better than to cross you. I am learning to live in fear of your wit." He spoke of her wit, but his eyes strayed, seemingly of their own accord, to her hair, which, he felt, was escaping its confines most charmingly.

Feeling his gaze, she put a hand up to feel that her curls were indeed coming loose. As usual, she felt flustered next to his cool good looks. "My hair will never stay put," she sighed.

"It's lovely," he replied softly.

Calista flushed with humiliation. Hoping to deflect attention, she said, "Thank you. For all that it does not curl nearly so admirably as your cousin's."

He slid her a sidelong glance. "Curl papers," he said.

"No!" she gasped. "But they are so lovely!"

"True. But sadly, he owes them all to artifice, as does, I'd hazard a guess, the lovely Sofie. I trust his secret is safe with you?"

"Of course." But honesty compelled her to add, "Sofie's, I assure you, are quite natural."

"Oswald will be consumed by jealousy. But I did not invite you out to discuss the coiffures of our various acquaintances."

"I wouldn't have thought so." She smiled, feeling suddenly exhilarated by the barely caged restlessness she could almost feel emanating from him. "Do you care to match your skills against mine, then?" she asked, knowing the answer.

He looked at her with interest, and she wasn't sure why, but she suddenly felt aware of the powerful, fluid lines of his body as he contained his restless horse with ease. "For speed or for distance?" he asked.

She grinned. "Speed."

"You will have an unfair advantage," he pointed out, "as you know the terrain."

"But I am sidesaddle," she countered.

"All the more reason for me to refuse."

Her glance was withering. "Should it be my understanding, then, sir, that the *Nonesuch* was afraid to race a simple country miss?"

"I see you are determined to be merciless, Miss Ashton. Where to?"

She thought. "Eversley Fell. Do you know the way?"

He nodded. "I do. It has been pointed out to me as one of the shining highlights of local geography in Miss Lyttworth's watercolour portfolio." At her grin, he asked, "Would you like a head start?" just for the pleasure of laughing at her look of pure outrage.

"I would not."

"You are not afraid, then, to be soundly beaten on your own turf?"

"Not a bit."

"Let us be off, then. Unless"—he fixed her with a challenging look—"you find you have lost your nerve?"

In reply, she offered him a bold grin and whispered something to the horse. She was off like a shot, clearing a daunting privet hedge. He quickly followed suit.

"Riding out with Calista Ashton!" Lady Lyttworth's voice was shrill. "Whatever can he be about?"

Sofie was holding various jewels up to the light. "Do you think he brought the Stanhope jewels? Perhaps I could wear the tiara to the engagement ball—"

"Sofie!" her mother chided. "You must concentrate more on bringing him up to snuff! There will be ample time to wear the Stanhope jewels after you are wed. It would not do to appear grasping—it is so *frightfully* common!"

Sofie put down her brush in horror. "Whatever can you mean by calling me common?" Her eyes pooled beautifully with unshed tears.

"I am sorry, my love," soothed her mother. "I am only concerned that things are not progressing as quickly as I would have wished. Remember that it is all that is essential for you to appear to advantage next to Amanda."

"Well, he can't mean to pay court to Calista," said Sofie with all the assurance of the young and beautiful. "The very notion is ridiculous. For one thing, she is *old*. And for another, she doesn't care a rap for fashion, whereas he is always dressed in the first stare of elegance—did you see the cut of his jacket this morning? He likely just needed someone to help exercise those precious horses of his. What else could they possibly have in common? She is likely reading him some prosy scold as we speak." She examined her perfectly arched eyebrows in the mirror.

Lady Lyttworth gazed fondly at her daughter's dewy countenance. "All the same, the sooner you have reeled him in, the better I will feel," she confided with a sigh. "Sometimes I think it is almost a shame he is far too much the gentleman to subject a gently born female to an excess of civility," she murmured, the beginnings of a thought glimmering.

Fourteen

The ladies of the Lyttworth household would no doubt have been horrified to learn that at just that moment Stanhope himself was wishing that he was less a gentleman. Dalliance with this particular gently born female was becoming a steadily more appealing thought.

"That was excellent. Really it was," Calista laughed as they slowed their horses. Her hair had come completely untied and cascaded down to her shoulders in most unladylike disarray. Her eyes sparkled and her cheeks were flushed a gentle pink. Her chest rose and fell rapidly beneath her hideous habit, Stanhope noted, swallowing hard.

"You do not even mind that I bested you?"

She fixed him with a hard glare. "That finish, sir, was neck and neck. Had I not so kindly saved you from coming a cropper by turning to warn you of the rocks, I should have whipped you handily!"

She looks about five years younger, Stanhope realized, feeling a jolt down to his toes and trying to remind himself that just a few days before he had thought her only passably attractive. "You are a formidable foe, Miss Ashton," he responded. "But loath as I am to point this out, as I am enjoying myself excessively, it looks to rain."

Calista mirrored his skyward glance and had to agree. "You are in the right of it," she said. "The weather at this time of year is capricious at best. We'd best turn back unless we want to end up with a drenching."

"I'm afraid so," he replied. And then, overcome by a sudden need to know that he would again be in her company before long, added, "But promise me another race. When we both know the course."

"Would you not prefer to ride out with some of the gentlemen?"

"I would not have asked, then. I can think of nothing I would enjoy more than another ride in your company, Miss Ashton."

She smiled, unable, despite herself, to hide her pleasure at his compliment. There was something much more approachable about the man on horseback. "Then, I accept with pleasure, my lord. No one in their right mind could turn down an opportunity to ride a goer such as this!"

"I am all to bits that it is not *my* company that attracts you," he replied in such wounded tones that she burst out laughing.

So it was that they were trotting along in perfect accord when the first raindrops fell. "I am sorry that we may be in for that drenching after all," he said, watching with fascination as a raindrop ran down her face toward her lips. She caught it on the tip of her tongue like a child. No, not at all like a child, he amended to himself as his pulse sped up.

"Don't be, sir. It is hardly the first, nor is it likely to be the last time I have been rained upon. And even the great Nonesuch—despite what Elmo believes—can hardly be expected to exercise control over the vagaries of the weather."

"That has long vexed me," he assured her, forcing his gaze upward from her lips, wanting, unaccountably, nothing more than to follow the trail of the raindrop with his own. "Alas, that power continues to elude me. But please do not tell young Master Lyttworth, as I fear I would plummet even further in his esteem. Yesterday I was forced to break the news to him that I have never fought a duel."

"Never!"

"Never."

"Well, that at least bespeaks more sense than I had given such a *sporting* gentleman credit for possessing."

"Miss Ashton!" Stanhope's expression was injured. "As I

believe I have mentioned previously, you do me a grave injustice!"

"And how did Elmo take the news?"

"He was crushed. But less so, I think, than his sister. Elmo was very consoling, assured me of his faith that there was no question as to who would emerge victorious when my time finally came, that it was only a matter of receiving the right insult, really. But Sofie said that that made me considerably less romantical than Robert Enright, even, who apparently put a bullet through the foot of some pup who dared step on her flounce at the Redingcote Assemblies. I think she would have said more on the subject, but just then Lady Lyttworth apparently suffered some type of attack as her elbow most mysteriously flew into Sofie's ribs."

Calista again burst out laughing, and Stanhope savoured the sound of it. "In point of fact, he did not. Robert's papa got wind of things and showed up on the field, threatening to turn them both over his knee as he was used to when they were lads. Trip Thorne, Robert's erstwhile opponent, was so terrified by the sight of Lord Enright in a towering rage that he discharged his pistol, nicking his own toe. I don't suppose either participant felt the episode reflected overly well on them, so they let the story stand that they had dueled. I imagine it was less wounding to Trip's pride to have been bested in a duel than scared senseless of a whipping from Lord Enright, who is sixty if he's a day, not to mention on the short and, uh, *rotund* side."

"Please, Miss Ashton," Stanhope gasped, wiping the tears of laughter from his eyes, "*you* might be able to control these beasts without a thought, but I need my wits about me." He looked again at the sky and noted with concern that the horizon was now looking ominously purple. "Is there somewhere between here and the vicarage where we may take shelter should the storm worsen?" he asked.

Calista shook her head. "But we are not long from the village."

They rode in silence, both concentrating on guiding the animals safely over the slippery ground. At first Calista enjoyed the rain on her face and the rich, loamy smell of the spring storm, but it didn't take long for her wet habit to start to feel leaden and cold. And when the first thunderclap rattled the sky, it took all her strength to control Aurelius's startled rearing. As Stanhope came abreast of her, he said, "We really must find some shelter."

She nodded. "It would not do to have one of these beauties injure themselves." He thought of telling her that his concern was more for her, but watching her valiant attempts to control the chattering of her teeth, he decided she would only cavil and insist on pressing on. "But I am unsure of where we should go. There is Lord Ardsley's hunting box just ahead"—her tone was doubtful—"though it is likely unoccupied and locked up tight this time of year."

"Sloane Ardsley?" Stanhope asked. "I've known him forever, and I am sure he would not begrudge us shelter even were it to necessitate breaking in."

"Is breaking and entering one of your many talents?" Calista queried through blue lips.

"Unfortunately, no. I am something of a novice, as doors are, of course, wont to fly open in the face of such a *sporting* gentleman."

The house was, as Calista had predicted, locked up tight. She huddled against the intensifying storm under the slight shelter offered by the overhang of the roof and murmured soothingly to the frightened horses. Stanhope left her and went around to check the back of the house for possible entry. Failing to find any, he returned and, removing his jacket and wrapping it around his hand, very capably broke the glass in a front window and then climbed through it. That he could look elegant even breaking into a house in the pouring rain, while she, Calista reflected, looked no doubt like a drowned rat—and a dowdy one at that—was a clear example of how unfair nature could be. A moment later he reappeared out the front door and relieved her of the horses. Her hand, where his touched it as he took the reins, seemed to tingle through the sodden glove she wore. She rubbed it against her side as he said, "I will see to these two. You go in and attempt to get warm. One of the advantages to breaking into a hunting box is that the horses, at least, are assured decent accommodations." He nodded toward the stable. "Judging by how long unoccupied the house appears, I am not confident that we will fare nearly so well."

But when he returned, it was to find that Calista had started an excellent fire in the hearth, and the dark kitchen seemed less gloomy. "Is there no end to your resourcefulness, Miss Ashton? I had thought to find you dissolved by the vapours and in need of a strong masculine arm to start a fire."

"Although it may surprise you, sir, I have never yet succumbed to the vapours." Calista lifted her chin a fraction.

"No, it does not surprise me at all." Stanhope turned away so she would not see his smile. "And I must say, it is a very lowering realization! Makes a fellow feel useless."

"Your ego, I am sure, can withstand such a trifling bruise, sir. Besides, I am not at all convinced I could have broken into the house by myself," she assured him.

"That is very generous of you, Miss Ashton, but something tells me you would have managed admirably. In the meantime, though, I think the wisest course of action would be if we were to raid Ardsley's clothes press and change into something dry. It looks to be a while before the storm will abate."

"If I recollect properly, Lord Ardsley is more of a size with me than with you, my lord. I hope you will find something suitable."

That her wet habit was making apparent some very pleasing differences between her figure and Sloane Ardsley's was something that Stanhope was attempting not to think about. For such a slight woman, she was surprisingly curved, he noted, stomping down his better judgment for what he assured himself was just a moment. "And then I will retire to the stables to keep watch on the horses," he said a shade too briskly.

"Surely they are fine?"

Her innocence somehow made her even more enticing. It was clear, he reflected, that she possessed no inkling of her own effect. He arched a brow. *"They* may be fine, Miss Ashton, but we must have a care for your reputation. What would be said if it became known that we were here alone?"

To his surprise, she burst out laughing. "I am a bookish country spinster of four and twenty, so far on the shelf that they need to take me off and dust me, my lord. And you are a regular out-and-outer, able to command the most beautiful women in London at the snap of your fingers. Everyone in town has known me since my cradle, and not only do they think I am absolutely incorruptible—"

"Surely no man, or woman, is incorruptible, Miss Ashton," Stanhope interrupted with a raised brow.

"But they know it is above all things unlikely that *you* would look to *me* for dalliance."

Oh, but how wrong they are, thought Stanhope, his eyes again wandering to her clinging habit as he valiantly fought down visions of just how enjoyable it would be to corrupt Calista Ashton. "But what of Greystock?" he asked. "What would he think?"

"Why on earth should I care what he thinks?" She turned a suspicious eye on him, but before he could delve deeper into her lack of concern for Greystock's opinion, she went on. "Besides, it would be considered a much greater sin in these parts were I to be responsible for the Earl of Stanhope—the Nonesuch no less!—taking his death of cold because I had sent him to freeze in a barn."

"I doubt that very much, Miss Ashton. But as sitting in front of your exemplary fire in dry clothing sounds infinitely preferable to shivering in the stable with Aurelius and Raleigh, who are excellent mounts but not much in the way of conversationalists, I believe I will accept."

"Good," she said briskly. "Now I think you should go in search of some dry clothes while I look for provisions."

"Yes, ma'am," he said meekly as he headed upstairs. When he returned a short time later in his too-small borrowed clothes, she had located brandy and tea. After shooing her upstairs to try her luck with Ardsley's wardrobe, he set about making the tea with surprising competence.

Although Calista had been hard pressed not to smirk at his impeccably tailored lordship attired thus, she was forced to admit ruefully to herself, as she looked in the glass, that she hadn't fared much better. She was rigged out in a white lawn shirt that reached almost to her knees, and pantaloons that she had to roll up to avoid tripping over. Having decided that the fabric of the shirt was too thin, she had topped off the ensemble with a highly patterned maroon satin dressing gown with a tasseled cord around the waist.

At her entrance into the kitchen, even Stanhope's legendary sangfroid deserted him. "Oh my. You do look . . . dry," he said.

"As do you, sir," she replied pertly. "Although for me, it is less of a comedown."

When they had finished laughing, he motioned her to the kitchen table. As she followed his directive, she tripped over the hem of the overlong robe, and Stanhope put out a hand to steady her. Again she almost jumped as his touch seemed to burn through her sleeve. With difficulty she kept her eyes down.

Stanhope noticed her nervousness and wanted to put her at ease. Truth to tell, he was feeling some unaccustomed nerves himself. "I shall certainly have a word with Sloane, when next I see him, about the paltry wardrobe he leaves for house-breakers," he said as he busied himself pouring them both lib-eral glasses of brandy. At her demur that she had never before drunk the stuff—indeed Hannah More warned most strongly against its consumption—he assured her in tones that brooked no argument that it was just the thing to ward off a chill after a drenching, and he doubted at any rate that licentiousness would overtake her from one glass. "So stop lecturing and drink up," he advised, raising his own.

She did, and when she was done spluttering found that she quite liked the spreading warmth the amber liquid left in its wake. "I can well see why gentlemen prefer this to ratafia," she said.

He shivered. "Vile stuff. It is perhaps the worst of the priva-tions your sex suffers."

"Hardly that, my lord," she responded with a look that made him regret his frivolous assertion. And then somehow or other all trace of awkwardness between them was gone as they were off on an impassioned discussion of Hannah More's work. Cal-ista professed complete admiration for that lady, but Stanhope countered that while many of her goals were worthwhile, her

Society for the Suppression of Vice as a whole was censorious and repressive.

Trying to focus on Calista's words rather than on the fresh lavender scent of her drying hair, Stanhope reached over and poured her another glass of brandy. He admired the high colour in her cheeks and the sparkle in her eye as she explained tartly that the reason he didn't *fully* agree with Hannah More was clearly due to his failure to read the entire transcript of the statement of proceedings read at the 12 November 1804 general meeting of the society. He replied that the more likely reason was his own conviction that vice was infinitely more fun than virtue but agreed to borrow her copy nonetheless. As she laughed, his hand reached out to refill her glass seemingly of its own accord.

She told him, wondering as she did why she was opening up to this man, of her early life in Deepdene and her parents' untimely death—the boat carrying them to a tour of Italy had sunk—and the subsequent discovery that her father's affairs had been in shambles. Walter Ashton had apparently been a fascinating, learned gentleman as well as a bruising rider but possessed of a lamentable head for business. Almost all the money was gone, the unentailed house had been sold, and Adolphus, woefully unprepared for employment, had been forced to enter the clergy. Stanhope was so touched by the way her eyes pooled with tears, which she self-consciously brushed away, that he had to fight his desire to take her into his arms and console her, instead pouring her what he assured himself was merely a steadying shot of brandy.

Before he knew it, he was confiding the tale of Oswald's disgrace at the hands of Sally Jersey's punch fountain and the dowager viscountess's decree and his own subsequent pursuit—feeling only a twinge of guilt at his omission of her own unwitting involvement.

"So," Calista said, "that is the true tale of how you came to find yourself here. I had thought your overweening desire to own that particular horse rather suspect! You must find Deepdene sadly flat after London?"

"Not at all," he said lightly. "In fact, I am finding it unexpectedly diverting." His mesmerizing eyes held hers. "Calista is a very unusual name."

Nonplussed by his change of topic, she said, "My father chose it. Mama was used to say he was in a Greek phase when I was born."

"Do you know Greek?" he asked with interest.

She nodded. "And Latin."

"Then you know it means 'most beautiful.' Suits you." His eyes were unreadable, almost black in the dim light, and his voice had taken on a husky note.

"I am hardly 'most beautiful,' my lord," she replied repressively, reminding herself that the thing that separates a mere flirt from an extraordinarily successful flirt is the ability to make one believe the flummery is sincere. "Although it is kind of you to say so."

"I take leave to disagree, Miss Ashton." He reached across and, somehow unable to stop himself, took her hand in his and began gently to stroke the backs of her fingers. She looked down at her hand, small in both of his large ones, and tried to will it to move. But it seemed curiously unattached to her body, except for the little tingling trails of fire that shot up it every time he moved the ball of his thumb. She shivered with the sensation, feeling as if every nerve in her body was suddenly centered in her hand. "In fact"——his voice was almost a whisper——"it is the damnedest thing, but the more I am in your company, the lovelier you seem to become."

Calista tried to think of a damping reply, but her voice seemed stricken by that same curious immobility as her arm.

Stanhope was suddenly conscious of an overwhelming and shocking desire to kiss Calista Ashton. And to run his hands through that luxuriant hair and bury his face in its fragrance. And then to kiss her again and elicit a sigh of pleasure from those lovely lips. And to remove that ridiculous robe and trail kisses down her graceful neck onto the creamy flesh that lay below the shirt. Unbidden, he thought of the huge, no doubt damp and musty four-poster abovestairs. How smooth her skin would feel under his hands. And she would be a delight to lie with afterward. We could laugh and talk of ideas, of literature,

of Mary Wollstonecraft and Robert Owen, he thought wistfully.
He looked at her startled eyes and was scandalized by his own
sudden violent longing. He was hardly in the business of seducing virgins, he reminded himself sternly. Gently, he disengaged his hands, leaving Calista feeling colder than her wet
clothing had.

Resolutely stoppering the brandy decanter, he said with an
enthusiasm he was far from feeling, "What *your* education has
clearly lacked thus far, and what you need, Miss Ashton, is to
learn to play cards and swear." Not meeting her eyes, he headed
to the back parlour and searched the drawers of a desk until he
was able to return with some equanimity and a pack of cards.

Fifteen

Next morning Calista awoke with a splitting headache. When Annie bustled in with a tray of chocolate and a mouthful of admonitions that it was time to rise and shine or else be late for the Venetian breakfast, she longed for nothing more than to pull the covers back over her head and erase her memories of the previous afternoon.

So engrossed had they become in their game of piquet that it had come as quite a shock to discover the storm had rained itself out and the sky was clear in the rapidly falling dusk. Although she had behaved like the veriest wanton—gaming, swearing, drinking brandy, and donning men's clothing—Calista was not so gone to all propriety as to think they could return to the vicarage together and announce where they had been. After changing back into her still-damp habit, she had insisted, brooking no argument from him, that they ride back separately and put it about that they had parted just before the storm and waited it out in different shelters.

In the end, as it turned out, Calista's return went unremarked by anyone except Annie, Hermione having taken to her bed with a megrim, or possibly a spasm, and Adolphus having gone to dine with Squire Greystock. She had slipped quietly up to her room after telling Annie not to fuss, and taken supper on a tray, which Annie noted went back to the kitchen barely touched, and retired early. If Annie privately thought she detected fumes from strong spirits, she kept this intelligence to herself.

Calista had sought her bed more from a longing for privacy

than any real need to sleep, and unconsciousness had been maddeningly slow in coming. Stanhope's accusation that she had done him a grave injustice was true, she ruefully acknowledged. She had assumed that he would be empty-headed, dedicated only to the pursuit of sport and pleasure. Instead, he had turned out to be possessed of a fine intellect and a sharp, ready wit. Not to mention more devastating charm and good looks than any one man should reasonably possess. Cursing herself for a pathetic fool, she recalled how he had looked in the firelight, tilting his chair back on two legs and laughing as he dealt her a resounding defeat at cards. His eyes had sparkled and her own had been drawn to that mesmerizing, finely etched mouth as a moth to a flame. She had noticed, despite her stern warnings to herself, the way his muscular body filled out his too-tight borrowed clothes and the way his silky dark hair fell slightly over his forehead as it dried.

Sleep the previous night had also eluded His Lordship, the Earl of Stanhope. If anything, he had spent even more restless a night than Calista. He had lain staring at the bed hangings until, as the night thinned into the small hours of the morning, he had thrown the covers aside and risen. He paused to pull on a pair of trousers and a shirt, then strode restlessly to the French doors that led to a balcony off his room. Pulling them open, he walked out and gratefully inhaled the cool, misty air. He stood staring out at the grounds in the waning moonlight and relived in his mind for what seemed like the hundredth time the afternoon he had shared with Calista Ashton.

He had been so close to kissing her, and then God knows where he would have stopped. The fact of it was that the spinsterish, inexperienced Miss Ashton, with her abominable dresses and her lively mind, had awakened something in him. He had wanted her with a longing so fierce, he had almost succumbed to it there and then. And whatever scandalous transgressions had been his to claim in his lifetime, taking innocents to his bed had never been among them. But this desire for her . . . suffice it to say, he had never felt this way before.

And he had seen an answering hunger in her eyes that he knew she did not yet understand. But he certainly did.

The damnable thing was that instead of feeling relief that he had not taken advantage of their situation, he felt . . . *regret*. Making love to Calista Ashton, he reminded himself, is not the same as bedding someone more worldly wise. It would have repercussions. *Marriage,* for example, he told himself harshly. But to his surprise, that thought did not fill him with dread. In fact, it did not seem to diminish his yearning for her in the least.

It is only lust, he had told himself at first, a simple result of having pensioned off Rosamunde and Amanda. But as the night had worn on, he had been forced to concede it was more than just the effect of his self-imposed celibacy.

As much as he wanted to be the one to awaken the passion he knew Calista was capable of, he was also conscious of the deep desire to hear her laugh, to smooth her curls away from her face when she was tired, to feel the bite of her wit, and to learn her no doubt lively opinions on a great many more topics. He wanted to introduce her to his mother. *Introduce her to his mother?* The thought brought him up short, and he stood up straighter as he contemplated the thought of what such an introduction would mean. Here he was, brushing up against the idea of marriage. Again. And still no sense of crushing doom. Actually, come to think of it, it sounded rather nice. The thought of marriage to Calista seemed to have aroused a tenderness in him that felt foreign but, somehow, pleasant. He suddenly wanted desperately to give her the protection of his heart and his name. To rescue her. From her odious brother, her shockingly inappropriate fiancé, his own idiot cousin, all of stuffy, unimaginative Deepdene, anyone, in fact, who could not appreciate her true uniqueness. Why not? None of them, after all, would hold any power over her if she were my countess, he thought with a trace of arrogance. Then he grinned. This was definitely one maiden who would hardly appreciate his chivalry.

There was, of course, the slight problem that he hardly knew the lady. And if he were to refine on *all* the negatives of the thing, she *was* engaged. And if she didn't know about his own bogus alliance to Amanda, she surely would soon. Not to mention the fact he was no doubt expected to offer for the radiant Sofie at any moment. And, of course, there was also the small issue of her being the unknowing subject of thousands of pounds worth of wagers at the hands of his cousin. The thought of all the difficulties brought a groan to his lips.

But in his heart he knew. *My heart,* he thought in surprise, having always assumed that particular organ to be impenetrable. She was the woman he had waited his entire life to meet. And whether he had known her an hour or ten years made no difference.

Under other circumstances, his impulse would be that she needed to be courted slowly. But considering the obstacles, sweeping her off her feet might be the smarter choice. He would need to cut Greystock out, and it was all but urgent that he release them both from the cloud of danger presented by Oswald's attempts to right the situation. He would start immediately by sending over some of his valet's hangover remedy, which, he thought, should at least show her that he was a suitor with a serious and practical turn of mind. Another man, or even himself under different circumstances, would have sent expensive bouquets, which his beloved was bound to find frivolous. Then, at the Venetian breakfast, he would lure her to a secluded spot and kiss her. Preferably until they were both senseless. It was not at all the reasoned type of decision he was used to making, but truth to tell, he was clearly lost to all reason where Miss Ashton was concerned. And, he had to admit, enjoying it thoroughly.

Feeling better now that he had at least settled on a course of action, Stanhope had returned inside, stripped off his clothes, and fallen into bed. He had been asleep in a time that would have made the Baron Lyttworth envious.

She was naught but a foolish old maid, Calista reminded herself harshly under the lowering effects of her headache the next morning. Stanhope was disgraceful. He was a rake. He was engaged. And were he not, she told herself bluntly, a man who could command Sofie Lyttworth or a hundred such beauties in an instant would surely look elsewhere for a bride or even real diversion. But for one blissful moment when she had thought he was about to kiss her . . . The thought brought her up short. Was she truly willing to provide diversion for him? Hopefully, it was the brandy, she thought, as she stood in front of her clothes press, or next I will be damping my petticoats and flirting with every eligible gentleman in town from behind a fan. Stanhope undoubtedly thought her a dull elderly spinster with whom to while away a rainy afternoon, and nothing more. And she, anyway, had no use for this type of flirtation.

Calista was still standing, woolgathering, in front of the clothes press, when Annie knocked on the door. Wearing her best I'm-not-saying-a-word expression, for which Calista was supremely grateful, the maid handed her a bottle and a note.

Seeing Stanhope's seal on the letter, Calista schooled herself to appear expressionless. "My Dear Miss Ashton," he had written. "I have found this draught to be remarkably efficacious for the aftereffects of an overindulgence of spirits and any associated headache. Your Servant, Stanhope. P.S. I have decided to forgive your gambling debts."

Calista surmised from the tone of his letter that their idyll had meant even less than nothing to him. Some women probably receive flowers and love letters she thought wryly, taking a sniff of the evil-smelling stuff. And I was not foxed! Nonetheless she took a swig of the liquid and choked at the vile taste. It did seem to help, however, and she managed to say, "The yellow wool today, I think, Annie."

"Oh, Miss Calista, not the yellow wool!" Annie gasped as though Calista had apprised her of plans to go abroad in her shift.

"The yellow wool, Annie. I shan't attend the breakfast. I plan, instead, to give the schoolroom a thorough cleaning." She adopted as imperious a voice as she was able. "And do be gentle when you brush out my hair."

Ignoring Annie's mulish expression, Calista took a seat before the mirror. "Ouch," she shrieked a moment later as a brush was dragged through the tangles a shade more briskly than might have been strictly necessary. "Whatever are you about?"

"Just brushing out your hair, Miss Calista."

"Well, be more careful!"

"Sorry. I guess my mind was wandering as to how Lady Enright said if you were to try to weasel—and that was her exact word, weasel—out of any entertainments, I was to send a message straight round to her. I'm guessing that Jim can be spared to run it over."

"You are in league with her? Against me?" Calista gasped.

Annie was imperturbable. "Yes, miss. I'm afraid so."

"Well, of all the—" Calista brought herself up short before one of the new words she had learned from Stanhope could have a chance to escape her. "Uh, never mind! Very well, then, Annie. I know when I am outmaneuvered, but," she said, clutching the last shred of independence she could, "I will wear the yellow."

"Yes, Miss Calista." Annie too knew when she had pushed as far as possible.

"And the olive pelisse, if you please," Calista added. And resolutely ignoring Annie's expression, she climbed into the bath.

Sixteen

As it turned out, Stanhope's resolved course of action did not fall out exactly as planned.

He was in the breakfast room, partaking of a cup of coffee, feeling, despite his lack of sleep, energetic and, even in the sobering light of day, well pleased with his decision.

"Is my cousin about yet?" he asked Neville as he helped himself to some coddled eggs and a slice of ham from the sideboard.

"He is making his toilette. *Still*," sniffed Neville, who was delicately consuming a piece of dry toast.

Squibby carried over a heavily loaded plate. "Stubble it, Nev," he mumbled, mouth full, as he tucked in. "You rose at five of the clock to make yourself ready. Not," he continued as, still chewing, he raked an eye over Neville's capucine pantaloons, waistcoat, and nip-waisted coat, "that your care is the least bit apparent. Too sleepy to see what you were putting on, I collect?"

"Coming from a coxcomb such as yourself, that ain't exactly stinging," Neville retorted.

Stanhope, who felt not even their sniping could ruin his good mood that morning, but who privately felt some sympathy with Squibby's expressed opinion, broke in, hoping to defuse the situation. "And where, if I may inquire, is Elmo?"

"Abovestairs blacking his boots with a bottle of his father's best champagne. Heard that's what you use," Squibby supplied.

Stanhope lifted a brow. *"That's* what you young bucks spend your time discussing?"

"Been known to," admitted Squibby, loath to reveal just how many hours he personally had spent in thrall by talk of that very topic. "It is said, you know"—he lowered his voice—"that your mixture is a carefully guarded secret, sir."

"Is it?"

Squibby was scarce able to believe his good fortune that on his return to town he would be able to boast of having chatted tête-à-tête about bootblacking with the Nonesuch. *How do I get such a shine?* he could hear himself saying. *Why, just a little secret I picked up from the Earl of Stanhope.* "Do you use champagne, sir?" he ventured to ask.

"Waste good champagne on boots? I certainly hope not."

At their crestfallen faces, he took pity on them. "In truth, I've no idea what my man uses," he confessed. "Bootblacking, I should think. Why don't you ask him?"

They looked across the table at each other. *He didn't know!* Wait until word of this made the rounds at White's!

" 'Morning, fellows," said a heavily brocaded Ossie, strolling into the dining room, followed shortly by Elmo in boots that emitted a suspicious squishing sound.

I hope he at least has the sense to keep his distance from the fire, thought Stanhope, edging away ever so slightly. Having committed in his mind to having fallen in love, he had no desire to be flambéed by a pair of rogue boots before even broaching the topic with the maiden of his affections.

"Well, well, if it ain't fat Oswald." Neville raised his quizzing glass.

"Stow it, Neville," Ossie retorted.

"Shouldn't eat all that if I were you, Oswald." Squibby offered as he eyed Ossie's laden plate. "Might bust some buttons."

"Not with that corset, he won't," Neville recovered enough to snap. "Didn't you hear him creaking his way down the stairs?"

Stanhope turned to Elmo. "What have they fallen out over?"

"M'sister," Elmo replied in gloomy tones. "Capital fellows, all of 'em, until they laid eyes on her," he complained.

"Ah, the fair Sofie," Stanhope murmured. "Sort of the Helen of Deepdene."

"Pardon?" Squibby thought that Ossie's cousin was really too clever to be a *comfortable* sort of fellow.

"Er, nothing. So you are all three of a mind to court Miss Lyttworth, then?"

They nodded vigourously, and Elmo rolled his eyes heavenward.

"And Oswald, of course, as befits his obligations, is also courting Miss Ashton," added Squibby primly.

Ossie sighed. "Has eyes only for the Greystock fellow."

Stanhope raised a brow.

"But I have plans," continued Ossie hastily, mindful of his cousin's impatience to have the entire business brought to a speedy conclusion. "I intend," he explained, "to suggest that she might look less peaky in a daffodil-yellow bonnet."

"I'd have thought cream would be more her shade," Neville replied, deep in thought. "Doncha think with those gray eyes, daffodil might be overwhelming?"

Ossie eyed Neville with disdain. "And at the Venetian breakfast today I plan to press her hand in a *speaking* way."

"Ah. Well, certainly, *that* can hardly fail to put her under your spell," Stanhope said, thinking with a strictly inward grin that with a little luck Miss Ashton might be very much otherwise engaged. "But back to Sofie for a moment. Do you suppose that she might be put off all of you by this sniping among yourselves?"

The three of them stared at him in incomprehension. "Why?" Ossie finally asked.

"Er, never mind. Forget I said anything. Best of luck to all of you. Now, if you would excuse me"—he stood, placing his napkin on the table—"I—"

It was then that a carrying voice, rapidly approaching the breakfast room, interrupted his words. He momentarily froze at the sound. *"Where,* oh, where, is that *rascal* Stanhope? I declare, I am all in a pelter to lay eyes upon him once again. I have even composed an ode to him on the journey. Well, almost. Do you know of a rhyme for 'fevered'? Ah, the trials of being an *artiste."* On that note Amanda Prescott, accompanied by a trotting Lady Lyttworth, who was clearly trying to get a word in edgewise, burst through the door.

That Amanda was indeed a stunner even Lady Lyttworth was forced to admit. She was dressed in the very height of fashion in a stylish navy blue traveling suit topped with a fitted spencer that was obviously the creation of the best seamstress London had to offer. Her glossy, dark curls were dashingly cropped, the better to highlight her perfect, even features and set off her graceful neck.

Oh, my Lord, I thought I was in the basket before; now I am well and truly done for, thought Stanhope, something akin to panic rising in his chest. He instantly decided that there was no moment like the present to begin his campaign to win Miss Ashton—never mind luring her to a secluded spot at the breakfast, he would kiss her senseless on the way. Nothing of his thoughts was visible on his face, however, as he made his bows. "You, as usual, are in looks, Mrs. Prescott," he said politely as he smiled down at her. "I must confess it is quite a surprise, a delightful one, of course, to find you acquainted with the Lyttworths."

Out of the corner of his eye he saw Lady Lyttworth flush. "Mrs. Prescott's mama was used to be quite a bosom bow of mine, and I thought"—she gave an uncomfortable-sounding giggle—"that as we are so many gentleman and so few ladies, she would make a charming addition to our little party."

"Indeed." Stanhope's smile was fixed. "Mrs. Prescott makes a charming addition to any gathering. But forgive my keeping you standing here, I'm certain you two must have a great deal to catch up on," he said. "As I was just explaining to these gentlemen, La—Cousin Gladys, I am on my way to the vicarage as I had, er, promised Miss Ashton, a chance to . . . drive my curricle. I doubt my company will be missed, as I know you will be eager to be left in peace to renew your friendship." He again made his bows and strolled from the room.

The ladies stood, staring after him, and Amanda lowered the hand that she had extended for his kiss, which had somehow failed to materialize.

Seventeen

Calista arrived at the bottom of the stairs to find her sister-in-law in a foul mood. She was turned out in a flounced, high-waisted, pea-green morning gown topped with a fur-trimmed spencer. Accessorizing were a high-crowned bonnet lavishly adorned with plumes and a furled pea-green parasol, which she was, at that moment, tapping impatiently on the ground as she berated a woebegone Adolphus, who was nursing a worse head even than his sister. At the sight of Calista, her lips tightened further and she removed her attention from her spouse. "That getup, Calista, is not in the least bit suitable," she said.

Calista picked up her bonnet, which was considerably worse for having been worn on the day she scrubbed the outside windows of the schoolhouse. "What a shame," she replied, her accents calm, "as it is what I shall be wearing."

"It is a slap in the face to the consequence of Lady Lyttworth's guests. Whatever will his lordship think?"

"What the Earl of Stanhope thinks, especially with regard to my wardrobe, is of less than no interest to me," said Calista with spirit if not complete truthfulness. "You may continue to tax me on this, Hermione, but I assure you, it will be a waste of breath."

Hermione, however, planted her kid slippers firmly on the ground and settled in to do battle. Adolphus, having spotted a rare opportunity to curry his wife's favour, was just joining in the chorus, when they were interrupted by Annie.

"His Lordship, the Earl of Stanhope," the housekeeper announced, so relishing her role in this drama that she was barely able to suppress a smirk as she ushered the gentleman into the hallway.

"Er—Stanhope, old man, ah, my lord," Adolphus said in bluff tones as he stuck out his hand. "Unexpected pleasure."

"My lord," chirped Hermione, sinking into a curtsy so low that Calista feared she would be unable to rise altogether.

"Stanhope," acknowledged Calista with a nod that positively bordered on incivility.

She was attired this morning in possibly the ugliest gown he had ever seen, in a sort of brownish-yellow shade that defied classification, topped off by a hideous olive-green pelisse. Neville would no doubt need a vinaigrette when he caught sight of it. She was pale, the dress bringing out sallow undertones in her skin, and had dark circles under her eyes, he noted. And his newly discovered heart seemed to flip within his chest. Never, he reflected, had a woman looked more desirable.

"I trust I find you well, Reverend Ashton," he said, clasping the proffered hand. "And you, Mrs. Ashton," he said, turning to bow over her hand, "look especially charming this morning."

"Oh, my goodness. Why, thank you, my lord," Hermione fluttered. "We have a very fine dressmaker just over in Little Elm, not a Frenchie, you understand, but very talented all the same. She studies *La Belle Assemblée* most assiduously—"

"Hermione!" Adolphus interrupted. "It is plain that Stanhope did not ride over to discuss ladies' fripperies!" He turned to Stanhope. "Came to sample some of that 'eighty-nine I mentioned, eh? Just decanted her last night," he said, warming to his favourite topic. "I think you'll find her quite a bold little minx. Not too cloudy. Fine tawny colour. Far, far superior to the shipment of 'eighty-seven Enright's just laid down, if I do say so m'self!"

"Very kind of you, sir, but I am afraid it's a bit early in the day for such a fainthearted sort as myself. I am actually come to collect Miss Ashton. Did she forget to mention that she was engaged to travel to the breakfast with me?" The shocked expressions on the vicar's and his wife's faces were almost comical, he thought.

"I don't recall—" Calista began to object, only to be interrupted by her brother.

"You are under no obligation, my lord, to put yourself out to humour my sister in any of her odd starts, I assure you," he said. "You, like myself, are a busy man. No one expects you to trouble yourself to escort local spinsters about!"

"It is my pleasure entirely," replied Stanhope, inwardly seething at such dismissive treatment of his beloved. He could hardly wait for the moment when he would be able to offer her protection from such repellent people. "I confess, Miss Ashton, I am all that is injured that you seem to have forgotten so soon that you were to accompany me." He clasped a hand over his heart. His green eyes danced at her, willing her to share a private joke, and his finely chiseled lips turned up in an intimate smile that made a warm feeling steal over her whole body. It was most unfair for a man to be so handsome, she thought as he continued. "Only yesterday you were positively *begging* for the chance to tool the ribbons on my curricle!"

At his words, an answering gleam came into her eyes, and he realized how very much he looked forward to discovering what type of payment she was devising in return for his manipulations. "It is very poor of me. I confess I *had* forgotten, but I do recall *positively begging* now that you are so ungallant as to mention it." She smiled a sickly sweet smile as she took his arm.

"It has been a pleasure, as always, Mrs. Ashton, Reverend Ashton." Stanhope bowed and steered Calista smoothly toward the door before they could object. "I give my word that I shall deliver Miss Ashton safe to the Stanleys', but I am afraid the horses will become restive if we are not on our way."

" 'Bye, Hermione. 'Bye, Adolphus," Calista couldn't resist calling over her shoulder as she was swept out on Stanhope's arm.

The instant they were out the door and beyond her relatives' hearing, however, she turned on him, as he had known she would, demanding, "And exactly *what* are you about with this odious, high-handed behaviour, my lord?"

He fixed her with a steady look. "I should think you would be grateful. Sounded as though I saved you from a most tedious scold. I suppose the delightful confection you are sporting was conceived and rendered by the not-quite-Frenchie over in Little Elm?"

"I suppose those are details of import to a man-milliner such as yourself."

"Do you by any chance have the headache this morning, Miss Ashton?" he inquired with a raised brow. "From your surfeit of brandy, perhaps? You are not of your usual sunny disposition."

"I *never* have the headache," she snapped.

"Of course not," he replied cheerfully. "Up you go, then, my dear."

She looked askance at the high-perched red vehicle into which he was handing her, the same one he had driven at their first meeting. "What *are* you doing? You don't truly expect me to drive this thing? Have your wits gone begging? And stop calling me 'my dear,' " she demanded as he helped her into the driver's box.

"Yes, I do, to the first, no, they haven't, to the second, and 'why?' to the third. Don't worry, my love. I shall explain all once we are under way," he promised, springing lightly into his seat.

"I am not your love."

Stanhope sprawled in an irkingly relaxed manner over the bench, and Calista could not resist sneaking a look at his long, muscular legs stretched out in front of him. "Just drive before your brother drags me in and forces me to sample an entire shipment of the 'eighty-nine—which, if memory serves, is not a particularly good year."

She shrugged as she took up the reins, and Stanhope had to bite back his words as she urged the horses into a gallop around the sharp corner at the bottom of the drive. The precariously sprung vehicle swung wildly from side to side. The scenery blurred. But it was not until they winged a tree that Stanhope, unable to contain himself any longer, yelled over the noise of screaming metal, "Are you insane? Slow down!"

"If you insist," Calista screamed, reining in the horses to a speed that was merely terrifying while managing to hit what seemed like every rut in the road. Stanhope had just slowly released his death grip on the side, when she swerved suddenly to miss a particularly large pothole. The left horse's startled rearing in the traces brought the carriage terrifyingly up on two wheels. But after teetering in midair for a moment, it righted itself.

"Miss Ashton," he bellowed when they were once again settled on all four wheels, the horses still flying along at a gallop that he was inclined to believe made his own legendary London-Brighton speed seem a mere trot. "I am shocked"—he raised his voice further so it would carry over the shriek of the wind rushing past—"no, make that appalled and horrified, to discover what a dreadful driver you are. I would never have thought it. It is most unusual to find someone who rides so well and drives so very poorly."

"Had you asked before so high-handedly ordering me about, I would have warned you," she yelled back, turning to glare at him.

"Please! Keep your eyes on the road!" he begged. "Of course. I do not know how I could have forgotten to inquire as to whether you were the worst whip Sussex has ever seen." Despite the volume necessary to make himself heard, he sounded amused. "But would you object to pulling over before you kill us both or maim the horses? Else, I'll just hang on and prepare to die."

"Gladly," she snapped as she bumped them to a shuddering halt. Stanhope managed to duck his head just in time to miss being scraped off the vehicle entirely by the low-hanging branches of a beech tree. "I have never made any pretense of being able to handle the ribbons like a fribble," she complained.

He sighed with the sheer relief of not moving. "Do you realize that you have called me both a man-milliner *and* a fribble in the space of a quarter hour! I am beginning to think that despite your denials, you must have the headache after all."

She sighed. "Did you kidnap me to harangue me? Or may I suppose you had another reason?"

"Me? Kidnap you? I like that! And *I* never harangue. But now that you ask, yes, I had numerous other reasons," he said, his voice sliding into huskiness as he decided that Neville for once was in the right of it, her eyes were more gray than hazel. "But they all seem to escape me for the moment, save one. Do you know what was running through my head when I thought we would both surely die?"

"Something improper, I am sure."

"I must confess that of late I have had many improper thoughts where you are concerned, Miss Ashton," he said softly, looking at her in such a way that her heart began to trip. "So improper, in fact, that I am not even going to inspect the damage to my rig or my favourite horses until I've attended to them." His voice was so caressing that Calista could have sworn he was touching her.

"I would assume that is the usual state of affairs for you, sir. Meet an aging spinster, attempt to seduce her." Her voice was tart to cover the pounding of her heart, but she blushed. Delightfully, Stanhope thought.

Cupping her face with the utmost gentleness, he murmured, "I was thinking how unbearable it would be to die without ever having kissed you." He looked into her eyes for a long moment.

This time he *is* going to kiss me, thought Calista in a dizzying mixture of terror and anticipation

He leaned closer. His mouth, when it did come down on hers, was warm and feather light and tasted vaguely of mint as he slid firm lips gently across hers. Calista, who had never even allowed herself to imagine such an experience, reveled in the kiss for a moment, unwittingly breathing an ecstatic sigh before recalling herself.

Then she pulled away. "You must stop this on the *instant,* my lord."

He pulled her gently back. His eyes, she noted, looked darker than usual, but his tone was light when he said, "Absolutely," before pulling her harder against him and deepening his kiss most agreeably. "It is *entirely* wrong," he murmured against her mouth.

Colours seemed to burst behind her closed eyelids. Calista felt burning hot, but she was shivering. She took a deep, ragged breath. Her pulse was racing, but she felt deliciously languid, powerless to stop him as he continued exploring her mouth. So, *this* is what it's all about, she thought. No wonder he is so good at this raking business. "I have been properly raised, my lord," she murmured back, not quite able to bring herself to pull away but trying vaguely for some propriety.

In reply, he stopped kissing her mouth and trailed light kisses down her jaw to her ear before pausing to whisper in a voice that sounded so intimate, Calista felt herself grow warmer still, "I will do my best to make you forget that. Call me Tristan."

"Tristan," she whispered, lost in the moment as he stroked his fingers down the line of her jaw, sending shivers through every part of her body. "How romantical."

He leaned his forehead against hers. "Is it not disgraceful? I bore no end of teasing as a child."

"I will not tease you, sir," she replied, pulling away slightly and wishing that she did not long so for him to begin kissing her again.

You already are, my love, he thought, unable to resist bending his lips to hers once again. Her kiss was not by a long shot the most practiced kiss he had ever experienced—in fact, he'd go odds it was her first. How peculiar, he reflected, that Greystock, for all his lascivious talk, had left her so untouched. And so hungry, he thought, feeling the fieriness of her response.

"We really must stop," she said a moment later when she had once again forced herself to gain mastery of her voice. "Anyone could come upon us."

"Let them," he replied, his lips against hers still, intoxicated by her kiss.

She gasped and pulled away hard, and he cursed himself for speaking so carelessly. "Discovery might mean nothing to you, sir. But to me it would spell ruin among the people I have known all my life—which, I grant you, is no more than I deserve after my disgraceful behaviour. I knew you to be a rake, sir. But that you would ruin me for a spot of dalliance is insupportable."

"At Ardsley's hunting box you insisted that your reputation was beyond blackening."

"True. But taking shelter from a storm and carrying on like a wanton in an open carriage are not at all the same thing."

How can I possibly go another day without knowing this woman is mine? he wondered with a sense of urgency he had never known before. "Marry me, Calista," he said before he could think. The words came out easily enough, but his voice sounded hoarse and unfamiliar to his ears. His hands, he noted, were shaking. Odd, he thought in a detached way, and I am reputed to have the steadiest hands in London.

"What?" she gasped as though she had just been drenched in cold water, which was not at all the reaction he had been looking for.

"Marry me," he repeated, liking the sound this time. "Be my wife."

"You are worse than I ever could have imagined," she accused, as though her darkest suspicions had been confirmed.

"Soon." He fixed her with a crooked smile that was made up of beguilingly equal parts seduction and sweetness. And she instinctively knew it had gained him entrance to many hearts. And, no doubt, beds, she reminded herself severely before he continued. "Each day I have to wait for you is agony, Calista."

"And insulting too!"

"No, my love, I—"

"Don't call me that. I have heard enough. Set me down," she cried, making to jump down.

"Calista." Stanhope jumped down after her. "My sweet— damn!" he swore as the Enrights' barouche lumbered into sight.

As it drew to a halt, Lady Enright stuck her head out the open window and, seeing them standing in the road, inquired mildly as to whether they were in need of assistance. Calista ran to her, yellow dress flapping, and said with a strangled sound meant to pass for a laugh, "I find I overestimated my own stamina and have become quite ill from the swaying motion of such a high-sprung conveyance, Roberta. Is it possible there is room for me in your carriage?"

Emily Enright shot her a puzzled look. "That's not like you, Calista. I've never known you to be travel sick in your life!"

"Well, I was this time, Emily," she replied in a tone that effectively stifled all further conversation on the topic.

Accepting that he had made a hash of his first marriage proposal, and that perhaps next time a little advance planning might not go amiss, Stanhope helped Calista into the barouche.

"You poor dear," Roberta Enright clucked as she moved over to make room. "Do you need to return to the vicarage?"

"Well, I—"

"Good, good. I knew you were made of sterner stuff than that, my dear!" interrupted Lady Enright, having made her own assessment of Calista's rapid breathing and feverish-looking cheeks.

"Perhaps we *should* take her home, my love," said the kindly Lord Enright. "You do look a trifle done up, Calista."

"Now that you mention it, I *am* feeling a bit—"

"Nonsense, Frederick. She is fine," said his wife briskly. "Some lighthearted entertainment will no doubt put her to rights in no time."

Accepting that she had, for the second time that morning, been outmaneuvered by a mistress of strategy, Calista, under the guise of travel sickness, leaned her head back against the squabs. A picture of her own shocking conduct intruded behind her closed eyes. I, she thought with horror, was both improperly wanton and foolishly awkward—a pitiful combination—especially for an eccentric ape-leader. Why, oh, why, didn't I slap his face? Hard?

But even as she asked the question of herself, she knew that the answer was that she would have been incapable of it. And then the ultimate humiliation of his making sport of her with that joke of a marriage proposal! He was *truly* reprehensible! She pretended to sleep for the rest of the ride.

Eighteen

By the time Calista had pulled herself together and brushed off her hosts' concern, the party was well under way. Stanhope was occupied fetching Sofie a cool drink and seeing her settled in a shady spot. As Calista made her way down to the broad expanse of lawn, he threw back his head and laughed at something Sofie said. The sudden feeling of pure misery that overwhelmed Calista turned her even paler. Mr. Stanley, who was watching her go, turned to his wife, Elleanor. "I wonder what has come over Calista," he said, "not at all like her. The gel is usually the hardiest of souls."

"I was just thinking the same thing, my dear," she replied, a slight frown creasing her pleasant, plump face. "Let us keep an eye on her. But for now, we must attend to the rest of our guests."

"Peter! What on earth are you doing here? God, it's good to see you," Stanhope said with genuine delight as he looked up from Sofie and saw Lord Peter Gresham making his way over. "But I thought you didn't much fancy a trip to the country?"

"Suddenly overcome by the desire to pay a visit to my god-parents, doncha know," Peter said so casually that Stanhope knew for a certainty that the gossip had made the rounds.

His heart sank. "Excellent," he replied, nothing of his distress showing. "May I introduce you to Miss Sofie Lyttworth? Miss Lyttworth, Lord Peter Gresham." As Peter gazed down on Miss Lyttworth, a confection today in a long-sleeved, high-waisted peach froth, his face bore a thunderstruck expression and Stanhope mentally added yet another name to her list of admirers.

"My godmama has asked if I could assist the footmen in bringing some boats around in case people desire to row out on the lake, Tris," Lord Gresham pulled himself together to say. "She would never ask an exalted guest such as yourself to assist, but I have no such reservations."

Stanhope laughed. He excused himself from Miss Lyttworth and said, "By all means, then, Peter, lead the way."

"Well?" Peter demanded as soon as they were out of earshot. "I thought that was why you'd come."

"Couldn't resist. I must confess, though, I was a little surprised to learn of your upcoming nuptials with the, ah, delightful Mrs. Prescott. Didn't seem as though that was the way the wind was blowing when you left town."

"She showed up this morning, and I beat perhaps the hastiest retreat of my life. I trust it is too much to hope that she did not mention to anyone that she is expecting a marriage proposal from me?"

" 'Fraid so."

"Everyone?"

"Everyone and then some."

"Blast!"

"What the devil, if I may be so bold as to ask, is going on?"

"I daresay, Peter, that for perhaps the first time in my life I am well and truly in the suds," Stanhope explained with a trace of a rueful grin before proceeding to fill him in.

"So your cousin *invented* an engagement and Amanda got wind of it and showed up to claim your hand?" Gresham sounded disbelieving.

Stanhope nodded. "I've a hunch that my hostess, Lady Lyttworth, invited Amanda though. Even she wouldn't be bold enough to show up uninvited."

"But, Tris." Gresham frowned. "Why on earth would she do that? Invite Amanda here, I mean. Doesn't seem at all the thing."

"It's not," Stanhope, well used to matchmaking parents, explained, "but I'd hazard a guess it's so I have a chance to compare her to the lovely Sofie."

"No comparison, if you ask me. But what are you going to do? Not about to get shackled to Amanda, are you?"

"Of course not. I barely even enjoyed our, er, liaison. I am sure I can contrive a way out, but the devil of it is that for the first time, I have, oddly enough, found myself in love."

Lord Gresham's face shuttered. "With the beauteous Sofie, I trust?"

"Good Lord, no!" Stanhope looked so appalled, his friend had to laugh. "As fate would have it, with Calista Ashton."

Peter's jaw dropped. "The ape-leading bluestocking who's odds on to marry your cousin?" he demanded.

"The thing of it is that she didn't turn out to be exactly the elderly spinster we were given to understand. And what do you mean, *marry my cousin?"* he demanded.

"The, er, bets have escalated a tad," Gresham said mildly. "Although they've all but been obscured in the books by those about you and the divine Amanda."

Stanhope groaned. "Well, she'll marry my cousin over my dead body," he said. "See for yourself. That's her talking with your godfather and Elmo Lyttworth."

Gresham thought perhaps his friend was having a little joke at his expense. "What an, ah, *unusual* dress," he said carefully.

"I know," said Stanhope, sounding almost proud, and Peter shot him a puzzled look. "But is she not lovely?"

"Indeed," replied Lord Gresham, thinking that she *was* quite pretty, although not much more than that, and all but eclipsed by the shining star that was Sofie Lyttworth. "So what d'you plan to do?"

"Marry her, apparently." Stanhope shook his head as if in disbelief at his own words. "I've already asked her, in fact."

"You've *what?"* Lord Gresham stopped and stared at his friend.

Stanhope kept walking. "Asked her."

Gresham hurried to catch up. "And?"

"She refused me." Stanhope allowed himself a sigh. "But in truth, Peter, I think I made a sad mull of it."

Lord Gresham barked with laughter when he had heard the tale of the curricle ride and subsequent proposal. "Will you ask again?"

"Of course. I can barely restrain myself from running to her and doing it now. But it's been borne in upon me that I should do it more carefully next time. Down on my knees and all. The thing was that at the time I was not at my most levelheaded. All I could think about was making her mine so I could, um, make her mine, and it just slipped out," he finished lamely.

"If you felt that way with her in that getup, you *are* in love," Gresham said.

"Completely and irrevocably, it begins to dawn on me," Stanhope agreed. "Also a bit of a problem in that she is apparently already spoken for, or is about to be."

"What?" Lord Gresham reflected that for a man whose existence had always been completely ordered, Stanhope's seemed to have slipped curiously out of control.

"See that gentleman over there?" Stanhope pointed to Squire Greystock in conversation with Adolphus Ashton.

"Which one?"

"The one who just crammed a whole sausage into his mouth."

"Yes, I see him," Peter said with fastidious distaste.

"That is Squire Everard Greystock, widower and father of seven. I am given to understand, although the lady herself has not spoken of it, that Miss Ashton is shortly to become affianced to him. The other, by the way, is her brother."

Peter sounded dubious. "Doesn't look the most attractive sort."

"Which one?"

"Either."

"You have ever had keen powers of observation, Peter," replied Stanhope dryly.

"Cut line, Tris. I am on your side. Does she love him, do you think?"

"I have yet to take up the topic with her. However, judging by his general lovability, I would tend to doubt it. In fact, my guess is that she's being pressured into it." His voice was bland, but Gresham could discern a grim expression behind his eyes.

"You certainly have my sympathy, old man." Peter sounded genuinely concerned. "If there is anything I can do to help, let me know. I find I just might tarry in the neighbourhood a few days after all."

Stanhope laughed. "Well, perhaps if you could see your way clear to distracting Miss Lyttworth . . ."

"A horrid task, Stanhope. A horrid task. But as you are a friend"—Lord Gresham shrugged—"what can I do but your bidding?"

Stanhope's tone was dry but amused. "Thank you, Peter. I knew I could rely on you even if it meant undertaking such an unpleasantness. There is just one more problem."

"Do tell."

"Calista, er, Miss Ashton, doesn't exactly know about Amanda." Stanhope fiddled with his impeccable cravat in a most uncharacteristic way.

Peter stopped and faced his friend. "Do you mean to say that Amanda thinks you wish to become engaged to her, you want to wed Miss Ashton, Amanda is here, and they don't know about each other?"

"Once again an astute summation. Yes."

"And may I also suppose Miss Ashton has no knowledge as yet of the fact that she is the subject of numerous wagers at the hands of your cousin?"

Stanhope nodded.

Peter threw back his head and laughed. "A royal summons couldn't drag me out of this neighbourhood."

"Your support is much appreciated, Peter. Now, where are those blasted boats?"

They headed off to the boathouse with Peter still laughing.

On another corner of the well-manicured lawn, Lady Lyttworth was in hushed conversation with Hermione Ashton as they sat, comfortably ensconced in chairs by the side of the lake. "Travel sick! What fustian," she exclaimed. "That gel has never been unwell a day in her life!"

"I don't mind telling you that she has been positively *uncivil* at home," returned Hermione, snapping her fingers to summon a footman for another glass of iced champagne. "When I had a spell yesterday—I had been to order new gowns in the morning, so fatiguing!—and found it necessary to rest instead of calling on the Plovers, she told me it was my *duty* as the vicar's wife. Imagine! As if I don't know my own duty. I mean, old Mr. Plover was eighty if he was a day." She paused to refresh herself with a sip. "It's not as if his passing could have come as a *surprise* to the family. What was *I* going to say?"

Lady Lyttworth sighed into her glass. "I fear the earl's attentions have given Calista ideas. The way she has been throwing herself at his head is most unbecoming."

"He *did* call to collect her this morning. Perhaps he enjoys her company?" Hermione sounded dubious.

"Nonsense. In fact, I should not be at all surprised if he was forced to give her a sharp set-down before this day is done," sniffed Lady Lyttworth. "She is sure to come a cropper if she has set her sights on *him*. I don't know what Stanhope is playing at—likely he is too polite to put her in her place, but if we let her get ideas above herself, not only will you end up losing the squire's blunt, but Calista is sure to wind up a disappointed old maid."

"What should we do, do you think?"

"*I* will take her down a peg or two by introducing her to Amanda Prescott—if she ever arrives. How long can it possibly take her to finish her toilette? Once Calista gets a taste of the type of woman Stanhope is accustomed to associating with, she will no doubt slink away, her tail between her legs. And *you* have a talk with Everard. Tell him to take some action, for heaven's sake."

Calista longed for a moment of solitude to allow herself to admit how wretched she was feeling. But no sooner had she managed to excuse herself from listening to the exhaustingly earnest Mr. Arthur Price expound on his plans for the summer theatrical—no laughing eyes or sensuous lips there, she thought before gasping at the realization that she never would have entertained such uncharitable thoughts just a few short weeks ago—when Sir Ossie appeared at her side, begging, to her astonishment, the pleasure of escorting her for a stroll around the gardens. With no choice but to accept, Calista took his arm, and he began to promenade her back and forth across a small stretch of grass, puffing slightly from the exertion. To venture farther afield, he explained, might muddy his boots.

"I hope my sartorial splendour does not intimidate you, my dear Miss Ashton," he began. "I can understand that you might feel quite the dowdy country mouse with me, but I would have you know that underneath the finery, I am a humble fellow, really."

For once Calista found herself at a loss.

"Even many of the town belles find themselves cast in the shade by me," he said kindly, "so I quite understand your shyness."

"Thank you, sir. Your words are greatly reassuring."

"Amelia Farham, as I believe you are aware, has told me that my curls are finer than Byron's."

"Er, yes. And Miss Farham, I am sure, must be considered a very astute judge of such things."

He waved this away modestly. "Regardless, there is no reason I should be considered above your touch. You are, despite your straitened circumstances, of good birth, after all."

"Er, thank you."

"Good. Yes. I trust you won't think it impertinent of me to say that it seems that your colour sense is not what it could be."

"That has ever been a source of great distress to me, sir."

Ossie failed to recognize the dryness in her tone. "Perhaps I can help." He grabbed her hand between his two pudgy ones, which, Calista registered, felt damp and clammy. She was unable to stop herself from comparing them to Stanhope's long, elegant fingers. After shooting a furtive glance at the rest of the company, Sir Ossie pressed a wet kiss into her palm before scurrying away.

Calista stood, watching his retreating back and attempting to make some sense out of their encounter as she wiped her hand on her skirt. Shaking her head, she decided that she could not possibly understand anything today, so it was best not even to try, and slipped down toward the woods.

Having at last gained privacy, she walked in the cool shade of the trees for a few minutes until, feeling chilled, she sat on an old stone bench set in a sunny clearing.

Her first reaction when Squire Greystock came upon her there a few moments later was one of exasperation that her hard-won peace had been disturbed.

"Good afternoon, Calista," he said, advancing upon her bench. "Lovely day, ain't it?"

"Very fine. I bid you good afternoon, sir," she replied guardedly as he sat down beside her, his large frame forcing her partway off the small bench. Why didn't he just go away?

"Tried the sausages?"

"I have not found myself overly hungry," she replied, watching his right hand, which seemed to be making its way toward her leg.

"Pity. Excellent spread. Elleanor has always set a marvelous table. Quite an example for any woman," he said, directing a meaningful look toward her. "Yes, quite an example." Calista avoided his eyes, but he continued. "Given any more thought to my little proposal?"

She sighed. "It is most kind of you, sir, and as I said before, I am deeply sensible of the great honour you do me, but I am convinced we should not suit at all."

"Brats, er, the children like you well enough. And you could handle 'em a damn sight better than those fool nurses and governesses I keep employing. Waste of blunt. Two quit last week alone. Imagine!"

"Again, I must thank you for your kind words. I—I am very fond of them also," she said not altogether truthfully, "but still, I must decline."

"Ain't as if you're going to get many more offers, y'know," he said, pressing his thigh against hers and placing his hand on her knee.

She inched away, a shiver of revulsion coursing through her. "Be that as it may," she replied in what she hoped were repressive accents, "I am still convinced we should not suit."

"Perhaps I should show you how well we could suit," he whispered, his hot breath, a mixture of port, onions, and strong cheese, in her face.

She rose to flee, no longer caring whether she appeared impolite, but before she could make good her escape, he reached out a stubby hand and pulled her back toward him. "Sit back down, my girl," he said, "don't be in such a rush. It is past time we got to know each other better." He was stronger than she was, and Calista had no choice but to sit back down beside him. And when she did, he snatched the opportunity to pull her close. She could feel his corset pressing through his clothing.

"Let go of me," she hissed. "This instant!"

"Not likely," he smirked before his thick, wet lips came down on hers. "And you'd best learn to enjoy this."

Her eyes open wide as she struggled fruitlessly to free herself, Calista looked around for help. The only thing close to hand was a thick length of fallen tree branch. To her relief, she was able to stretch far enough down to grab it. The squire was too well occupied trying to grope her bosom to notice, so, closing her eyes, she raised it in the air as best she could, one arm pinned as it was, and brought it down on his knee with a resounding crack. The squire howled in pain and released her. Not sparing him a backward glance, Calista fled. Trying desperately to hold back the tears that threatened, she ran blindly out of the woods, stumbling through the low-hanging branches and smack into Lady Lyttworth, who was in conversation with a stunningly beautiful stranger.

"Calista!" Lady Lyttworth looked at her with obvious distaste. "Surely you cannot be aware of the picture you present. Your hair is disheveled—why, I do believe there are *twigs* in it!"

"Yes, Gladys," she said, mustering as much composure as she was able under the circumstances which, since she was shaking and gasping for breath, was remarkably little. "I met with an accident in the woods."

"Well, you look unharmed to me, just messy," snapped Lady Lyttworth. "In any event, I would like to introduce you to our new guest, Mrs. Amanda Prescott. Mrs. Prescott, Miss Calista Ashton."

Amanda Prescott. Stanhope's fiancée. She had come to join him. Calista felt the blood drain from her face, and she almost swayed on her feet. Of course, she thought wryly, regaining her equilibrium, what else could she have expected today? But did the woman have to be so very beautiful?

"The two of you have much in common!" Lady Lyttworth chirped.

Only that we are both in love with the same man, Calista wanted to wail. Instead, she forced a smile. "It is a pleasure to meet you, Mrs. Prescott," she said politely as she surreptitiously tried to remove a few of the larger twigs from her hair.

"Calista," Lady Lyttworth said, turning toward Mrs. Prescott as if she were announcing something of great moment, *"reads.* In fact, she is known in these parts as being quite unfashionably blue, the naughty puss. Mrs. Prescott is a poetess, Calista!"

"Charmed to meet you, Miss Ashton," said Amanda lazily. "Perhaps you've heard of me?"

"Er, no, I'm afraid not," Calista replied, struggling to hide her discomfiture. "Although I am sure the fault is my own. I must beg some ignorance when it comes to poetry. I am not nearly so well read as I should be. Perhaps you could recommend some of your favourites to me during your stay?"

"Oh, I don't *read* poetry, I only write it. So fatiguing to read other people's poetry, and so muddling to have it rattling about in your head, don't you think? Of course, only another *artiste* could truly sympathize with that viewpoint."

"A very interesting theory all the same," Calista replied.

"I just *knew* you two would be fast friends. And now you must excuse me. Honestly! Anyone would think Sofie was *trying* to ruin her complexion," Lady Lyttworth said with a little frown.

The moment she had departed, Amanda demanded, "Are you the young woman who became ill in Tristan's curricle this morning?" Her voice dragged lazily over the syllables of his name, investing them with an unmistakable intimacy.

"I'm afraid so," replied Calista ruefully. "I do not know what came over me, as I am very rarely so delicate."

"No matter." Amanda waved the issue away. "He can be perfectly terrifying in that thing. Why, I recall once on a weekend jaunt I became so ill that the entire journey was *ruined.*" Her meaning was so unmistakable that Calista felt a blush rising.

Across the lawn, Calista had spotted Stanhope making his way toward the duo, a grim look on his face. "Please excuse me, Mrs. Prescott, but I find I am not feeling at all the thing even now," she choked. And then, knowing that she was being rude, and not caring, she fled as fast as her shaking legs would allow.

Calista hurried to Hermione, who was reclining on a chair, sipping delicately from yet another cup of iced champagne. She looked up. "Calista! My goodness! You look a fright."

"Squire Greystock attempted a . . . a familiarity, Hermione," Calista whispered in the most composed tone she could muster.

Hermione cast an eye over her. "Surely you are mistaken. The squire is a man of unimpeachable character. You are inexperienced, Calista. Doubtless you misconstrued a simple friendly gesture."

Calista gave up hope of an explanation, and said simply, "I am unwell. May we depart?"

"Absolutely *not!*" Hermione hissed. "If you are indeed unwell, you have only yourself to blame. You have no doubt contracted a fever from one of the villagers you are so insistent upon visiting. I have warned you numerous times that no good can come of that. Women, as I do believe I have explained often, are called the fairer sex for a *reason.* Our constitutions cannot ward off the illness that is the inevitable consequence of consorting with those beneath our stations. In the future, you would do well to recall that and keep to our own type, but for today you will need to make the best of it."

Realizing that Hermione was to be of no help, Calista appealed to Lady Enright. This time that lady took one look at her stricken face and said, "I'll take you home, my dear. Let me collect your things and tell Frederick and Emily that they are to make their own way home."

Nineteen

Calista leaned back against the cushions of the barouche and let a sigh escape. Closing her eyes, she reflected that this was quite possibly the worst day she could ever remember.

And it was all that dreadful Nonesuch's fault! Life had ever been well ordered and meaningful until his arrival had disrupted her entire existence. Gentlemen had never previously been known to assault her in the bushes. Nor had they ever condemned her taste in clothing—at least, she amended in the name of fairness, not to her face—before pressing revolting kisses into her palm. And never had they had such very green eyes or made her heart turn over just by their very presence. Or kissed her. Or had hands that with the slightest touch seemed to drug her mind and set her body on fire.

Now, in the space of just a few days, everything was turned upside down. She had all but lost interest in her work, come dangerously close to indulging in the sin of vanity, coveted fine horses and other women's fiancés; and today, she had found herself the recipient of unwanted attentions from three different men! Well, most of the attentions were unwanted, she amended to herself as she fought down the memory of her body's treacherous response to Stanhope's kisses. Then she imagined him doing the same thing with the glorious Amanda Prescott and slumped even farther down in her seat.

It was just too much to be borne. She sat up straighter. Surely if he would only leave, life would return to normal. It was time he took that collection of bad points he said he had come for, and, along with his loose screw of a cousin, departed this little town for good and left them all in peace. It was the right thing, she knew. So, why, then, did the very thought leave her feeling so bleak?

Lady Enright did indeed collect Calista's belongings and inform her husband that she was escorting the girl home. Then she approached Stanhope, who was in conversation with Amanda.

"As I was saying, and I am not at all convinced that you are attending," Amanda was saying, "I have decided to compose a poem on a country house party. I am certain it will be my finest work to date. I suppose those are elm trees?"

Stanhope followed the direction of her finger. "Beeches, actually, Amanda."

"That destroys my entire rhyme scheme!" She looked as though she considered it his fault. "Now, Stanhope, *do,* please, pay attention. Those—would you call them bushes? Over there—"

"Please excuse my rude interruption," Lady Enright cut in, not sounding in the least bit apologetic, "but I am leaving, and I had most especially wished to have a word with his lordship."

"Lady Enright." He smiled as he bowed over her hand.

"I had hoped we would have a chance to converse this afternoon, my lord, but I am departing early, as Miss Ashton has taken ill—"

"Very odd girl!" said Amanda. "I met her earlier, and do you know, she had *twigs* in her hair!"

"Miss Ashton is ill?"

There was something in Stanhope's green gaze and a note in his voice that Lady Enright found greatly reassuring, although, she reflected, he was not a man to give much away. She hastened to reassure him. "A trifle. If I know Calista, she will be over it before we reach home. But as she is waiting in the carriage, I must depart." She put on her most imperious tone. "I desire a word with you, however, young man. It will be acceptable for you to pay me a visit at eleven of the clock tomorrow."

He bowed. "It will be my pleasure."

She tapped him with her fan. "Be sure that it is," she said, and then grinned to herself as she heard Amanda demand shrilly, "Whatever can you be thinking? Surely you don't intend to allow that old *harridan* to order you about?"

In the carriage she looked at Calista. "You are coming home with me."

"I can't, Roberta. I've things to do."

"They will wait. You are obviously in no state to do anything except recline in my sitting room with a blanket over you, drink hot tea, and tell me the whole of it, my girl."

Very interesting, she thought a short time later when she had had the whole tale and dispatched a much calmer Calista home in her barouche. Tomorrow's interview would tell. If Stanhope is truly interested in Calista, she thought, I will do my best to ensure a happy outcome. But if he's trifling with her— No, that didn't bear thinking about. Not at all.

Twenty

It was four days before Calista next saw Stanhope. The party at Moreford Park progressed, and Calista politely but firmly refused all invitations to join them. She turned down dinner, refused a picnic, said thank you very much but no to a musical evening, and, when a note was delivered requesting her company for another ride with his lordship, the Earl of Stanhope, the footman was immediately dispatched back with firm regrets.

Which did not mean, Deepdene being a small village, that she was not informed of Stanhope's every waking movement—and some of his not-waking ones also, as Annie had it on good authority—and felt it necessary to pass the information on to her mistress—from the underhousemaid at Moreford Park, who had it straight from Sofie's abigail, who had it *directly* from his lordship's valet that the gentleman suffered no nasal obstructions and had never been known to snore. When awake, the earl was seen—according to Annie, who'd had *this* on good authority from Joan Trent, who had been delivering eggs to market—strolling through the town square with Sofie Lyttworth on his arm. His presence was duly noted the following day as he picked up a picnic hamper from the Horse and Castle for an outing to the ruins of Colford Castle that he had arranged to please the ladies. "He ordered cold pheasant and champagne!" reported Annie, in alt at such extravagance. His great reserve of patience was remarked by all the day he escorted the ladies shopping for fripperies. And rumour had it that he made many witty com-

ments that seemed to delight Amanda at the Searles' rout. Therefore, it hardly came as much of a surprise when Hermione reported back after the Enrights' musical evening that Stanhope
was the best dancer ever to be seen in these parts—"Such natural grace! And he stood up with Sofie *twice!* And favoured his
own intended bride only once! Surely the tide is turning."

It was also remarked in the village, to the puzzlement of
many, that the Squire Greystock was noted to have suddenly
developed not only a pronounced limp but a nastily blacked
eye, both of which he refused to discuss. That the blacked eye
had appeared not long after her interview with Stanhope, during
which she might have let slip a morsel or two of information
about Calista's encounter with the oaf, was a development that
Lady Enright could not help but find highly gratifying.

Honestly, thought Calista with some asperity, couldn't a person get some relief from the exploits of the man? This uncharitable thought came on the heels of a meeting of the sewing
circle. The conversation centered entirely on the Earl of Stanhope. His lack of airs. His excellent address. His perfection of
countenance. His witty conversation. His unparalleled grace on
the dance floor. Until Calista, who felt that her self-imposed
exile had restored some measure of sanity, wanted to scream.
Even Elleanor Stanley giggled like a schoolgirl, and Roberta
Enright appeared to have lost all her customary good sense as
she fretted over the dinner she was giving the following evening.

It was not that Calista had ceased to think of Stanhope, but
at least she had managed to avoid seeing him. And as long as
he stayed out of sight, her brain might be traitorous, but her
heart did not thunder and her hands did not shake. And she
never, but never, thought of his outrageous proposal of marriage. Or of his kisses! Or even of the mysterious treacherous
heat he seemed to have awakened in her. Surely those things
must have had some bearing on the fact that all the activities
in which she had previously found such fulfillment seemed curiously flat. But she didn't think about them.

Calista was not entirely without fashionable company, how-

ever, as twice during her withdrawal from society Sir Ossie rode
over, once to offer her a sample of a special hair pomade his
man had whipped up, and once to show her a new emerald and
pink waistcoat with turquoise piping that had just been delivered. Both times he gazed meaningfully, if inexplicably, into
her eyes before leaving.

It was on that fourth day that Lady Enright managed to drag
her back into the social fray. It was the day before her dinner,
to which Calista had, naturally, sent regrets.

The girl had been shaken up, true, but enough was enough—
she'd had time to settle herself, Lady Enright had decided, and
so had put her all into coercing Calista's attendance. "If you
will not attend, at least say you will do the flowers. You have
such a way with them," she had begged. And Calista, knowing
full well she was poised at the top of a slippery slope but uncharacteristically lacking the will to argue with the immutable
force of nature that Lady Enright seemed of late to have become,
had reluctantly agreed.

Next morning, when she arrived to arrange the armloads of
hothouse roses and tulips in silver bowls, Lady Enright was
lying in wait. She followed Calista about the huge dining room
as she worked. "I shall refrain from resorting to high-handed
tricks, Calista. I must, however, point out that your mother was
one of my very dearest friends, and it would gladden my heart
no end to have her daughter's support in this most *trying* hour
as I prepare to entertain such an *exalted* visitor to the neighbourhood."

Calista snipped a stem with an economical motion. "Roberta,
you are doing it far too brown, you know. I know for a fact that
you could entertain the royal family on fifteen minutes' notice.
Without a staff if necessary. And as I am already lending my
support by doing the flowers, surely my presence is not necessary?"

"But without you we shall be an odd number at table. So
unlucky!" Lady Enright wailed. When Calista continued to snip
stems, unmoved, she switched tactics. "It pains me greatly, of
course, to have to bring this up, my dear, it is only"—she
paused, allowing her eyes to pool with tears—"that your mama

most specifically asked me to watch over you should anything happen to her. And I cannot truly be comfortable that I have fulfilled that office knowing that you sit home with your knitting while the rest of us make merry. Only think how it would grieve her, that poor, gentle soul!" A not entirely convincing tear ran down her cheek.

"It pains *me* that you would stoop to such depths. But you win, Roberta." Calista threw up her hands figuratively, if not literally, filled as they were with irises at the moment. "Do not think for a moment that you have deceived me with your underhanded tactics, but I know you'll not rest until you've had your way. However," she said as she looked at the older woman, "I do not expect to find myself seated next to *him*. No meddling, Roberta."

Lady Enright looked offended. "Seat you next to Stanhope? I wouldn't dream of it, my dear!"

"Good. See that you don't." Calista put the last flower on the table and stood back to check her handiwork. "I shall see you this evening, then."

After walking her to the door, Lady Enright murmured to herself, "Seat you next to Stanhope? Honestly! That is for amateurs like Gladys. When I meddle, my girl, I really meddle!"

Stanhope was with Peter Gresham in the taproom at the Horse and Castle. "Nice place, this," he said a tad wistfully, looking around at the polished wood wainscoting and cheerful fire as they settled themselves into two comfortable chairs. "I wish I could get myself out of Moreford Park and ensconced here, but every time I mention it, Lady Lyttworth flies into the boughs."

"You've tried?"

"Daily. The house party is enough to drive anyone to distraction. Ossie and his cronies are constantly on the verge of fisticuffs. Elmo follows me about, asking endless questions on the style of my cravat. Amanda is growing steadily more bold—she draped herself all over me when we found ourselves alone in the breakfast room this morning." He shook his head as if to clear it. "Sofie pouts if an hour goes by during which I fail to pay her an extravagant compliment. And Lady Lyttworth is so determined to prove Sofie a worthy countess, she actually forced the poor girl to brew a posset when I sneezed once. I had to drink half the damned thing before they left the room and I could send Enders to dump it on the lawn and, do you know, Peter, when I left—I swear it—the grass was *dead."*

"It does sound cozy," said Gresham, laughing. "But, I confess, I wouldn't say no to dancing attendance on Sofie myself."

"I pray you will, old fellow. Take some of the heat off me," Stanhope said as he glanced at his friend. "I am fairly exhausted with the effort of thinking up new flattery. In fact, I suppose it would be too much to ask that you have a friend for Amanda."

Gresham shook his head. *"Most* of my acquaintances are far too intelligent to become mixed up with her!" They laughed companionably at that, and then he added more soberly, "Dashed rackety thing for Lady Lyttworth to have invited her here though."

Stanhope nodded. "I agree. And I've been extremely craven when it comes to disabusing Amanda of the notion that there is any possibility that the two of us might make a match. It is not, may I say, a task I am looking forward to."

"I can certainly understand that. Will she have hysterics, do you think?"

"I doubt it. She's had practically scores of lovers, and she understood from the first exactly what our relationship was. And I'd already told her before I left London that we were through. What I am more concerned about is that she will compose one of her execrable poems on heartbreak and I will be forced to listen to it."

"Hysterics," Gresham, who had been present for readings of Amanda's poetry at several *salons,* said with conviction, "would be *infinitely* preferable."

"I'm glad you're here, Peter," said Stanhope gratefully. "It's done me a world of good to talk to another reasonable person—I was beginning to feel that everyone in this town is mad, with the exception, of course, of Calista, who doesn't want to talk to me half the time anyway."

"You're glad *I'm* here! You must be jesting!" Gresham said

with a grin. "Seeing the Nonesuch humbled this way! I plan to dine out on tales of this for years to come."

Stanhope grinned in return. "I shudder to think of it. The rumourmongering that is sure to result from this mess only serves to make me more determined than ever to take my bride away on an extended honeymoon before any of this party returns to town."

"Will she have you, do you think?"

Stanhope turned his glass slowly with his fingertips, looking at it intently. The firelight played against the hollow of his cheek, and his eyes, when they met Peter's, were dark. "Well, a less optimistic man might refine on the fact that since I kissed her and asked her to marry me, she has been assiduously avoiding any contact with me. But I had an interesting interview with Lady Enright. She is convinced that Calista is anything but indifferent to me. She also thinks that Calista doesn't even *know* that she is about to be married off to Greystock—some scheme her foul brother and sister-in-law have cooked up to get their hands on his blunt, apparently." He gave Peter a sudden grin, saying, "It may be misplaced vanity, but I can't convince myself that given a choice between the two of us, she'd rather have him."

"What if she should decide not to have either of you?"

"Knowing Calista, that is precisely what she will decide. I'm worried, though, that her brother could make her life a misery."

"Is someone going to tell her about this plan of theirs?"

"Lady Enright thinks I should be the one—play the role of rescuer."

"She is not concerned that this will be a case of kill the messenger?"

Stanhope laughed. "Apparently not."

"And to think," mused Gresham, "if you survive imparting this bit of news, you can go on to the wagers."

"Good Lord, no. Even I am not brave enough for that. Ossie will tell her himself."

"You'd best work fast, Tris. She's bound to hear soon."

"Lady Enright, who apparently is not averse to a scheme or two, thinks I should just compromise her and be done with it."

Peter's eyebrows went up. "Well, she'd have to marry you then. Goodness knows it's been done. You, I trust, are not best pleased with that solution."

"No . . . Not that it wouldn't answer. I do think she has feelings for me under all those years of Sunday school and self-imposed spinsterhood, but she's afraid to let herself go with them. She's also confused, and thinks I'm a licentious rake—"

"Are you not?"

"Those days are over," Stanhope replied in frosty accents. "I'm as good as settled. *And* she thinks I'm engaged to Amanda. Although I am not supposed to know that she knows that, as it is secret intelligence from Lady Enright."

"It does sound like the devil's own mess. I no longer seem able to keep track of who knows what about whom. In fact, I'm not even certain what I just said."

Stanhope nodded with a trace of a smile. "I'm coming to believe, though, that in time it can all be sorted out, but that it would be disrespectful of her strength and intelligence to force her into a situation she cannot like. She needs time to learn what a lovable fellow I am. And I'd have all the time in the world except that Lady Enright fears—servants' gossip—that the good vicar plans to announce the match with our squire soon." He grinned suddenly. "I have, on Lady Enright's advice, however, sent for a special license so we need not lose a moment when Calista realizes just how badly she wants me."

"So this is love at last." Gresham shook his head wonderingly. "I confess I am almost envious."

Stanhope laughed and leaned back in his chair. "So far it has been equal parts misery and exultation. I am not entirely sure I can recommend it."

"Let us see what you have to say after that extended honeymoon," Gresham said, pouring out more wine.

Twenty-one

Lady Enright's "little dinner" was a sad crush. Or, in other words, a triumph to turn Gladys Lyttworth green. It seemed to Calista, as she sipped the glass of sherry that had been pressed upon her, as if everyone in the county had been invited, and, indeed, they sat down to dinner thirty people.

She was not, as she had feared, seated next to Stanhope. Instead, she was between Lord Peter Gresham and Sir Oswald. Stanhope, who had been *hoping* for some interference from his hostess, found himself disappointingly seated between Amanda and Sofie.

Calista glanced around at the assembled company in the glowing candlelight and felt a perfect dowd in her straw-coloured wool gown. Amanda Prescott was, as usual, the epitome of the stunning town belle in navy blue silk with diamonds in her hair. And Sofie, in exquisite counterpoint to her dark sophistication, positively radiated innocent blonde beauty. Even the Searle twins looked nice. And no one, Calista had assured her, would have dreamed that Emily Enright's white gown with a rose satin overskirt was *local*.

Stanhope, from his place between the two most stunning women in the county, gazed down the table at Calista—who was toying with her turtle soup—and willed his heart not to show in his eyes. The dress was hideous, but the colour looked good on her, bringing a soft glow to her cheeks and making those gray eyes look huge under sooty lashes. Gresham leaned unnecessarily close and elicited that unaffected laugh. She should have worn the yellow, he thought as a savage arrow of jealousy tore through him. When we are wed, he decided, I shall insist that she always wear yellow. And Peter shall never, ever, sit next to her.

Amanda, on his right, interrupted his musing. "You know, Tristan," she said, "we really must start to spend more time in the country. For I vow, I am coming quite bucolic."

He laughed with genuine amusement despite his irritation. "You? Bucolic? I do not believe such a thing for an instant."

"I have come to see," she said, gazing at him with meaning, "that there are ways to *occupy* oneself in the country. Ways that could prove *most* diverting."

He shot her a look, warning her to watch her tongue in front of Miss Lyttworth.

"It is most amusing to hear you say so, Mrs. Prescott," tittered Sofie, sapphire eyes open wide as she leaned in from his left, "as you have thus far declined to participate in almost all of our country pursuits. And, though one, of course, hates to make a point of it, have positively failed at those you *have* attempted."

"Oh, I am convinced I should find *some* to my liking," Amanda replied.

"Amanda!" Stanhope said sharply, hoping that Sofie was unaware of the risqué undertone to the conversation. "Tell me, how does your poem progress? An ode to a country house party, is it not?"

"Well, you may sing the praises of the country all you like, but I for one am positively agog to go to London," interrupted Sofie, fluttering her eyelashes at Stanhope in an attempt to keep up with Amanda's lures. "I am convinced that despite your kind condescension, you must find the country dull." Stanhope was about to protest, with perfect honesty, that he was finding it anything but dull, when Sofie continued. "Tell me of Stanhope House in London, my lord. I have heard it is exceedingly grand."

"It is *divine*," replied Amanda, sounding proprietary. "With a prime Grosvenor Square location. However, being a *town house,* it has only smallish grounds. Why, a rustic could become quite homesick!"

Sofie put on her sweetest smile. "My dear Mrs. Prescott," she said. "You mistake the matter. It is *you* who have professed an affinity for the countryside. *I* for one cannot wait to be surrounded by nothing but pavement. And shops," she added.

"There are horses in town, you know," Amanda replied with a smile as sweet as Sofie's. "And even there ladies are expected to ride them."

"By 'ladies' do you mean the female sex, or ladies as deemed by birth and behaviour?" inquired Sofie silkily, leaning across Stanhope, who sat apparently completely at his ease between them, consuming his turtle soup and listening with an expression of interest. "Because if it is the latter, I fail to see what that is to do with you."

"I—" Amanda began, but she was interrupted by a commotion on the other side of the table as Sir Ossie choked loudly and had to be hammered on the back by Lord Gresham before he could regain his composure.

"Dreadfully sorry," he said, bowing to the assembled company. "Please forgive me. It is only that Miss Ashton has just said that she does not know the difference between the Byron and the Irlandaise."

Neville gasped in horror and fanned himself with his hand. Hermione looked embarrassed at this lapse in education.

Lord Dunn, who was just a little hard of hearing, bellowed, "And quite right too! Don't hold no truck with those fancy French sauces m'self. Cause gout and flatulence, if you ask me! Look at the Greystock fellow!" All heads swiveled to do just that, but the squire, apparently unconcerned, merely stared back and continued cramming lobster patties into his mouth at top speed. "That's right, my dear," Lord Dunn boomed approvingly at Calista. "Stick to plain English cooking as the good Lord intended!"

As Lady Dunn shushed her husband, Stanhope looked across the table at Calista. The candlelight made his hair seem very dark, and his eyes were vividly alight. Everyone at the table was trying not to snicker, so why did the blasted man have to make her feel as if it was their own private joke? As much as she wanted to, she couldn't resist, and had to drop her head to hide her smile.

"The difference, you see," Ossie began to explain in a painstaking manner, as if to a very dense student, "is not only in the *knot!*" He paused to make sure she was taking this in. "It is also in the stiffening, or starching, if you will, of the fabric of the cravat. Are you with me thus far?"

Calista nodded, thinking that the room seemed unnaturally close. So many bright colours, all fading into each other. But truly it was Sir Ossie's eau de cologne that was positively overwhelming, she reflected fuzzily in the moment before her head hit the table.

Twenty-two

Where am I, and who has stuffed cotton wool in my mouth? were Calista's first thoughts on awakening in a darkened bedroom that was clearly not her own.

Sir Ossie had been giving her a most tedious lecture on cravats and gesturing wildly in demonstration of his finer points, which had the effect of sending wafts of his cloying eau de cologne into her face. She had met Stanhope's eyes, which had been alight with mirth and something else that she had not cared to define. The next thing she knew, the room had dimmed, but no one else seemed to notice. Then her cologne-infused world had begun to spin, and she had, for the first time in her life, fainted.

How very odd that I fainted, she thought in a detached sort of way, when I have never done so before. Surely even the Nonesuch could not with a mere gaze induce fainting spells? The thought of everyone he greeted falling over in a faint made her giggle, which set her head to spinning again, and she groaned. Altogether it was a rather tedious sort of experience, she decided, wondering why Hermione indulged in it so often. Looking down, she was somewhat surprised to see that she was clad in a white silk nightdress and had apparently been put to bed for the night.

In that case, I might as well enjoy it, Calista decided, and rolled over into the plump goose-down pillows—which were infinitely fluffier and more luxurious and lavender-scented than her own rather spartan ones at the vicarage, owing to her belief

that too much attention to the creature comforts diluted moral
purity. She stretched luxuriously against the silky sheets. I could
about get used to this were it not so extraordinarily decadent,
she thought drowsily. Stanhope, no doubt, bedded down in such
luxury every night. She blushed at the realization that imagining
gentlemen in bed was not a fit occupation for an unmarried
woman. And then the miserably disturbing picture of him bedding down in such sinful luxury with Amanda Prescott intruded.

Before she could refine on the thought, however, there was
a brief scratch at the door, and Stanhope himself, as if conjured
by her improper thoughts, entered the room.

"You," she gasped, snatching up the counterpane to her chin
as he crossed the room and settled himself on the bed next to
her. He said nothing, but propped his head comfortably on several of the aforementioned down pillows, and crossed his booted
feet negligently on the coverlet.

"What the devil—" she began to demand, but stopped, as her
parched throat seemed incapable of delivering anything beyond
a strangled croak.

He cocked a brow. "Water, my heart?"

She nodded, which set her head to spinning once again, and
collapsed back against the pillows. Stanhope lazily sat up and
poured out a glass from the jug on the night table. He handed
it to her in silence and, looking mistrustfully at him over the
rim of the glass, she drained it. He had untied his cravat, she
noticed, and it hung over the back of his coat. He looked utterly
relaxed and almost unbearably handsome.

"Better?" he asked, accepting the empty glass and replacing
it on the bedside table.

"What are you doing here? Are you insane?" she hissed.

"It relieves me no end that you seem to have found your
voice again," he drawled, sounding every inch the bored town
beau.

Mixed with Calista's alarm at his appearance was perhaps
the tiniest trace of pique at his indifference to her virtual naked-
ness, but she was not about to let him know that. "Of all the
rackety, no-brained ways to behave—"

His brow went up again. "However, if you don't watch what

you are saying, Calista, I may regret having given you the water. It is possible I underestimated the merits of having you silenced."

Her mouth opened and closed as she tried to think of a retort. Unable, she contented herself with "Get out!"

"But I am so enjoying our proximity." As if of their own will his eyes wandered to her almost bare shoulders. His hand itched to reach out and feel the silkiness of her skin. "Can you honestly say you aren't?"

She drew a shaky breath. It is just the fainting spell, she assured herself. This has nothing to do with his nearness. "I certainly am not," she replied in her most repressive schoolmarm tone. "So forget whatever it is you have in mind! And do not try to gammon me by telling me that you fainted also. The room is dim, to be sure, but you do not appear in the least bit pale."

"Your nearness makes me light-headed, Calista," he whispered, suddenly perilously close.

She drew a shaky breath. "What are you doing here? Please just tell me and go. This is extraordinarily improper. While it is likely commonplace for unwed couples to share a bed in your circles, it is not considered at all the thing here, Stanhope."

"Then let us bring it into fashion here in Deepdene, you and I, Calista," he suggested softly.

The husky promise in his voice was almost too much for Calista. She repressed the shiver of longing that his words caused. "No!" she forced herself to say.

"No? What a shame. I can think of few things more enjoyable. But since you are determined in your decision, I shall have to settle for speaking with you."

"Have you never heard of a morning call? Civilized people make them. At civilized hours."

"Would you have been at home to me?"

"Likely not."

"My point exactly. Besides, it is unlikely that I would enjoy our conversation half so much were you not in such a charming state of dishabille." His eyes wandered again to her shoulders.

"So you waited for me to faint and then sneaked around

looking for me?" Calista retorted, somehow heartened by his look.

"Well, not exactly. I stayed after the dinner to discuss some breeding experiments with Lord Enright—at his request, might I add—"

"Breeding?"

He looked at her. "My herds—"

"Of course. Your herds," she echoed.

"Well, what did you think I meant? I own a property in Scotland, where the terrain is—"

She held up a hand. "Enough!" Really, this conversation almost defied belief, reflected Calista. Whatever she had expected would transpire if they were alone in a bedroom, it was not a discussion on the vagaries of cattle breeding. "Just tell me what you are come for. And then do go away." She put a hand to her head. "This is all to much for me," she complained. "As I have mentioned before, I am not at all accustomed to fainting."

"The thing of it is that I am not at all certain that you fainted." Here he had the good grace to look a tad uncomfortable.

She gave him a questioning look.

"I'm almost certain there was laudanum in your sherry."

"You are saying that I was poisoned?"

"Not poisoned, my love, drugged."

"Naturally. And to think I thought it was the cologne! I gather you know who bears responsibility for this treachery?" she asked, thinking that he was clearly having a joke.

He nodded. "Lady Enright."

"Of course. I don't know why I didn't think of it myself." She faced him directly. "You are asking me to believe, sir, that a woman I have known all my life—a respectable matron, a doting wife and mother, my own mother's closest friend, in fact—drugged me. All the while hosting thirty of the county's most august citizens at her dinner table?" She almost laughed at the sheer ridiculousness of it.

"Well, yes."

"Why would she do that?"

"So I could compromise you."

Calista was so angry at his implication that she jumped off

the bed, heedless of the immodesty of her attire and the dizziness that followed her action, and stood.

Oh, my! Stanhope thought, getting a good look at the nightgown for the first time. He tried to concentrate on her words as she stood glaring down at his reclining figure. "Are you suggesting, sir, that she was helping me trap you?" she demanded. "Because I can assure you that no such thing—"

"Calista," he interrupted, gently taking her hand and pulling her back onto the bed. "Please, sit down before you faint again. And no, I am suggesting that she was trying to help *me* trap *you.*"

"What?" she whispered, wishing her head would stop this inconvenient whirling. Stanhope had somehow forgotten to release her hand, which wasn't helping.

"She thought she would speed matters along between us," he said quietly.

"There are no matters between us! I do not suppose that she was in possession of the intelligence that you are already promised at the time she was drugging my sherry?"

"Calista—"

She freed her hand. "No! You seem to manage to conveniently forget that you are engaged whenever the notion enters your head! It is bad enough that I allowed you to take liberties—I assure you I can feel nothing but shock and disgust at my own conduct. But that you would not only toy with me but mislead and enlist Lady Enright in your schemes to seduce me for your entertainment is beyond anything I could have expected. Even from you!" The unshed tears in her eyes made his heart sink.

"Calista, listen to me for a moment," he said gently. "I am not engaged to Amanda, and Lady Enright knows that."

"I realize it is more of an understanding, but surely—"

"There is no understanding." He sighed, disliking to shock her but knowing that honesty was called for. "I had hoped to spare you the particular details of this, my sweet, but the truth is that Amanda is—*was* actually—my, er—"

The light dawned in her eyes as she saw his discomfort. "Mistress? Fancy piece? Bit of muslin?" Her tone sounded bit-

ter to her own ears, and tears burned in her eyes as she acknowledged to herself that they owed as much to jealousy of Amanda
Prescott as to disgust with his profligacy.

"Yes, my love."

"Miss Ashton!" She shook her head, disgusted at herself for
the feeling of relief that had gone through her to learn that
whatever Amanda was, she was not to be his bride.

Stanhope looked at her pale face and decided that his only
hope was to make a clean breast of things. "The thing of it is,"
he began, feeling awkward and wanting only to smooth away
her frown, "that I have not lived an exemplary life, it is true,
and Amanda was one of my mistresses, but—"

"One of your mistresses? How many do you have? Or do I
dare ask? No, wait." She held out her hand to stop him speaking.
"It is none of my business."

He took a deep breath. "Two."

I am in love with this man, Calista realized with perfect clar-
ity. Foolishly, irreversibly, in love. And he has two mistresses.
She was careful to keep her voice steady, *"Only* two, my lord?
How tedious for you."

"I *had* two. I had parted ways with both of them before I left
London."

Her eyebrow went up. "Then, why is one of them here?"

"Well, that's just the thing. Oswald, fool that he is, thought
to get me out of the suds with Sofie by inventing an engagement
to Amanda. And then Lady Lyttworth, who, as you know, is an
old crony of her mother's, invited her to join our congenial little
party."

"How odd of Lady Lyttworth to have invited her," Calista
started to say, when the import of his words hit with the force
of a blow. "You are *using* me!" she gasped, the tears coming
in earnest now. "I understand now. To fob off your mistress!
You don't want to marry her. But now that Sir Oswald landed
you in the soup, you thought to get rid of her by wedding a
quiet, mousy nobody who will remain in the country breeding
and look the other way while you pursue your other—" She
broke off, looking put out when Stanhope effectively took the

wind out of her sails by throwing back his head and barking with laughter.

"Oh, Calista," he said as he put an arm around her and drew her close. She knew she should resist but somehow seemed powerless to stop herself being drawn into the warm circle of his arm. "I have never heard a less apt description of you than 'quiet mousy nobody.' " With the pristine white of his shirt cuff, he gently dried her eyes. "I have made a mull of this from the very beginning, but I have never tried to declare myself before."

She sniffled a little, and just for a moment, she assured herself, allowed herself the luxury of relaxing against him.

His arm tightened. "Tell me, are you feeling any better?"

"A little."

"Good." He nodded. "Then let us talk of Greystock."

"Did you black his eye?"

He nodded again. "Lady Enright told me what he did to you."

"It was not necessary, you know, but thank you."

"I don't suppose you desire me to call him out?" he asked, a hopeful note in his voice. "I can think of nothing that would give me more pleasure—well, perhaps one thing," he said with a glance that brought warmth to her cheeks, and suddenly the feeling of him next to her went from comforting to something else entirely as the heat of his arm seemed to burn through the thin fabric of the nightgown, "than putting a ball through him."

"You," she reminded him, "do not duel."

"Perhaps Elmo was in the right of it," he said, avoiding her eye, "and it is simply a matter of the proper insult."

"You were not insulted, sir," she reminded him.

"No," he replied. "But I find that you are the only thing on this earth I have ever thought worth dueling over, Miss Ashton." With his free hand he reached over and took hers.

His hand was beautifully shaped. Like the rest of him, she noted, studying it as if from outside herself. It was warm, with slightly callused palms and long, capable-looking fingers. He wore a heavy gold signet ring that felt smooth and warmed by his flesh. She firmly pushed away the memory of those hands stroking her face when he had kissed her on the way to the Stanleys' breakfast. "That will hardly be necessary," she managed to say with a reassuring amount of spirit. "As you can see, I am well able to take care of myself."

He raised their hands and gently stroked the back of hers. She ignored the sweet sensations his actions provoked. "I am more than aware of that, Calista. But would it not be pleasant to allow someone else to care for you for a change?" His thumb caressed the inside of her wrist, sending little quivers through her arm.

"No." She snatched her hand back, and he promptly encircled her with his arms. "I value my independence far too much for that. By the way, your boots are making the bed dirty."

"So they are," he agreed pleasantly as he reclined against the pillows again, this time taking her with him. "The Enrights will no doubt think you a most inconsiderate guest. And," he added, a grin lighting his face, "one with extraordinarily large feet."

"They are much more likely to be disturbed by the sudden penchant I seem to have developed for rendezvousing with gentlemen in bedchambers," she said, leaning her head against his shoulder.

He laughed, and his arms tightened around her. "As they arranged it, that is doubtful."

"Have I asked you to go away?" she retorted, starting to enjoy sparring with him, especially as she was so firmly and so very improperly ensconced in his arms. "Because if I have somehow overlooked it, I am asking you now."

He buried his face in her hair and inhaled the clean scent of it. "I am convinced you would miss me!"

"You, as usual, are incorrect, sir!"

"Calista," he said gently, looking upward at the bed hangings and ignoring her last riposte. "If you wed Greystock, you will of a certainty lose the freedom you so value."

"Marry him?" she gasped. "Why on earth would I do that? Just because you have been engaged to nearly everyone in this town, including, briefly, a horse, is no reason to insist I follow your lead. In fact, for a man who has spent goodness knows how many years assiduously avoiding the married state, you seem most eager that I enter it."

"Suppose I reminded you that I no longer wish to avoid that particular state?" His tone was quiet, but his body was tense.

"Is that not what rakes always say to their prey?"

"I have given up raking, Calista." A lock of hair had fallen across his forehead. His tousledness was somehow endearing and so very intimate. "It seems that all I want is home and hearth these days. And you."

She forced her voice to steadiness. "How very dull your tastes are become, sir."

"My tastes are not become dull at all, my heart," he said in a tone that made Calista think the Enrights kept their bedchambers overwarm.

"I am not in your style."

"I doubt that," he said with conviction, propping his head on one elbow so he looked down at her. He could see by the depth of her eyes that his nearness was affecting her. There was no question that hers was affecting him. Opting to press his advantage, he bent and placed his lips against hers. Gently, very gently.

In the first instant, Calista decided that she had clearly run mad. But at this point, she reasoned, no further harm could possibly come of one more kiss. So she closed her eyes and gave herself over to sensation as she allowed his lips their gentle exploration.

All too soon he pulled away, and the feather-light sensations stopped. "Am I kissing another man's fiancée?" he asked.

His words brought her momentarily back to reality. "No! Why do you keep asking that? Not," she remembered to add, "that you should be kissing me at all."

"Actually, I had intended to get back to that in just a moment," he said with a look that made a shiver run through her.

She frowned. "I have firmly refused the squire's offer."

"The prevailing belief seems to be that your brother may have made arrangements without your consent," he said carefully, not forgetting Gresham's warnings about killing the messenger.

All traces of softness were gone from Calista's eyes in an instant. She sat up like a shot and stared at him. "Are you saying they went behind my back?" she demanded. "They would actually do that to me?"

"We don't know that for certain," he started to say, but she went on as if she had not heard him.

"No wonder that muttonhead thought he'd a right to maul me in the woods! Blast them! Damn! I'll put a stop to any notions they have that *that* will ever come off, you can be certain!"

Stanhope lifted a brow, but all he said was, "Marry me. It would provide a way out of your dilemma."

She faced him. "To escape one unwanted alliance? That is no good reason for marriage, my lord."

"I suppose not. And I wish you would call me Tristan," he complained as he pulled her down so she was leaning over him, her loosened hair curtaining his face. "It is so hard to make love to a woman who insists on calling you 'my lord.' Which is exactly what I intend to get back to now that I know that neither your heart nor your hand belong to another. This time," he said, pulling her against him, "you can do the work and I will relax."

He spoke in jest, but to both their surprise she did just that, kissing him, tentatively at first. This is wrong, absolutely wrong, Calista told herself. Besides which, it solves nothing. Stanhope made a little noise in his throat, and when his firmly muscled arms pulled her closer, she kissed him harder.

"Oh, Calista, Calista," he groaned as the blood pounded through his veins. He pulled her body on top of his and lay, feeling her through the thin nightdress, so slight and yet so deliciously curved in all the right places, stretched out along the firm, lean length of him. Lady Enright knew what she was about with her meddling. "God help me, I have never wanted a woman the way I want you," he whispered hoarsely against her lips.

She lifted her head slightly and looked down into his eyes. She felt as though her body were inhabited by another person. A wild, wanton person with no qualms and no regrets. "And to think I have never wanted a man before," she heard herself say.

At his appreciative crack of laughter she blushed, as much shocked by her words as her actions.

"You," he said, still laughing, "should know nothing of these things."

"I don't really," she admitted as she gazed down at the contours of his face. His eyes were dark and his cheeks flushed.

He said nothing but reached for her again. This time when he pulled her back down, he rolled them over so he was almost on top of her. With absolute gentleness he caught her full lower lip between his teeth, and she gasped with pleasure, her lips parting for him. His hands went to her hair and then traveled down her back, stroking her, molding her body closer. When she looked into his eyes, there was an expression she had never seen there before.

Flames seemed to course through her body, and her limbs felt strangely heavy. I am powerless to stop this. I know it is wrong, but I want it and this may be my only chance, she thought.

But suddenly he stopped. Rolling over onto his back, he lay next to her, breathing raggedly. He has come to his senses and realized that he could not possibly want me, she thought, numbness flooding her where there had been only heat a moment before.

His next words sent feeling through her again. "You enchant me, my heart. I look forward with great anticipation to the day when we will not have to stop ourselves. However"—his smile was slightly twisted—"one of us has to behave with propriety, and you—properly raised, though you claim to be—do not appear to be about to." He rolled to his side and lay gazing down. Her throaty laugh prompted him to continue in a more serious tone as he traced the line of her cheek with his hand. "Make no mistake. I want you more than I have ever wanted anything, but I want you to come to me on your own terms. Not because you are compromised."

Suddenly his nearness was too much. The last thing she needed was for that blasted light-headedness to engulf her again. She pulled herself up to sitting and hugged her knees to her chest. "Surely that was done several days ago," she said.

Stanhope sat up also and with gentle care tucked a pillow behind her back. "Yes," he replied, still serious. "And as a gentleman, I am ashamed of myself," he said, putting a finger to her lips to stop her speaking. "Although as a man I cannot bring myself to regret anything that has passed between us. But I can promise you that should you so choose, no one need ever know anything that has occurred. Were things to progress further, I would be unable to live with myself. I am not, despite what you may believe, in the habit of seducing innocents."

"I did not truly think that you were," she said, looking down.

"Calista." He tilted her chin up so he could see her eyes. "Tell me that you are completely indifferent to me."

She shook her head, refusing to be drawn into that line of conversation. "What of Amanda?"

"Amanda," he said carefully, hope surging through him, "was a mistake from the first moment. Nothing more, nothing less."

"A rather cavalier treatment." She shook her head. "I do not know how I can feel about a man who could cast her aside so easily. Unfortunate women who are forced by circumstances to—"

He wanted desperately to laugh but knew she would be furious. "Calista, sweetheart," he said gently, "I know this is foreign to everything you understand, but Amanda was not forced into anything by circumstances. She married the oldest, wealthiest man who offered. And when he died, she set herself up in grand style. She has had a string of lovers longer than my arm and has often voiced the opinion that it is infinitely preferable to marriage."

"But perhaps she fell in love with you," she said, thinking that it would hardly be possible not to. "You would break her heart without so much as a second thought?"

"I will endeavor to do the thing without causing her undue pain—not that I am convinced she can actually *feel* pain, though heaven knows she can't *write* about it—but I've no intention of being forced into marriage with a woman for whom I feel nothing, by some half-baked scheme. And don't talk yourself around to believing that she loves me, because she doesn't, any more than I love her."

"And Sofie?" she asked, her eyes not quite meeting his.

"Sofie is a beautiful, empty-headed widgeon. She is everything I have always thought I would find in my bride, which is why I am still unwed."

"You do not offer solely as a chivalrous gesture to save me from an unwanted alliance?" Calista looked up through her lashes. In another woman it might have smacked of coquetry, but from her Stanhope found it enormously appealing. So appealing, in fact, that he was hard pressed not to pull her back into his arms.

"I am not nearly such a saintly fellow as that." His voice was dry but his face was grave. "While I must own to some revulsion at the idea of a union between you and Greystock, I credit you with the good sense and resourcefulness to extricate yourself. Make no mistake, Calista, there is very little altruism in my gesture." He paused, and when he continued, he sounded less sure of himself. "I am asking because I want you beside me. I want you in my bed, but I also want your mind and your laughter and your sharp wit. I am constantly surprised by you, but at the same time I feel that I've known you forever."

"Thank you, Stanhope," she replied, genuinely touched.

"Only say that you will think about it?"

"My head is spinning so," she complained. "I doubt I can."

"My presence, no doubt."

"More like the laudanum, no doubt," she said with a smirk.

"Let us put that assertion to the test," he whispered as he pulled her closer. "This time, however, I promise to keep my baser appetites in check."

Indeed, she immediately felt herself melting once again under the sweetness of his expert mouth. "What a shame," whispered back that mysterious wanton person who seemed once again to have taken her over as his lips found the hollow of her throat.

He barked with laughter. "I rest secure in the conviction that we will spend many happy hours attending to those in the future. Once you accept me"—there was a husky promise in his voice—"I will teach you everything I know about baser appetites."

The very notion should have been shocking. Why, then, did

it sound so very appealing? He was so close that she could feel his heart beating beneath the linen of his shirt. She pulled away with effort, wanting nothing more than to remain in his embrace forever. "Do you know so very much?" she asked.

Her words were sharp, but when he pulled her back, her body seemed to melt against him, making him waver in his resolve.

"Enough anyway to keep us busy for a long, long time," he murmured as his lips found her earlobe. Just as the languorous heat threatened completely to consume her, he disengaged himself and stood, leaving her once again cold and alone. She wrapped her arms around herself for warmth. "But as I am so intent on clinging to propriety," he explained, "although I am finding it vastly overrated, I will take my leave now, before we are discovered."

"Thank you," she replied, wishing she didn't feel so bereft. *I could say yes to his proposal, and he would get right back on the bed and finish what we started. And then I would never be alone again,* a traitorous voice whispered inside her head. *Except when he was with his mistresses,* whispered back another.

"Get some rest," he advised. "And please remember that you only need say so and I am yours to command." He bowed and gave her a last lingering look that left her heart pounding in her ears before he vanished out the door.

After his departure, Calista put her face against the pillows, still warm where he had lain against them, and breathed in the scent of his soap. Was it truly possible, she wondered, that such a man could want her? She had trouble believing it, but she also couldn't truly believe that he would say such things only to deceive her. *I am a rational person,* she thought. *I will list the positives and negatives.*

On the positive side, he was not at all what she had imagined he would be. Despite his lightheartedness, he had a deep intelligence, which spoke well for him. He was well read and concerned with issues other than fashion—an area in which, to own the truth, he never indulged in excess. Even Elmo's cravat had of late been of a manageable height since Stanhope had taught

LORD STANHOPE'S PROPOSAL   171

him how to tie it. His presence in the area had been curiously
free of the sort of larks and rackety capers she had expected to
accompany the Nonesuch. There had been no wild wagers or
mills or any signs of drunken debauchery. If anything, his presence had a stabilizing influence on the local Nonesuch aspirants,
to whom he had made it clear that a genuine top-of-the-trees
fellow is unfailingly polite, even when cornered by the Dowager
Lady Dabley. Then there was the sense of humour that seemed
to bring out her own. And that private smile that seemed as if
it were for her alone. And, oh, those kisses and those hands!
Who would have imagined what sensations those elegant hands
could awake within her? She smiled to herself with the memory
and fell into a deep sleep before reaching the negatives.

Twenty-three

Calista wasn't sure how long she would have gone on sleeping the next morning, if not for the maid's exceedingly noisy arrival at the shockingly late hour of eleven of the clock. She accepted the cup of steaming chocolate proffered and informed the girl that she wished an immediate audience with her mistress. Not ten minutes later, when Lady Enright tripped blithely in, she found Calista dressed in a wrapper and seated at the dressing table.

"Calista, you poor dear. You must on no account tax yourself today!" she cried.

"Doing it too brown, Roberta," replied Calista, folding her arms and tapping her foot. "Do not come the innocent with me."

"I don't know what you can possibly mean by that, my dear. I can only assume you were overset by last night's events," her hostess replied, assuming a mien of injured innocence.

Calista raised a brow. "And what last night might have happened that would overset me, Roberta? Having my sherry drugged? Waking to find a man in my bedchamber?" Lady Enright, she noted, at least had the good sense to blush, but when she opened her mouth to reply, Calista forestalled her. "Do not bother denying it. I know of your part in the scheme."

"Well," began Lady Enright frostily, "if you think—"

"Roberta!"

"Oh, very well. I admit my part in it." She threw up her hands and sank into a luxuriously upholstered slipper chair next to the dressing table. "I am only trying to assist the course of true love! Stanhope loves you, and it is plain that you, my girl, love him! I can see it even if you don't, and *I*"—she glared defiantly—"have done only what is right!"

Calista turned to her, her face glowing. "Do you truly think he loves me, Roberta? Could such a thing be possible?"

"Of *course* it is," Lady Enright replied, glad to be let off the hook so easily. "I am not so old or so unromantical that I no longer recognize the signs, you know."

"You do not think he is toying with me?" Doubt was creeping back into Calista's eyes. "Why would he want me? He breaks hearts like, well . . . I don't know, but he breaks hearts! And needless to say, he is quite skilled in the business of seducing females. His morals, you know, are completely reprehensible. In fact, he—" She dropped her head.

"He what, love?" Lady Enright leaned forward.

Calista could feel her cheeks burning. "He had *two* mistresses," she blurted out.

Lady Enright laughed. "I'd wager he's had a long sight more than two," she replied bluntly.

"No, Roberta, you mistake my meaning. He kept two at once."

"Likely because each one bored him silly." She shrugged away Calista's concern. "A man like Stanhope needs a woman who will challenge him with her mind as well as her body. He's just never understood that before now."

"I-I cannot believe we are talking of such things. It is not at all proper," Calista said, pressing her hands to her face, which felt aflame with embarrassment.

"You are a woman of great intelligence and common sense, Calista, not some die-away debutante. It is one of the things, I am sure, that attracted Stanhope to you in the first place, and it is the reason I feel able to speak with you with a certain frankness. His past is his past, and he seems ready and pleased to put it behind him and look to a future with you."

"But I've behaved so wantonly with him," Calista wailed. "Surely it can only give him a disgust of me. I am so ashamed."

"Calista," Lady Enright said, handing her a lace-trimmed

handkerchief, "there is nothing to be ashamed of, and I am certain your behaviour has not given him a disgust of you. Quite the opposite, in fact, unless I miss my guess."

"I cannot believe we are speaking of this," Calista said.

"Forget propriety," Lady Enright commanded. "There is no need to be missish with me, Calista. Now," she said briskly, "did he apprise you of my suspicions regarding the situation with Everard?"

"He did."

"Good. Then I did not misjudge the man! It is one thing, seducing virgins under my roof. But to do it without talk of a future would be entirely reprehensible!"

"I am glad that you have your morals." Calista was unable to make her face as severe as her words.

"Morals are all well and good, except, of course, when they're not," Lady Enright replied obliquely.

"You are a baggage, Roberta." Calista laughed despite herself. "But do you truly think Adolphus would agree to a betrothal without my consent?"

"Yes," said Lady Enright decisively. "Absolutely I do. Especially when Everard's blunt is at stake. Will Stanhope challenge him, do you think?" she asked hopefully.

"Of course not!" Calista began in her most damping accents, before breaking off. A note of interest entered her voice. "Who? Adolphus or Squire Greystock?"

"Either would be nice, but I was thinking of Everard."

Calista shook her head to clear it. "I cannot believe that I am participating in this conversation. It is surely a measure of how far I am sunk. *I* shall handle this by speaking with Adolphus about it!"

"What a shame. I, for one, think it would be excellent above all things were Stanhope to at least *threaten* to kill him. A favour to the neighbourhood, in fact!"

"Honestly! There is no doubt from where Emily comes by her lack of common sense, Roberta."

"Well Adolphus had hoped to announce your engagement to Everard, and Gladys had planned to announce Sofie's to Stanhope, and it seems neither event shall come to pass. Although, mind you, Gladys will not have given up hope of bringing that one about. She never could accept the obvious!" Lady Enright frowned, saying with a sniff, "In fact, I detect *her* meddling hand in this entire matter. Neither Adolphus nor Hermione, odious though they are, has the brains or backbone to go ahead with this on their own."

Calista raised a brow, but under the circumstances deemed it appropriate to ignore this slight on her closest living relatives. "And you, Roberta, are in a position to accuse others of meddling?"

Lady Enright raised her chin defiantly. "I cannot be sorry for drugging your sherry if it speeds a happy conclusion!"

"But can he really want me, Roberta? Whatever could he gain from such an unequal match?"

"I would hazard a guess that he is in love with you," said Lady Enright dryly, "just as you are with him. He is, you know, more than old enough to know what he wants, and it appears, my girl, that he wants you."

"For the moment. And mainly because he can't have me, I would guess."

"Pshaw! And only think how out of joint Gladys's nose will be when you snatch this prize right out from under the familial chin, as it were!"

"Roberta!" Shocked laughter warred with Calista's tears.

"Enough of your scruples," Lady Enright insisted, firmly changing the subject. "Now, tell me, what had you planned for today?"

"I don't understand what that is to do with anything," answered Calista with a suspicious look, "but I've many duties that I've sorely neglected of late."

"Forget them," said Lady Enright in firm tones. "You are looking tired and far too thin. Stanhope will want you with some curves left, so today you will forget duty and loll around my house, reading in front of the fire for most of the day, until this evening, when, attired in one of Emily's best gowns—locally purchased, I am afraid—you will accompany us to the Redingcote Assemblies. And do not bother protesting," she said, anticipating Calista's demurral, "as you know now the means

I am prepared to employ, should they prove necessary, to get my way."

"I shall not find poison in my tea or laudanum in my lemonade?"

"Not if you do as I say! Now," she said briskly, "may I send a message to your repellent brother informing him that you will meet them at the assembly?"

Calista was suddenly put in mind of the swimming lessons her father had given her. If you should ever find yourself caught in a strong tide, do not attempt to fight it, he had explained, as that is the surest route to drowning. Let it carry you until it diminishes and then swim for shore. The only problem with that, she reflected, was that she was not at all sure where the shore lay anymore. So, she nodded her acquiescence and hoped she was headed toward solid ground.

"Excellent! There is nothing wrong with allowing yourself some happiness, you know," Lady Enright called airily as she departed.

Twenty-four

The Redingcote Assemblies offered the highlight of what was admittedly a less than stellar social whirl in Deepdene. In the ordinary run of things, on the second Friday of every month, without much regard to birth or rank, much of the citizenry turned out for dancing and a late supper. But tonight with the expected presence of the Earl of Stanhope, an unprecedented crowd had the small rooms crammed almost to bursting. Those unfortunates who had failed to garner invites to the entertainments in honour of his lordship were positively agog to catch a firsthand glimpse of the exalted visitor, and those able to claim his acquaintance were deeply desirous of making that fact clear to their neighbours.

A wave of hushed conversation went through the room at the arrival of the first of the Lyttworth house party: Ossie, Neville, and Squibby got up in their finest, accompanied by a stunning, but extremely haughty-looking, Amanda Prescott.

These four were followed a few minutes later by the familiar and considerably less interesting sight of the Baron and Lady Lyttworth, nodding regally to the assembled company as they made their way toward the cloakroom.

Lord Gresham, arriving not long afterward with the Stanleys, was generally agreed upon to be an extremely handsome young man.

"And he has eighteen thousand a year! So stand up straight and try not to look so spotty, gel!" bellowed the Dowager Lady

Dabley at her granddaughter, who had the ill fortune to be visiting from Windsor.

The next to arrive, to no one's great excitement, as Adolphus was wont to drink all the spirits and lecture tediously on the evils of dancing with partners of unequal birth, were Adolphus and Hermione, followed closely by Squire Greystock.

There was an actual hush for a fraction of a minute when Stanhope entered with Sofie Lyttworth on his arm. The earl, generally accounted to be the best-looking man ever to visit the town, was positively stunning in evening dress, it was universally agreed. The severe black and white he wore stood out starkly against all the colours in the ballroom, highlighting his dark hair and those amazing eyes. And Sofie, too, was more beautiful than anyone could ever remember seeing her before, in a demure white gown with a peach net overskirt. Her hair was arranged in a deceptively simple froth of ringlets. And the pearls she wore highlighted rather than detracted from the creaminess of her skin and the whiteness of her teeth. And if few in the room felt much liking for her, well, that was completely beside the point.

"I feel privileged to be here to witness a match surely made by the angels," sniffled the Dowager Lady Dabley in a sentimental moment. "Now, get off your fat derrière and make one of your own, since there obviously ain't no angels watching over you, missy!" she thundered at the hapless granddaughter.

Stanhope did the proper, greeting people with whom he was already acquainted and putting the newly introduced at their ease. But beneath the casual exterior, his entire body felt taut as he scanned the room for Calista while scratching his name on a good many dance cards belonging to a good many hopeful young misses. His eyebrow rose as he realized that the prospect of even one night without seeing her felt virtually unendurable.

So occupied with Calista were his thoughts that he responded to one of Sofie's remarks with a smile so dazzling and genuine that she felt her heart in her throat as he led her out for the opening dance. Her mother also noted it and smiled to herself. The figures of the lively country dance offered little opportunity for conversation, but it seemed to both ladies that when they did come together, Stanhope had a different look in his eye.

When Calista did arrive, Stanhope could have sworn that he actually felt her presence rather than saw it.

Lady Enright had ruled over her preparations with an iron hand. "I was under the happy impression, Calista, that I had made you properly afraid of me," she had said menacingly when Calista had caviled at borrowing one of Emily's gowns. "Besides, I'll not allow her to wear it. It is perfect for an elegant young woman such as yourself but far too sophisticated for a girl of fifteen. She bamboozled the dressmaker into making it in the first place, and I do so hate to think of it just hanging in the closet."

So for possibly the first time in her life, Calista was perfumed and pampered and creamed and buffed practically to a sheen as she had wryly observed. The gown was a high-waisted chemise in a deep sea-green watered silk tied under the bust with gossamer silver ribbons. Emily was a little shorter than Calista, and a trifle heavier, so Lady Enright's maid, who was a dab hand with a needle, had done some quick alterations, and it now sported an elegant underskirt in a creamy ivory satin. The short puffed sleeves and décolletage had left Calista feeling self-conscious, so Lady Lyttworth's maid had draped a filmy silver shawl over her shoulders. Her hair—even Lady Enright had been unable to convince her to allow them to cut it—was dressed simply in a loose knot on the back of her head with some tendrils allowed to curl about her face. A silver silk rose anchored the knot, and low-heeled slipper shoes completed the toilette. Truth to tell, she had barely recognized herself in the glass.

As she stood with the Enrights, she had one ear on their good-natured bickering—as to whether Lady Enright would consent to leave in time to be home by ten of the clock, after which time Lord Enright had declared he would lie down and go to sleep wherever he happened to find himself—and one ear on Emily's prattle.

"Oooh, there is Sofie dancing with the earl," said Emily. "Do they not make a handsome pair? I confess I hope I will be able to find a man half as handsome during my season."

At the sight of them moving so gracefully together on the dance floor, Calista stopped, unable to tear her eyes away.

"D'you think I will, Calista?" Emily asked, not at all sure what to make of such behaviour on the sensible Miss Ashton's part.

"I am certain that when your affections are truly engaged, Emily, you are bound to find the gentleman's countenance pleasing as well," replied Calista a trifle absently, trying but seemingly unable to look away from the glowing couple on the dance floor.

Sensing that she was watching them, Stanhope cursed the fact that he had been obligated to fill so many dance cards. He would be unable to claim her until the supper dance, but at least he had been able to leave that free. And then hopefully there would be time for a stroll on the terrace. People would talk if he were to single her out, but so what? He had no objection to staking his claim publicly. He was so busy thinking of ways in which they could take advantage of the dark corners of the terrace that he almost missed a step. Sofie gave him an odd look, and he forced his mind back to the dance.

"I say, is that *Calista?*" Elmo squinted across the ballroom.

"Well, well. If the frog hasn't turned into a princess," said Neville, handing his snuffbox to the footman and raising his quizzing glass, the better to peer across the ballroom.

"Ha!" crowed Ossie. "Not as if I need anything else to tell me which way the wind is blowing."

Neville arched an exquisite brow. "Excuse me?"

"It is plain that Miss Ashton has gone to great pains to capture my attention," explained Ossie, shooting him what he hoped was a withering glance.

"Your head has become positively swelled since our arrival in this town," accused Neville. "Not," he drawled, "that any part of you was small before."

"How else do you explain it except that she realized that she would never catch my eye as a dowd?" Ossie demanded.

Unable to do so, Elmo shook his head. "I've known her all my life and I've never seen her rigged out like that before. Looks smashing," he added.

"Passable," sniffed Neville.

"The important thing is that Oswald turn the situation to our advantage, since this entire charade has a purpose, if you recall," Squibby reminded them. "I for one shall be rolling in the ready!"

The uncomfortable thought of what his idol would say about dragging the name of an innocent miss into a wager entered Elmo's mind. The past few weeks in Stanhope's company had served to convince him that a top-of-the-trees fellow, awake on all suits, might hesitate to use a lady thusly. "Not altogether sure this is quite the thing, fellows," he said, feeling his throat tighten. "Calista'll be ripping mad if word of the wagers gets back to her."

"Elmo!" said Squibby in what he felt was a marvelously controlled tone. "It is already in the *books*. To back down now would be ruin!"

"He's right, for once, you know, Elmo," Neville said as Ossie nodded his agreement.

"If you say so," said Elmo dubiously. "But I cannot like it all the same. Couldn't it mean ruin for Calista?"

"Don't trouble your head over it, old fellow," said Ossie with a reassuring clap on the back. "It's already done. Besides, I've a mind to bring her into fashion after all."

"And exactly how d'you intend to do that, old bean?" inquired Neville coldly, eyeing him through his quizzing glass.

"I intend to do it," replied Ossie equally coldly, "by favouring her with my attentions. Once she is seen to have attracted *me,* the fashionable world can hardly help but embrace her," he explained with a modest shrug.

"Not too sure she cares overmuch for the fashionable world," quibbled Elmo, still dissatisfied.

Fed up with Elmo's scruples, Ossie snapped. "Not as if the other bluestockings and radicals will shun her, and she don't exactly move in the best circles as it is."

"Not yesterday you were favouring Sofie with all of your *attentions,* Oswald," Neville felt called upon to remind him.

"Still want to, of course," Ossie replied with a plaintive sigh, "but with the way m'cousin and Gresham are monopolizing her, a fellow can't even fetch her a cool drink."

"S'truth," sighed Neville. "If you're certain about wanting to bring Miss Ashton into fashion, I suppose it couldn't hurt to divert my own attention for a while, although"——he brushed his sleeve fastidiously—"I cannot forget the habit she wore the day we went out riding. It is branded in my memory. Why, I have had *nightmares* about the thing."

"I wish you *would* court her, as *your* suit can doubtless only serve to drive her into my arms," snapped Ossie.

"Hah! We'll see about that, my fat friend," Neville sneered.

"Think I'll have a dance with her myself," Squibby said.

Elmo shrugged. "Why not, if you think it could help her in the long run."

And so they converged on Calista, who was already surrounded by local friends and well-wishers. The news of her fainting spell had made the rounds of the village gossip mill instantly. She was without question the village's best-liked citizen—not to mention one of its most notoriously healthy ones—so everyone had been concerned, and sentiment ran uniformly that it was wonderful to see her up and about. And looking so well! Everyone had known that Miss Calista was a right one, but who'd have thought she could be a stunner?

The three dandies barged through the crowd to their surprised quarry. Promenading her, dancing with her, fetching refreshment, and offering up what passed for witty conversation until Lord Gresham, having decided earlier that he should make an effort to get to know his best friend's true love—since she had done a facer onto the table the last time he had tried—came to claim her for the supper dance.

Stanhope and Gresham crossed paths at the punch bowl following supper. Calista was engaged in a lively minuet with Elmo, and Stanhope, having been forced to spend the supper dance with Sofie, was in as foul mood as Gresham could ever recall seeing him. "Look at the way those ridiculous fops are clustered around her!" he complained. "Every time I approach, one of them cuts me off."

"They are doubtless unaware of the direction in which your interests lie," said his friend reasonably. "She *is* lovely—charming, intelligent, and unaffected. And she looks it tonight."

"Of course," said Stanhope impatiently.

"No, Tris," said Gresham, rolling his eyes with some amusement. "I meant lovelier than usual."

"I suppose so," said Stanhope grudgingly. "D'you mean the gown and hair and all?"

Peter's tone was amused. "I do."

"I am not at all sure I can like it."

"That is because you, my friend, are hopeless."

Stanhope smiled. "I know."

"I enjoyed supper immensely," said Gresham with a grin. "And not only because I am enjoying taunting you so very much." Stanhope glared at him in such a way that he hurried to say, "The dance is over. Look." He pointed as Elmo delivered Calista to a chair and went to answer an angry summons from his mama. "Go to her," he urged.

"Can't," replied Stanhope gloomily. "I must go and atone for my misspent youth by bringing this punch to Amanda." He held aloft the filled cup in his hand. "And listening further to her idea for a musical theatre piece about a lame milkmaid—to be written in rhymed couplets, naturally."

"Naturally!" said Gresham with a look of sympathy.

"Perhaps I can convince her to dance. At least then I won't have to *listen* to her. And then I'm to lead out the giggling Searle twins, one after the other."

Calista, breathless from dancing endlessly, not to mention fending off compliments so ridiculously overblown as to defy belief, watched Stanhope as he made his way across the room with that easy, athletic grace. He somehow seemed to occupy more space than his physical size warranted. He couldn't have been more than a few inches above six feet, but he seemed to stand above all the other gentlemen in the room. Watching him go and solicitously hand the punch to Amanda, who smiled possessively up at him, she felt a wave of longing so overwhelming that she had to hold the edge of the chair to steady herself. Her heart seemed to sink to the very soles of her little satin slippers as she observed the way he bent his head to Amanda's until, laughing, he led her out for a waltz, his hand curved intimately around her waist.

Calista was not the only person to observe Stanhope's attentions to Amanda with dismay.

"The time has come to take drastic action, my love," Lady Lyttworth was whispering in urgent tones behind the potted palms.

"Why, Mama?" Sofie asked

"Smile while we talk, Sofie, in case we should be observed." She waited until Sofie had a smile on her face before continuing. "I had hoped that Stanhope would have fixed his attentions by now. He is attentive, and all that is proper, to be sure, but he is the same with everyone from that dreadful Amanda to Calista."

"His lordship is, I think, somewhat dazzled by me," Sofie assured her mama, smoothing her skirts. "He did give me a most *particular* look tonight, but it is true, he has never been in the least loverlike toward me."

"Sofie!" her mother commented in exasperated accents. "Earls are not known for being overwarm in their affections, and I for one say thank goodness! It is extremely déclassé to treat one's intended bride with too much warmth!"

"Lord Gresham seems quite warm," ventured Sofie—who was greatly enjoying life as the center of so much masculine attention—with a slight pout. "As do Ossie, Neville, and Squibby."

"That is the Honorable Mr. Cravanndish, Lord Ffolkes, and Mr. Stoneham to you, Sofie." Her mother's tone was unusually reproving. "And I said to *smile*. Those three are naught but children with, I daresay, no serious intent toward matrimony. And as for Lord Gresham, I am sure he is a most unexceptionable young man, but may I remind you. He is no earl."

"Yes, Mama. You are right," Sofie replied, remembering how very nice it would be to be a countess. Especially when the earl in question was so very handsome. "What do you think I should do?"

"I have refined upon this at length, my love, and it seems to me that Stanhope is a man, and as such is weak in matters of the flesh—that is an annoyance you will no doubt have to put up with briefly after you are wed, my dear, but there is no need for you to trouble yourself about such unpleasantries just yet. I have observed him carefully, and I also have detected a certain softening of his manner this evening. So I have decided," she continued with a firmness of tone, "that the best course of action would be for you to sleepwalk into his bedchamber tonight."

Sofie gasped in shock. "But that would waste precious sleeping hours. What if I were to arise with *dark circles* under my eyes in the morning? And besides! It can't be proper!"

Her mother fixed her with a gimlet eye. "Of course it is not proper. That is the very point of the thing. But drastic times warrant drastic measures. It is not as if I am suggesting that you allow him to take *liberties,* after all! I will be certain that you are discovered together before such a thing could possibly take place."

A slight frown marred Sofie's ivory brow. "But, Mama," she said, "suppose he does not wish to marry me?"

"I had not thought to find you making such a cake of yourself, Sofie." Lady Lyttworth's chin wore a determined tilt. "You cannot afford to give in to this excess of sentiment if you intend to marry the earl. As to whether or not he *wishes* to marry you—that is entirely beside the point. It is absolutely the correct course of action! He may merely require some assistance in realizing it. These things often need some helping along, you know. Men, and I point to your dearest father as an example, are often in the dark as to where their best interests lie."

"Very well, Mama. I am certain that you, as usual, know what is best."

"Good girl." Lady Lyttworth patted Sofie's hand. "You shall be a credit to the Lyttworth family if you only do what you are told. Now, I am vastly relieved that is settled."

Twenty-five

At long last, Stanhope spied Calista standing alone. Approaching, he bowed formally, and brushed her fingertips with his lips. As he straightened, he saw the happiness in her eyes. It was one of the things he loved most about her, how utterly without artifice she was. But at the same time, her look caused him a stab of pain. *Even after last night, she doesn't quite trust me,* he realized. *She cannot believe in my constancy.* He cursed the necessity to do the civil with the rest of the world. "Miss Ashton," he said in that husky voice that made her feel as though they were quite alone, "could I claim the last dance of the evening?"

"Honestly!" exclaimed Lady Lyttworth, who was just wrapping up the details of her plan with Sofie when she happened to glance up and observe Stanhope in conversation with Calista. "I must go speak with Hermione about Calista *yet again*. I shall make it abundantly clear to them that Adolphus *must* announce the banns this very Sunday. I know it is more hurried than we had planned, but will you look at that girl? She is positively *throwing* herself at all the gentlemen present! If Hermione and Adolphus have a brain between them, they will get her bracketed to the squire before she brings disgrace on them! Only look at how she is making up to *his lordship* now! Oh the mortification," Lady Lyttworth wailed. "What will he think of our little town if desperate spinsters accost him at every turn?"

* * *

Stanhope reached for Calista's hand, but before she could reply, a voice behind them drawled, " 'Fraid you're too late, Coz." Ossie bowed with a great flourish and rose, saying, "My dance, I believe, Miss Ashton."

Stanhope raised a brow in a manner that would have caused any young buck in any ballroom in London to cede the dance to him. This, however, was not any young buck. This was the singularly, stupidly, oblivious Oswald, he reminded himself savagely as his cousin minced her off in the direction of the dance floor.

When the dance, at long last, drew to a close, and the musicians began to pack up their instruments, Lady Lyttworth ambushed the couple as they were coming off the floor. "Calista," she said, "I have told Adolphus that I will escort you home, as I most specifically wish to have words with you. I hope you don't mind giving her up to me, Sir Oswald." She smiled as she took Calista's arm. "I refuse to take no for an answer, and have taken the liberty of fetching your wrap, my dear. Come, let us go." And so saying, she tugged a bewildered Calista behind her.

Stanhope, in the meantime, was engaged in a little plotting of his own with Lord Gresham.

"Am I to assume you are desirous of a word?" Gresham asked as his friend whisked him behind a pillar.

"Less a word than an alibi."

"Pardon?"

"I have arranged for you to escort Miss Lyttworth home!"

Gresham raised a questioning brow.

"You may thank me now."

"Thank you. I trust there is a price to be paid?"

"Well, now that you mention it . . . You will return Sofie, I will drive Amanda, and then you and I will set out, ostensibly to have a drink together at the Horse and Castle."

"Ah, yes. And you will be where, exactly?"

"Courting."

Gresham expelled a long-suffering sigh. "I do not suppose it has occurred to you that your beloved might well be fast asleep by the time you arrive. Not to mention, the taproom closed. It is gone past one of the clock already."

"Not to me, they won't be," Stanhope replied with unconscious arrogance. Then he grinned. "And there is no need to make yourself a damping presence, Peter. It would be above all things a shame if people started to think of you as a priggish, gloomy fellow."

Lord Gresham laughed. "You are right. I'm all too happy to aid your intrigue—I vow, it is almost as if we are back at school!"

"That is much more the spirit."

"If I remember anything about those days, it is of the utmost importance in avoiding a whipping—or, worse, getting sent down—that we ensure in advance that our stories match. At the Horse and Castle, what were you drinking?"

"Brandy. It was very old and very good."

"And what time did you set out for home?"

"I don't know," replied Stanhope looking at him with some exasperation. "That depends on whether my luck is running."

Twenty-six

There was no question at the moment that Calista's was not. Lady Lyttworth, who had wasted not a moment after settling herself in the carriage, was currently occupied in subjecting her to a most unpleasant harangue.

"It is no secret that you are in my black books, my girl!" she began before the horses were even under way, and then, lest Calista try to get a word in edgewise, rushed on. "The way you have been carrying on is beyond anything, and is, I daresay, *most* unbecoming! You have no doubt been egged on in this disgraceful display by Roberta Enright, and that woman never did have so much as a *grain* of common sense. But there you are! All decked out in ridiculously unsuitable clothing, throwing yourself at every man in sight. No good can come of this night's work. Mark my words."

"I have not thrown myself at anyone, ma'am," replied Calista through stiff lips.

"Well, that is certainly how it appears, and trust me, you are making a complete *cake* of yourself. The gentlemen all no doubt think you a figure of ridicule! Tarted up like some over-the-hill debutante! And to have the *temerity* to flirt with his lordship!" She broke off, breathing hard.

"If that is what you think, you are sadly mistaken—"

"Do not attempt to gammon me, Calista. I have seen the way you look at him and seize on every opportunity to monopolize him in conversation. That he is not at all high in the instep has been much discussed, but, I tell you, it might be better if he was. Perhaps then he would not be so hesitant to give you the set-down you obviously need—and I said as much to Hermione at the Stanleys' Venetian breakfast! 'Tis apparent that all he wants from you is someone to help exercise those precious horses and, yes, perhaps your bizarre notions and bluestocking tendencies provide him a few moments' entertainment. But you! You are making up shamelessly to the man!" she finished accusingly.

"I am doing no such thing!"

"Well, you cannot possibly hope to look that high for a match, my girl, and you would do well not to forget it!"

Enraged, Calista replied coldly, "I have not looked at all for a match, but my mother, I would remind you, *was* the daughter of a marquess."

"An *impoverished* marquess! And anyway, that connexion has stood you in little stead, has it not? Your brother, after all, has been forced to *make a living* as a curate. Not, mind you, that I malign his need to work, but it has surely put you beyond the pale as far as hoping to find a match in *those* circles goes! Never mind your age and ridiculous intellectual tendencies! And if you've any radical ideas of setting yourself up as his mistress, I would advise you to forget that also. To be blunt, you haven't the looks to turn his head from Amanda Prescott if a mistress is what he wants."

"What is the point of this scold, my lady? If I am such a figure of ridicule, I can offer little obstacle for your plans for Sofie."

"Calista." Lady Lyttworth's voice gentled. "Don't be foolish. I am not in the least worried about Sofie. There is no question that he will come around where she is concerned, and I don't believe for a moment that nonsense about him wedding Amanda. It is obvious just exactly what she is to him! I am merely trying to save you and your family from the embarrassment that shall be the inevitable result of getting ideas above your station. As I've pointed out, you can hardly be considered an *eligible parti* where an earl is concerned."

"I thank you for your kind intentions."

Sarcasm, however, was lost on Lady Lyttworth. "You are

most welcome, my dear," she said. "I am sorry to have spoken harshly. I daresay, I do not hold you entirely accountable, you know. You are at an age where unmarried females are likely to develop unrealistic notions—even when their heads are not stuffed full of all kinds of radical nonsense, and goodness knows yours is! Adolphus and Hermione are as much to blame as you are for allowing you access to such drivel."

All Calista wanted was for the ride to end so she could seek the solitude of her bedchamber, but she forced a response to her lips. "I am greatly comforted," she said acidly.

"There is a fine match for you right here in Deepdene! You could do much worse than to accept Everard, you know, my dear. And perhaps in time there would be children. Not that Everard's brood will not keep you well occupied in the meantime! Well, here we are. Arrived already! I am so glad we have had this chance to chat. I vow, once Sofie becomes a countess and removes to London, I will no doubt positively come to dote on you as a daughter!"

"No doubt," Calista replied in as even a tone as she was able before escaping the confines of the carriage.

Inside, she climbed blindly to her room, where she allowed Annie to undress her, replying in uncharacteristic monosyllables to the maid's gay chatter. The moment Annie left, Calista walked to the window and looked out at the familiar moonlit lawn of the vicarage without really seeing it. Finally she was able to give way to the tears she had held back since Lady Lyttworth's first words. Surely, despite her disagreeable manner, that lady had spoken only the truth.

Last night scandalously ensconced in Stanhope's arms, and tonight in her borrowed finery, she had almost allowed herself to believe that she was entering the charmed circle that seemed to surround Stanhope—where there was laughter and glitter and waltzing. And passion. And warm, tender security. But tonight, practically cut by him at the assembly, Lady Lyttworth's scold ringing in her ears, dressed in her utilitarian flannel nightgown, she knew. This was where she belonged. In Deepdene, with her feet planted solidly on the ground, her moral principles in place, and her head firmly in her work.

There is nothing wrong with allowing yourself some happiness, Lady Enright had said. Well, in this case there was. It had not been true happiness, Calista assured herself, the kind born of hard work and proper living. It had been a fleeting, evanescent drunkenness with no substance. Despite his assurances to the contrary, and her lamentable tendency to believe them when he was close by, it was obvious that Stanhope's motives for proposing marriage to her were less than respectable. The man clearly wanted to set up his nursery in the country while maintaining his veritable stable of *chères amies* in London. Lady Lyttworth was right, else he would have chosen a beauty like Sofie to wed.

But what if that arrangement would be preferable to not having any part of him at all? asked a traitorous voice in her head. At least then I would have his children, she thought wistfully, and I would see him sometimes. How pathetic I am become, she scolded herself the next moment, the tears flowing in earnest now. Where is my self-respect? But still, the idea of never seeing him again felt unendurable.

I no longer know myself, she thought. I am like a feather in the wind. He whispers that he loves me and wants me, and I am so besotted with his presence that I cannot help but believe it. Lady Lyttworth tells me he cannot, and I am sunk in despair. I, who have always had such clear ideas about my life, have no control anymore. She shook her head sadly, knowing she could never live that way. It was time to put an end to this folly and take up the reins of her life again.

With not much joy but a sense of purpose at least, she picked up the Hannah More tract that had been gathering dust on her windowsill since the day after Stanhope's arrival. Tonight she would finish it. Then she would get a good night's sleep. And tomorrow morning she would have a firm word with Adolphus to be certain he understood that she would under no circumstances—even if the announcement was inserted into the *Post,* the banns were cried, *and* a special license procured—wed Everard Greystock. Then she would put on an old dress and finally finish cleaning out the schoolroom.

An hour later saw her only three pages further into the book, which, for some reason, did not seem to engage her attention. The shocking idea that perhaps Miss More did in fact approach things from a perspective that was overly black and white, as Stanhope had charged, seemed to have gained a foothold in her mind. Perhaps it *is* possible to be concerned with equality and the plight of the less fortunate, and to better it, without seeing all comforts and pleasures as decadent and evil. No! she told herself. That I could even entertain that notion is a measure of just how far my values have fallen.

In time, she heard Adolphus and Hermione retire, and eventually the house settled into quiet. Her candle burned lower in its holder, but she forced herself to read on. She had somehow determined that if only she could finish the thing, it would put to rest those traitorous, niggling doubts for once and for all, and she would be able to reclaim her life.

Twenty-seven

At Moreford Park, Sofie was impatient. "When do you suppose he will be back from the Horse and Castle, Mama? I cannot wait all night, you know," she complained. "I am already certain my complexion will be dull tomorrow and quite possibly *blotchy,* which, as you are aware, *does* happen when I am extremely tired, and—"

"Stop complaining, Sofie, and let us go over this again," her mother snapped as she adjusted the neck of her daughter's robe to a more modest drape. "It is imperative that this be done properly. One misstep and all will be lost. You remember what to do?"

"Yes, Mama. Once he is asleep, I am to go into his bedroom and climb into the bed. As soon as he wakes and notes my presence, I open my eyes and, pretending to be shocked, scream," she recited dutifully. "You will come running on the instant."

"Good," Lady Lyttworth nodded. "Now all we need do is wait."

Amanda Prescott sat at her dressing table and looked at herself in the mirror as her maid brushed out her glossy curls. Dismissing the girl, she selected a filmy gold peignoir that would have shocked her hostess by its very immodesty and, after slipping it on, admired the picture it made against her creamy skin. She dabbed some scent on the insides of her wrists.

The perfume had been a gift from Stanhope in better days, which she recalled as she held her wrist to her nose for a moment. As she crossed to the door, the delicate silk whispering against her skin caused her a moment of delicious anticipation, and strengthened her resolve. Opening the door, she peered down the hall and, certain that she was unobserved, slipped out, closing it gently behind herself.

Twenty-eight

The night was clear and starry if a bit cool, and Stanhope felt a sudden surge of high spirits as he parted company with Peter Gresham. A few minutes later, he was following the fork that led off Deepdene's main street toward the vicarage. At the bottom of the drive he expertly guided Raleigh onto the grassy strip that bordered the loose stone and slowed him to a walk. When the darkened house came into view, he jumped down and looped his reins over a fencepost.

"Wish me luck, Raleigh," he whispered to the horse, who whickered against his ear briefly before beginning to devour a portion of the vicarage lawn.

In truth, Stanhope could barely believe he had come. *I only want to be near her,* he thought, shaking his head at his own transformation from hardened cynic to besotted fool. It had been almost as much as he could bear not to hold her in his arms at the assembly. He stood for a moment, trying to guess which of the upstairs windows might be Calista's, and smiled when he spied a stack of books on an inside windowsill, illuminated by a faint candle burning within. Neither the Reverend Ashton nor his good lady struck him as being avid late-night readers. He picked up a pebble and threw it gently at the window.

Calista was propped in bed preparing to put pen to paper. Having given up on the Hannah More, she was addressing herself to penning a letter to the *Edinburgh Review* in support of Mr. Robert Owen's controversial views on private ownership.

In her letter, entitled *A Most Lucid Argument in Defense of Traveling as One Nation: Or, Abolishing the Private Coach, an Advocacy,* she was putting forth the proposition that if private ownership of coaches were to be eradicated, and all citizens, regardless of social standing, were to travel together on the public stage, it would eradicate a great inequality. Her theory was correct, even if her remedy was unlikely, she knew. So why, then, was she suddenly engulfed by a feeling of sadness as she saw herself forever traveling on the overcrowded, frequently odiferous public stage, always doing what was right, while the Stanhopes and Sofie Lyttworths of the world were whisked easily about in luxuriously sprung and furnished comfort? She was about to berate herself for one more example of what she considered her moral decay, when she heard a clink at the window. When the same sound repeated itself a minute later, she climbed out of bed and padded across the cold floor. More irritated than frightened, she opened the window and put her head out to investigate. She might have known.

"Down here," Stanhope whispered, materializing from behind a tree and looking for all the world like a mischievous schoolboy.

"What on earth are you doing here?" she whispered back, willing her heart to slow down its sudden tumult.

"I wanted only to see your face, my love," he called quietly.

"You've seen it. You saw it at the assembly. Am I doomed never to be able to go to bed without you turning up? Now, get out of the shrubbery and go home. You're obviously mad, you know, Stanhope. You'll catch your death of cold or else disgrace us. Or likely," she concluded gloomily, "do both."

"Does that tirade mean you aren't planning to invite me up?"

"Yes!"

"Come down, then."

"No!"

"I've something to give you."

"Send it with a footman. Tomorrow," she said, but realized even as she did so that she was reaching for her wrapper.

"Please?"

She looked at him, almost unbearably handsome in the moon-

light, and felt her resolve slipping away. "Only for a minute."
Cursing herself for every kind of fool, she grabbed and pulled
on the sturdy boots that were close to hand. At least no one
could accuse her of dressing for seduction, she thought with a
wry smile as she added a heavy wrap and tiptoed—or, rather,
clomped as quietly as her boots would allow—down the stairs.
The front door gave a loud squeak of protest, and she froze.
When no answering noise came from inside, she continued cau-
tiously out toward Stanhope. "It is cold out here," she complained when she came abreast of him.

"I'll warm you," he whispered huskily as he slipped his arms
around her and pulled her behind a tree so they were out of
sight of the house.

She could smell brandy on his breath. It mixed with the scent
of his soap and the clean smell of the outdoors that always
seemed to surround him, in a way that made her stomach hurt
from longing. "You are drunk," she said accusingly.

"Only with need for you, Calista," he murmured into her hair
before setting out to prove his point.

"Stop," she gasped. But his arms felt like a warm, sheltering
haven, and his words were like balm to her battered psyche.
She had to force a note of severity into her voice. "How is it
that I keep finding myself in inappropriate situations where you
are concerned? No sooner am I finished engaging in the most
scandalous behaviour of my entire life, but I am slipping out
for midnight trysts." She shook her head. "I scarce know myself
anymore. Once you have departed this town—and it seems that
day cannot come soon enough to save me—and taken your London friends along with you—"

"They are hardly my friends," he said in a wounded tone.
"You may accuse me of many things, my love, but willingly
consorting with that motley collection is not one! You have been
crying!" he said, looking at her more carefully. "What is it?
What's wrong?"

She ignored him. "As I was saying, once you are gone I shall
no doubt become a painted woman in damped petticoats attempting to lure every young buck who crosses my path behind

the potted palms at the Redingcote Assemblies." Just as Lady Lyttworth predicted, she thought gloomily.

"I cannot allow that, my love. I was even jealous of Peter! Promise me that when we are wed you will wear only yellow."

The better to keep me tucked in the country, breeding every year, she thought, but felt flattered all the same. "I suppose you, as usual, *did* have a reason for this most improper tryst, other than to critique my wardrobe?"

"I have something for you, but I doubt I can leave without kissing you," he said simply. "I wish, though, that you would talk to me of what has upset you."

She felt tears prick again at his solicitousness but shook her head. "I don't wish to speak of it. It was nothing—just that I seem to be turning into something of a watering pot at this advanced age. And if you are determined to kiss me, you'd best get on with it," she said as snappishly as she was able, "as I have no doubt you will not leave until you get what you came for. And I for one would like to get some sleep this night."

He looked into her eyes for a long while, and then that irresistible smile tugged at his mouth. "Why, Miss Ashton, I do believe you are becoming a romantic," he said before bending his head to hers.

The instant he did, she forgot everything—Hannah More, private ownership of coaches, Lady Lyttworth's scold, Adolphus's perfidy, her own doubts—and clung to him as though they were fused together. Tonight there were no gentle, feathering kisses. He kissed her fiercely, almost desperately. And she kissed him back with an equal passion. She could feel the long, lean firmness of his muscles and the warmth of his body through the fabric of his coat. His right arm held her against him tightly, and with his left hand he loosened her wrap and gently rubbed her back. Then he brought his hand around and slid it caressingly up her side until he was almost touching the side of her breast. For just a second her mind screamed a protest that her voice refused to echo. Then his hand began gently to stroke and explore in earnest and her mind went absolutely blank. She moaned against his mouth, but was so lost she barely heard it. She had never imagined sensations like this. Ever.

Stanhope pulled her even closer. He continued to kiss her hungrily as he loosened his grip momentarily to shrug off his greatcoat. Without letting go of her, he dropped it on the ground and pulled her down on top of him. He tossed aside her wrap, and she offered not a murmur of protest. Gently, he rolled them over so she lay cushioned by his coat. Her heavy flannel night-gown had a row of tiny buttons down the front, and he expertly but impatiently began to unbutton them, kissing her mouth, her face, her hair. Murmuring words of tenderness and need that she had never thought to hear, he slid his hand inside and cupped her breast. She made a noise deep in her throat, and he pulled away for a moment to look again at her face and saw only invitation there. With a groan he began rebuttoning the tiny buttons.

"Oh, God, Calista." His voice was ragged, and his fingers felt clumsy. "I lose all reason near you. But I refuse to tumble you on the ground." She could feel the pounding of his heart. "When I make love to you, it will be the way you deserve. Not here. Not like this." He stood reluctantly and held out his hand to her.

Calista, who at that moment thought being tumbled on the ground sounded just fine, thank you, took the hand in silence and allowed him to pull her to her feet and gently enfold her once again in her wrap. His care and gentleness somehow made her feel all the more cherished even than his passion of a moment ago.

"I intended tonight, before I forgot myself to all propriety, to give you this," he said quietly as he pulled off the simple gold signet ring he wore. "To cement my declaration of last night. And I'd best do it and leave while I can still think." When she made no move to take it, he placed it inside her palm and curled her fingers around it, beneath his own.

She held the ring, surprised by the solid weight of it in her hand. It was still warm from his skin. She shook her head. "I cannot accept this, my lord."

"Of course you can. I have hopes of replacing it with a wedding band."

She looked at the ground. "It is only lust, Stanhope," she said bluntly. "We should not suit."

He looked at her intently. "I thought that at first also, Calista. But now I know otherwise, and I'd like a chance to persuade you too. It *is* lust. I'll not deny that my longing for you is almost more than I can bear. But it's so much more. Even should I fail to convince you of that, though, I would still like you to have the ring."

"It should be for your son," she said softly, tears threatening for the second time that night.

"I am optimistic that he will be your son too." He put his hand under her chin and tilted her face so she was looking square at him. "Marry me, Calista. I love you, you know."

She shook her head mutely.

"I know you doubt me. That my morals and my constancy in the past have not been everything that they could have been. But I am a changed man. I will talk to Amanda first thing in the morning. May I come to you then and ask again? Will you promise to think on it?"

She nodded, afraid to speak.

"Good. That is all I can ask," he replied, wondering if she could read the longing in his eyes. Suddenly embarrassed—he was not a man who was generally subject to excesses of emotion—he bent and picked up his greatcoat. His quick smile made her heart pound again in her ears. "When my valet sees me, he may resign to go work for Oswald—a man who knows how to care for his garments!"

Calista was made sharp by her own confusion. "He will doubtless know in an instant what it is you have been about. I take leave to doubt this is a first for you."

He stood closer and brushed her hair back from her face before gently pulling her wrap about her more tightly. "Oh, but it is, in so many ways, which is what I keep trying to tell you, my sweet. Now go back inside before you get too chilled or I get too warm. We will talk more of this when I come to call tomorrow—an unencumbered man—and ask you again to marry me." He dropped a gentle kiss on her lips, and resisting the overwhelming temptation to linger and try his hand again at those intriguingly tiny buttons, turned her in the direction of the door.

She walked in without looking back, as if in a daze. He watched her disappear inside and then, feeling a sense of peace despite his overwhelming frustration, turned and headed back to his horse.

Inside, Calista climbed into bed. When she leaned over to blow out the candle, the Hannah More book fell unnoticed to the rug.

Twenty-nine

"Go!" whispered Lady Lyttworth, giving her daughter a gentle shove. "It has been above an hour since we heard the door to his room close. Surely he is asleep by now. And should he be a trifle foxed, so much the better."

"But, Mama—"

"No buts. *Go!*" Lady Lyttworth pointed to the door of the unused bedchamber where they had kept their vigil, and Sofie obediently glided out. After her daughter left, she paced the length of the room, finally pausing at the window and tapping her foot impatiently. It was critical that this go as planned. She refused even to think of the consequences should things go awry.

When Sofie's scream came a few moments later, it sounded positively genuine. And so did the next. And the next. Her eyes quite welled with pride at the girl's performance. Affixing her haughtiest you-have-trifled-with-my-daughter-and-I'll-not-stand-for-it expression, Lady Lyttworth strode the few steps to Stanhope's room and threw open the door.

"What the devil?!" she gasped at the sight that met her astonished eyes.

Sitting on the edge of the bed, clutching the coverlet to her modestly covered bosom, her eyes wide with horror, was Sofie. On the other side of the bed, comfortably ensconced, not bothering to conceal her extremely immodestly covered bosom, her colour high with outrage, was Amanda.

A confused babble of voices came as the rest of the house

party—with the exception of the baron, who could and did sleep through anything—awakened by the commotion, converged on the Royal Chamber.

"I heard—"

"What on earth—"

"Screams—"

"What the deuce—"

"There has been a misunderstanding. Do, please, everyone, go back to bed," said Lady Lyttworth. But her words, for once, fell on deaf ears.

"This, this . . . *tussy*— " began Sofie in high dudgeon.

"I am no such thing!" interrupted Amanda in offended accents.

"What's a tussy?" inquired Neville.

"Obviously, some type of girl talk, you fool," replied Squibby helpfully.

"Think she meant hussy," supplied Elmo.

" 'Course!" Ossie nodded wisely.

Sofie sniffed. "I did. But I am not skilled in the vocabulary of women of easy virtue!"

"How dare you call *me* a hussy when it was you creeping about in the dark like a little bit of muslin?" Amanda shrieked.

"I . . . I *sleepwalked*," said Sofie triumphantly as her mother nodded her agreement.

"In satin slippers?" Amanda smirked her disbelief. "We don't, of course, go to bed still shod in the city, but here in the *country,* I suppose one never knows what kind of odd starts to expect." She shrugged her elegant, scantily covered shoulders.

"My feet were cold!" Sofie's accents were as wounded as she could manage under the circumstances.

"My daughter," said Lady Lyttworth frostily, "wandered in her sleep. An occurrence we have had before without quite such dramatic results. And what is your excuse for this scandalous behaviour?"

Amanda took a deep breath and looked Lady Lyttworth square in the eye. "Tris," she said, "invited *me.*"

Sofie gasped in outrage and burst out before her mother could stop her, "He never did. What a banbury tale, you lying jade!"

"He certainly did," Amanda drawled. "He told me he wanted a woman, you see, not a *girl!*"

"Ooh, a direct hit," remarked Elmo admiringly.

"How odd. He told *me* he wants a countess, not a doxy!" riposted Sofie.

"Excellent return," approved Ossie.

"Actually"—Amanda crossed her arms over her barely concealed bosom and looked at Sofie consideringly—"you seem remarkably well versed in the vocabulary of the *demimonde*. I vow, I am beginning to positively doubt that you *were* sleep-walking."

"Facer!" Elmo crowed, looking not entirely displeased to see his sister so deep in the suds.

"Anyone care to wager that this descends into a mill?" inquired Squibby.

Ossie thought. "I'll go odds it don't."

"Three to one in favour," Elmo chimed in.

Neville shuddered and tied the purple satin sash of his robe more carefully. "No blood, please, ladies, is all that I ask. I shall likely faint and crease my robe if there is any blood."

"Gentlemen!" thundered Lady Lyttworth.

"Elmo! How could you?" wailed Sofie. "Wager on my misfortune?"

"I hadn't realized there was a gathering planned for my room this evening, else I should have made every attempt to join you earlier," cut in a cool voice, and all babble ceased as the occupants became aware of Stanhope leaning against the doorframe. His tones were amiable, but the green eyes had all the warmth of the North Sea. "I certainly seem to have missed something."

He looked at the little knot of people gathered inside the room. "Elmo, would you be so good as to remove these three, er, *boys* from the room?" He nodded in the general direction of Ossie, Squibby, and Neville.

"Er, yes, sir," stammered Elmo, flattered to be trusted with such responsibility by his idol but looking at him most oddly.

"Is something amiss, lad?"

"It is your cravat, my lord. It is . . . it is *crushed!*" Elmo replied almost in a whisper.

"Ah." Stanhope nodded. "I had a slight problem with keeping Raleigh under control—I think he was spooked by a rabbit." He tried to look rueful.

"*You* lost control? Because of a *rabbit?*" Elmo's doubt was writ clear on his face.

"Elmo!" Stanhope's voice was almost sharp, and he ran his fingers through his hair, which only had the effect of making him look even more handsome. "Such things do happen, and a true out-and-outer does not consider it good form to refine too closely upon others' sporting mishaps!"

"You are right, of course, sir." Elmo looked abashed.

"Now, please, take this motley trio out. I will be along to speak with you all shortly." He turned toward the ladies and crossed to the bed. Taking his robe, he tossed it wordlessly to Amanda, who sat holding it. "Put it on," he said shortly, and she did, knotting the sash and leaning nonchalantly against the pillows as if it were an entirely normal situation.

Stanhope took a steadying breath. All he wanted was to crawl into bed and dream of Calista, but this promised to be a long and trying night. He eyed the ill-assorted duo on the bed and folded his arms across his chest. "What, pray, is taking place here?"

"Sofie sleepwalked, your lordship—the poor child is positively *prone* to it, you know," fluted Lady Lyttworth, "and ended up here in your bedchamber. Quite, *quite* by accident, of course," she hastened to add.

"Quite," he said dryly. "We must consider ourselves most fortunate, Lady Lyttworth—"

"*Cousin Gladys.*"

"Yes, of course. Cousin Gladys. It is most fortunate you were so near. Sleepwalking, I understand, can be an extremely dangerous habit."

"Indeed." Lady Lyttworth looked only slightly abashed. "I had gone to her chamber, you see, seeking a word about . . . well, anyway, when I noticed she was gone, I started the search immediately, as you can well imagine."

He nodded. "And you, Amanda? How did you come to be here?"

She took a deep breath and, apparently deciding to brazen it out, drawled, "Why, you invited me, Tris, for a little *rendezvous*. Do you not recall?"

He raised a brow. "What a lamentable memory I seem to be possessed of these days. It is my age, no doubt, but no, Amanda, I do not recall issuing that invitation. At any rate, all I long for now is a peaceful bed."

"Of course you do, your lordship," babbled Lady Lyttworth, who personally longed to have strong hysterics at the thought of such goings-on under her virtuous roof but knew she was hardly in a position to do so under the circumstances. "I do not know what we can be thinking to keep you standing here jabbering away in the middle of the night. I know some say that the way to a man's heart is through his stomach, but the baron is wont to say that's a load of nonsense. Anyone with an ounce of sense knows it is through a good night's undisturbed sleep! Come, Sofie!"

They made for the door as Amanda, apparently fully prepared to stay, stretched like a cat.

"Lady—Cousin Gladys!"

"Yes, my lord?"

"Could you be so good as to escort Mrs. Prescott to her room?"

"It would be my pleasure, my lord." Never had Lady Lyttworth spoken truer words. "Come along, Mrs. Prescott."

"But, Tris—"

"I am tired, Amanda," he said with an expression that wiped the pout off her face. "My patience is thin tonight, and I am hardly in the habit of engaging in illicit trysts at house parties. We will talk in the morning, but not tonight."

After Amanda had removed herself from the bed and stomped out in the wake of a sulky Sofie and a vastly relieved Lady Lyttworth, Stanhope allowed himself the luxury of sitting on the edge of the bed and resting his head in his hands. The blame for Amanda's atrocious behaviour, he realized, could be laid squarely at his door—if he had only spoken frankly with her from the start, it could have been avoided. But he'd been so preoccupied with Calista and his own feelings that he'd scarce spared a thought to the proper way to handle things. Although, truth to be told, it was Amanda's brazenness that had been the saving of him tonight. Had she not had seduction in mind, he would have had little choice other than to offer for Sofie. He groaned aloud at the idea. Lady Lyttworth, he concluded, was an even bigger fool than he thought to risk Sofie's reputation with this night's work. For what was alleged to be a quiet town, there certainly were a great deal of middle-of-the-night machinations carried out in Deepdene. At least there could be no question of his remaining at Moreford Park after this little farce.

Now it was time to go talk with the three dandies. He would caution them strongly against mentioning the incident but, unfortunately, had little faith that they could be counted upon to be discreet. Three bigger gossips would be difficult to find in all the drawing rooms of London. Stanhope walked to the door, reflecting that he could not remember ever having felt more tired.

Thirty

It was a gray, gloomy Saturday, and the rain was sheeting against the windows when Calista got out of bed. Despite the fact that it was the type of day to give anyone the sullens, she felt as though her room were bathed in sunlight. Her heart told her to listen to Stanhope. Her head still told her to listen to Lady Lyttworth. And her hand, regardless of which body part she attended to, would not seem to let go of his ring.

I am a lovesick disgrace, she thought happily as she stood—her heart taking the upper hand in the struggle—mooning into her clothes press. A smile spread across her face as she espied the yellow wool. Stanhope had specifically said that he always wanted to see her in that colour. Today, when he came to call, to propose again, she would be wearing it. Their little private joke.

"Not again!" cried Annie, splashing the bathwater she was carrying in her horror. "You cannot think to go abroad again in that one so soon."

"Actually, I'd planned to stick close to home today, Annie. I've spent far too much time of late haring about, pursuing frivolity. I've household accounts to go over and knitting to catch up on." And a visitor to wait for, she added mentally. "Besides," she said aloud, "I think I am of an age to decide what I shall wear."

"Some people who stay up half the night, tromping around in their nightclothes, doing I can only guess what with I can

only guess who, might not have all the judgment they should,"
Annie muttered darkly.

Calista blushed to the tips of her toes. "I heard a noise and
went to investigate."

"I reckon you did. The goings-on around here would be
enough to make respectable folks shudder! I've never seen such
a thing in all my born days," scolded Annie, trying to hide her
delighted approval. This was just what Calista needed, if you
asked her. She turned so Calista couldn't see her smile. "I trust
you kept your wits about you?" she added brusquely.

"Not particularly," Calista sighed, realizing it was no use to
try to hide anything from Annie.

"Hrmph. Get into your bath, Miss Calista, before the water
gets cold."

Calista obeyed and lay back in the warm water. "When Adolphus rises, please tell him I desire a word."

"He's gone," Annie replied.

"Gone?" queried Calista. Adolphus was never gone by this
hour of the day. "Gone where?"

"Rode over to St. Mead," Annie said, referring to a nearby
town. "Something about parish business. He won't be back until
church tomorrow."

"Since when does he concern himself with parish business?"
Calista asked.

"I'm guessing since he started trying to avoid you," Annie
replied with some asperity.

Calista laughed. "Well, he won't manage for long, Annie. I
shouldn't worry about that!"

Paying Calista a proper visit, during which he would seek an
audience with her brother, had been Stanhope's plan for the day.
Following that, his intention was that they would go for a long
ride together. And if they should stop again at Ardsley's hunting
box, and this time give in to the temptation to finish what they
had started there—well, that was no one's business but their
own. But first he had two trying interviews to get through.

Lady Lyttworth, who did not apparently feel even one iota

of remorse or embarrassment for the high jinks the previous evening, professed horror at the notion that he could possibly want to remove himself from her household. She wept with distress that he might not find her hospitality all it should be. She stomped with fury that someone in her household should have caused him discomfort. She warned in her direst tone that there were rumoured to be *fleas* in the bed linens at the Horse and Castle.

Through the storm, Stanhope remained firm. Her hospitality had been all it could possibly be, and it pained him greatly that she could ever suspect he could think otherwise. Of all the hostesses he had ever had the great good fortune to have stayed with, she was by far the finest. The most concerned with the details of her guests' comfort. Her household was the smoothest run. He could not, in good conscience, however, impose even one more night on her good nature. *Despite* the fact they were family.

Somewhat mollified by this reference to their irrevocable tie, she gave her reluctant agreement to his plan to remove himself to town.

Amanda—smartly attired this morning in a cherry-red walking suit accessorized with a completely unnecessary but nonetheless captivating parasol and a delightful confection of a hat—was in fine looks as she strode into the library on the heels of Lady Lyttworth's departure. The two women, Stanhope quickly concluded, were clearly cut from the same bolt of cloth, as Amanda also evinced not one whit of conscience over the last night's escapade.

"Good morning, Tris," she said, her voice sultry as she strolled to where he stood by the mantel and held out her hand.

"Good morning, Amanda." He took the hand briefly but did not kiss it. "Shall we sit?"

Nodding, she moved toward a small love seat and took up her place at one end. She patted the seat next to her, but he chose instead a chair a little distance away and turned it so he was facing her directly. Stanhope was well accustomed to breaking off affairs, but rarely, he was ashamed to admit to himself, face-to-face. And never where hopes of marriage were involved. He cleared his throat, searching for a way to explain.

"Er, Amanda," he began, looking studiously at the Turkey carpet.

"Yes, my love?" she asked, smiling invitingly at him.

He looked straight at her face. "I wish to make clear that our liaison is at an end. Er, is *still* at an end."

She rose and purposefully strode to him, and he made to rise also, but she waved him to remain seated. She stood, looking down on him, her hands on her shapely hips. "Am I to assume, then, that you *do not,* in fact, wish to marry me?"

He smiled ruefully. "I'm afraid not, Amanda."

"Well," she said briskly. "I thought that was a bit off. So let us, then, by all means, resume our previous *arrangement,* which was"—she put down her parasol, draped herself across his lap, and wound her arms around his neck before continuing in her most sultry tones—"pleasing in the extreme. Much more to my taste, in fact, than marriage, which is so very conventional, don't you think? And all *artistes* know that it is conventionality that stifles the creative soul."

She was close enough that her glossy curls brushed his face and her lush curves were pressed against his chest. How overwhelming her perfume is. How overdressed she is. How could I ever have desired her? he wondered as he gently disengaged her arms. He shook his head. "No, Amanda, not even that."

She removed herself from his lap and paced to the window. When she turned to face him, she was crying, but only a little and very carefully, so as not to redden her eyes. "Why?"

He decided to be honest. "I have recently discovered, much to my surprise, that I am in love."

"With the little dreadfully dressed do-gooder?" she asked, her eyes narrowing with a perspicacity that surprised him.

He nodded wordlessly.

"Will she have you?"

"I don't know yet."

"Well, I'd best be on my way today, then," she replied airily. "I've better things to do with my time than loiter in this town.

Void of intelligentsia that it is. If your provincial sweetheart's charms begin to wane, do pay me a visit."

"Thank you, Amanda," he said soberly. "But somehow I doubt they will."

"*C'est la vie,* as we cosmopolitan types say. Not," she said, returning to him and running her fingers lightly down his chest, "that I've ever had a man like you before, Tristan. Your skills are going to be quite wasted on the little mouse, since I would wager she's had no basis for comparison. But life goes on, and monogamy is rather poor for one's art. Which reminds me, I have finished my poem. Would you like to hear it?" Not waiting for a reply, she jumped up. "I shall just run and fetch it. It is only a little over two hundred pages. I shouldn't think this will take above a couple of hours."

Thirty-one

As the morning stretched on and still Stanhope did not come, Calista's happiness remained undimmed. He had said he would be there, and he would.

When word finally came that there were visitors, she whipped off her apron and actually paused, before going down, to run a brush through her hair and retie the ribbon—she would worry about the sin of vanity tomorrow. She did, however, make an effort to prevent herself from rushing headlong into the drawing room, and thus entered at a dignified pace. In her efforts to restrain herself from falling immediately into Stanhope's arms, she forgot to tame the expression of radiantly unguarded happiness that suffused her face—which quickly turned to one of polite welcome as she entered the room to find Ossie, Squibby, and Neville draped languidly about the room on various spindly items of Egyptian furniture. They rose at her entrance.

"Your dress," gasped Ossie, eyes bulging. "It is . . . it is—"

"Dreadful!" supplied Squibby.

Calista forced a smile. "I was engaged in assisting Annie with some household tasks, gentlemen. Please be so good as to overlook my ensemble. And do be seated." She waved a hand, and they disposed of themselves on the furniture once again.

"That's a relief, I don't mind telling you! Whew!" Squibby fanned himself with a squeaky laugh.

"Thought you'd gone dowdy again," Ossie explained. "You *do* look a frightful quiz!"

"Vastly important you don't. Pockets to let and all, doncha know!" said Squibby somewhat obliquely.

"Er, we've come to pay a visit and to give you this," Ossie hurriedly explained, producing a book. "I recommend you give it a close reading."

Calista took the proffered volume. It was entitled *Neckclothitania, or Titania: Being an Essay on Starchers, by One of the Cloth.* "Thank you, gentlemen. I hardly know what to say. I shall certainly study it, and with its assistance I will doubtless remedy my appalling lack of knowledge in this area." She smiled. "Can I offer you some refreshment?"

"Thanks," said Squibby, looking grateful. "Thought we'd best make ourselves scarce from Moreford Park for as long as possible."

"Quite a dustup last night," Ossie said.

"Simply frightful!" exclaimed Neville. "Extraordinary, really."

"Sofie's still reclining in a darkened room."

"Lady Lyttworth's in a dreadful taking."

"Stanhope's been closeted in the library—with Amanda on his lap!—for *hours.*"

"You spied?!" Ossie demanded. "Tris won't like that by half."

"Did not."

"Then, how'd you know she was on his lap?"

"I, well, er, *peeked.*"

"Elmo's been ordered to attend his mama."

"Most *famous crim. con.*"

"Who'd have expected it in the *country?*"

"Gentlemen!" Calista, who was well used to dealing with children, quickly stemmed the confused tide of babble. "I am afraid I cannot make head or tail of what you're saying. Perhaps if *one* of you were to recount the tale?"

"Oh, *I* will," said Neville with a delighted shudder. "It happened last night, after we'd returned from the assembly. The entire household had retired for the evening. Stanhope was still out with Gresham. I'd just applied an eye restorative—bramble jelly and rosewater, a trace sticky but *très* effective on puffy eyes. My man makes it himself—"

"The story, Lord Ffolkes," Calista reminded him.

"Sorry, I digress. I was getting into bed, when I heard a frightful row. Ghastly shrieking and screaming coming from the Royal Chamber. I dashed out, pausing only to select the proper robe—purple you know, to match my lime-green and purple nightshirt. You'd be surprised at how many people think blue complements purple—Oswald!—but I—"

"Lord Ffolkes!"

"Sorry. Ran in with these two and Elmo on my heels to see if I could be of assistance, and you can never imagine what we found!"

"What?"

"Mrs. Prescott and Miss Lyttworth. *Both* in m'cousin's bed," pronounced Ossie, taking up the tale with relish. "Miss Lyttworth was shrieking to wake the dead and her mama was standing in the door, looking entirely done up."

"Looked a bit like a setup," explained Squibby.

"Except for the fact that such a veritable angel as Sofie could never have participated in such a scheme!" Ossie explained with authority.

"Never!" agreed Neville and Squibby in fervent unison.

"Turned out she'd sleepwalked right into his chamber! The poor thing was *horrified* in the extreme to realize where her somnambulations had ended. Fortunately, her mama had gone to *her* bedchamber seeking a word, noticed her missing, and gone in search of her," explained Ossie. "So disaster was averted."

"But Amanda!" said Neville with relish, drawing out the tale. *"Stanhope had arranged an assignation with her!* An illicit liaison right under Lady Lyttworth's nose!" he exclaimed with a moue of excitement. "Never would've guessed it, but Stanhope must be truly head over ears to do such a thing, as he is known for conducting his private affairs with a pleasing discretion. Came to us last night and threatened us with bodily harm if we told anyone of the incident. Didn't mean you, of course, Miss Ashton! And now he is removing himself to the Horse

and Castle! One can only assume Lady Lyttworth requested that
he do so!"

Ossie chimed in. "And he has been closeted with Amanda—
apparently on his lap—for *hours* in the library. They must be
planning the engagement!"

"Should've laid odds on *that*," Squibby said gloomily.

"No one could've guessed it was in the wind," Ossie pointed
out, "until *I* arranged it. Tris was in a towering rage when I
first came up with that engagement idea, but I told him it'd all
come about. D'you suppose they'll name me godfather to their
first child?"

"Why, Miss Ashton! Is something amiss?" Neville inquired,
peering at her through his quizzing glass. "You are decidedly
pale!"

"Not about to faint again, are you?" asked Ossie, edging
away.

"No, no. I'm fine," Calista managed to say around the huge
lump that seemed to have formed in her throat. "I'll just go see
Annie about sending in some tea."

Ossie nodded. "D'you think we might have some cakes? I'm
quite famished!"

"Of course," Calista replied automatically as she fled the
room.

Once she had achieved the relative serenity of the hall, she
leaned against the door she had shut behind her and closed her
eyes. Tears slid out from under the lids. So this is what they
mean when they talk of a broken heart, was her first thought.
Having always assumed it to be merely a figure of speech, she
hadn't reckoned on having a suffocating, squeezing sensation
in the middle of her chest, making it almost impossible to
breathe or move. I should have known, she told herself in anguish.

"Now refresh my memory," she heard Ossie say. "did the
wagers stipulate that Miss Ashton had to accept a proposal? Or
simply that she had to be wooed and her affections engaged?"

They're talking about me! she realized, thinking that she
might truly be about to faint again. There was a *wager!* Stanhope *was* using me. But instead of wanting me to rid him of

Amanda, as I'd accused him of, he was trying to win a bet, all the while planning to rendezvous with *her!* Of all his treachery, that was the worst part—that in the end he had turned out to be no better than she had expected. He had come here to take advantage of the trusting nature of a small town and seduce a prim spinster for his entertainment. And he had tricked Roberta Enright into aiding him in his scheme! But, oh, what a fool I am, she thought, her face burning with mortification. I have only myself to blame for this misery.

"Where do you suppose she's got to with that tea? How parched does a fellow have to be to merit refreshment around here?" she heard Squibby complain, and realized that she had to pull herself together. When she returned, followed by Annie with the tea tray, no one would ever have guessed that she felt as if her life were over. She managed a wan smile as she poured and thanked her luck that their conversation required only that she smile and, on occasion, contribute a monosyllabic response to their nonsense.

When they finally took their leave, arguing companionably as how best to spend their afternoon, she barely waited until they were out the door before rushing to her room and throwing herself facedown on her bed. Now is the time to cry my heart out, she thought. But oddly, the tears refused to come. It was as if her misery had squeezed even the ability to cry out of her body.

She wasn't sure which sent the biggest needle into her soul: the thought of Stanhope together with the beautiful Amanda, no doubt laughing at his great joke on the vicar's spinster sister; the realization that he was capable of such perfidy to win a wager; or the fact that despite all of it her traitorous heart and body still yearned for him. She had rolled over and was staring listlessly up at the ceiling, wondering how she could ever get up again, when Annie knocked at the door.

"Miss Calista?" she called, more gently than was her wont.
Calista's voice sounded colourless. "Yes, Annie?"
"His lordship is belowstairs, wishing a word with you."
"Tell him I am not at home," she said, willing her voice not

to break with the tears that uncooperatively seemed to be coming now.

"As you say," Annie said, closing the door behind her.

A few minutes later she was back, and Calista was sobbing in earnest.

"The gentleman says he will wait until you have returned, miss. He seems quite prepared to sit in the parlour all day."

"Very well, Annie. Please tell him that I will join him in a few moments."

There was nothing to be gained by putting off this interview. The least she could do, Calista decided, was to finish things with pride. She crossed to the bureau and splashed some cold water on her face, and wishing she did not look quite so dreadful, ran a brush through her tangled curls. If nothing else, I must keep my chin up, she thought, catching her breath. Then she picked up his ring with a shaking hand and headed down the stairs.

Thirty-two

Never had Stanhope been in better spirits. He had finally extricated himself from the Lyttworth household. Amanda was on her way to London. There was a special license in his pocket. Calista, he knew, had been on the verge of accepting him last night, and today their path was clear.

The look of pure happiness he bestowed upon her as she entered cut through Calista worse than any physical pain. He bent to kiss her hand, but she snatched it away as from a flame.

"Are you well, my love?" he asked looking at her face with a concern she now knew to be false.

She managed a brittle smile. "I am fine, thank you, my lord. And yourself? Please be seated."

Stanhope sat down on the backless sofa and she took a chair as far distant as possible. He frowned. This was not going at all as he had hoped. "I know I have asked this before, Calista, but today I am come to do it properly," he said as he rose and walked to her. Possessing himself of a cold hand, he went down on one knee. "I ask you to make me the happiest of men, Calista," he said, looking into her eyes. "Will you do me the honour of saying you will become my wife?"

Her stricken expression felt like a slap. "You cannot mean that!" she gasped, unable to believe that under the circumstances, he would still go forward with the charade. The man was an absolute disgrace! Why, he did not even plan to marry Amanda after last night's shocking escapade! As painful as that would have been, it would at least have been honourable.

"Of course I do. I have never been more serious about anything, love." He frowned in confusion. "I've a special license right here," he said, withdrawing it from his pocket. "We can wait and do the thing in style if you wish, although I confess a quiet ceremony is more to my taste." He was about to add in words to be used between lovers that all he could think of was making her his, completely and irrevocably, when she jumped up and turned to face him, her colour high with outrage.

"I am sure it is, considering what it is you are proposing!"

"I am proposing that we spend our lives together," he said in a raw voice, feeling as if his very heart was exposed. "I love you. And I am sure that it is nothing that having you in my bed for the next fifty years won't cure, but I am sick with the need for you—"

"No!" she said her voice, almost a whisper. "Do not speak to me of love. I have been a fool, but you may be certain I shall never be again." And before he knew what she was about, she grabbed the special license out of his hand and tore it into pieces. "We won't be needing this, sir, nor, for that matter, this!" she sobbed, flinging his signet ring at him and running from the room.

He remained, kneeling, wondering what on earth had happened. After a few minutes he retrieved the ring, stood, and went in search of Annie.

Initially, she was wary of such an exalted gentleman. But by the time he was taking his third cup of tea at the scrubbed-oak table in the kitchen, his hunch that she was the clearinghouse for information at the vicarage was paying off. She had unbent enough to remark that of a certainty, Miss Calista had been acting mighty queer of late. When his lordship had finished his second piece of gingerbread, which he praised as being even better than his own nanny's, she was in the palm of his hand. So it seemed perfectly natural to tell him of Calista's earlier visitors and of the gossip making the rounds of the servants' halls. And then when he smiled that smile—which, as she later told Joan Trent, *made even my crusty old heart beat faster and, Lordy, I thought I was way past such foolishness*—she spilled all, including how Miss Calista had been lying on her bed, sobbing fit to break your heart in two.

Feeling perhaps a stab of conscience at having given away so very much more than her mistress would have wanted, she inquired anxiously, "You do intend to do right by Miss Calista, your lordship?"

He smiled again. "Of course I do, Annie. Her happiness is as important to me as my own life. Don't you worry about a thing." He only wished he felt half as confident in his own ability to put things to rights as he sounded. "However long it takes. Don't you worry about a thing," he repeated. More, if truth be told, to himself than to her.

Thirty-three

Calista knew her situation to be truly dire when, the following morning, she actually considered skipping church. When Annie clattered in cheerfully to rouse her, she mumbled that she was far too unwell to leave her bed.

"Then I'll make haste about summoning Dr. Barlowe," clucked Annie. "It wouldn't do to have you carried off by something."

Actually, being carried off by something, as long as it was mercifully brief, had a definite appeal, Calista decided. But then she thought of the doctor and his insistence that leeching cured everything from a sniffle to apoplexy, which was enough to convince her that she might as well rise after all. It was not as though she was able to sleep anyway. She was only lying listlessly awake and dwelling on her folly to have fallen in love with a known rake. And she would have every morning for the rest of her life to lie alone in bed, examining her pain. Besides, she thought, trying desperately to summon something approaching her old common sense as she threw aside the blankets, there was nothing to be gained by lying in bed, wallowing in self-pity. At the very least she should stay busy.

So, she allowed Annie to bring her bath—through which she shivered, despite the warmth of the water—and then to dress her, not even raising an objection to the smartness of the navy wool dress picked for her. She descended the stairs feeling as though she was wrapped in a cloud of numbing misery but decided that numbness had its positive side. At least it was preferable to the consuming pain that had engulfed her yesterday, and perhaps if she was lucky, nothing would ever penetrate enough to have the power to distress her again.

Hermione, mercifully, also seemed distracted, and for once failed to find fault with her sister-in-law's dress. She also did not comment on the fact that Calista seemed to be shivering uncontrollably despite the warmth of the day. They walked the short distance to the church in silence.

"Miss Calista!" A young woman hailed her outside the doors to the church, and Hermione, displaying her usual aversion to actual contact with a parishioner, took the opportunity to scurry away.

"Good morning, Susan," Calista said. And to her own surprise, not only did her voice sound normal, but she even managed a small smile. She had been certain that pain such as this would be writ all over her. Encouraged, she continued brightly. "How wonderful to see you up and looking so well. And so soon after the baby!"

"Thank you, miss," said Susan, looking pleased. "We wanted you to be the first to hold her outside the family. She's right there with Sam."

Calista took the infant gently in her arms and admired her appropriately, telling the proud parents what a stunning baby they had. So much for blessed numbness, she thought as she cooed down at the tiny sleeping face. And the certainty that she would never hold her own baby—Stanhope's baby—in her arms tore through her with a savage pain. The infant woke up and promptly regurgitated all over the blue wool. Laughing off the parents' distress, Calista handed her back.

Less tentative now that she realized her misery was not apparent to others, Calista turned to greet Mrs. Searle. "Have you heard the news, Calista?" asked that lady, coming up next to her. "No? You must have just arrived, for the whole town is talking of little else."

"What is it?" asked Calista, suddenly anxious lest her humiliation be the latest topic on everyone's lips.

"Rose Cottage has been sold!"

My cottage! thought Calista. The last ray of hope had been

the knowledge that at least she would soon be able to buy the cottage and remove herself from the vicarage. "But to whom?" she managed to ask. "It has stood empty this age."

"I know that. No one seems to know who the purchaser is. The rumour, although I don't know that I would put much stock in that, is that it was the Earl of Stanhope's man of business who transacted the purchase. But what would *he* possibly want with that poky little cottage? The man must already own dozens of properties! You don't truly think it could be for his lordship, do you?"

"I don't know, Alice. He has hardly seen fit to make me privy to his plans," answered Calista through lips that felt frozen. But it was, she knew in her heart. It was for Amanda. He must have purchased it when he had thought to win his wager. He had not even had the decency to leave his amusements in London, but instead had planned all along to install his mistress right under her nose! I must take consolation, she thought, in the knowledge that this is, of a certainty, the lowest moment of my life. It simply cannot get worse than this.

As if trying to disprove that heartening idea, Squire Greystock appeared at her elbow. "Ho! Miss Ashton!" he said by way of greeting.

"Good morning," she replied, trying to squelch her dislike.

He bowed. "Mrs. Searle."

"Good morning, Everard."

"Heard the news about Rose Cottage?" he asked.

"Indeed. We were just discussing that very topic," Mrs. Searle replied in chilly tones. The bright sunshine highlighted the redness of the squire's countenance.

"Plans to install his fancy piece, I make no doubt, since he's developed *interests* in the neighbourhood," he said, guffawing loudly. "Fellow's a dashed lucky dog. Rich as Croesus, about to pop the question to a prime article like Sofie, *and* he's got himself a stunner for a little bit o' fluff on the side."

Marry Sofie and keep Amanda under his protection? The scenarios changed so wildly with every hour, it was virtually a full-time occupation keeping up with the latest, Calista decided. Then she shook her head. She no longer cared what he did, she reminded herself firmly as she became aware of Lady Searle scolding the squire.

"*Everard!*" that lady exclaimed in what was by far the most authoritative tone Calista had ever heard her employ. "Hush! What can you be about to discuss such things in front of an unmarried female?"

"Calista?" he replied, puzzled. "Nothing there to shock her at her age. And besides," he added smugly, "we have an understanding and she knows I abhor die-away airs. She'd best adjust herself to some good plainspeaking!"

Mrs. Searle gasped in outrage and would have said more, but Calista hurriedly interrupted as she spied Elleanor Stanley, closely followed by her godson, waving her handkerchief and bearing down in their direction. As much as she loved Elleanor, she was just not up to being the object of her solicitous concern at the moment. Nor, if she were to be honest, was she up to making polite conversation with Stanhope's best friend, who must have been, at best, an accomplice in their little caper, and, at worst, the instigator of the wager. "Come, let us go in. I think the service is about to start," she said, hastily heading for the open double doors.

"Getting dashed hot out here," said the squire, mopping his perspiring forehead with his handkerchief. "Starting to think that I should not have had that second bottle with breakfast." He belched wetly. "Think it might have disagreed with me on top of all those creamed kidneys. Certainly hope the gout doesn't flare up again. D'you see why I need a female's gentle touch about the place?"

"Such a thing can never go amiss," agreed Mrs. Searle dubiously, making to take Calista's arm.

"I shall escort Miss Ashton to her pew," said the squire, snatching up her arm in his perspiring, stubby fingers and steering her inside.

Calista longed to snap that she was quite capable of finding her own way, thank you very much, but decided that she hadn't the energy for a scene. So she allowed herself to be led through the archway made by the open double doors. For a moment the dimness of the church, with its familiar smell of ancient dust and candles and flowers, comforted her as she slid into their pew next to Hermione. She closed her eyes and prayed for strength and serenity. Prayers that were not to be immediately answered, as Squire Greystock slid in next to her, his large thigh pressing against her leg. Calista tried to escape this unwelcome pressure by sliding farther to the left, but Hermione, who after greeting the squire cordially had lapsed back into her distracted state, did not yield her any more room. From his proximity, Calista was unpleasantly reminded of the gentleman's aversion to soap and water. I *must* manage an audience with Adolphus before the sun sets today, she resolved.

Calista caught her breath as the Lyttworth pew, directly in front of them, filled. Stanhope, who had joined the party for services, did not look at her as he came down the center aisle with Sofie and her parents but merely acknowledged their party with a nod and slid into the pew so he was seated almost directly in front of her. Despite her loathing for the man, her impulse to reach out and touch the back of his neck was so strong that she had to fold her hands in her lap. He was so close, she could smell him. In direct contrast with her neighbour, his scent was of soap and clean linen and something indefinably him that made her stomach ache with longing. He was flanked by Sofie, looking gloriously innocent in a simple sprigged muslin, and a chattering Lady Lyttworth.

"The Lyttworths have *always* been seated here, as, I would imagine, you have guessed," that lady was saying in her carrying voice. "The pew, as you are well able to see, my lord, is worn smooth by many generations of Lyttworth—" She broke off, and even in her state of anguish Calista was forced to stifle a laugh as she imagined Stanhope's amusement.

Her brief moment of levity ended quickly as the oppressive presence of Squire Greystock made itself felt. "Stanhope. Your lordship," he said, leaning forward and tapping him on the shoulder.

Stanhope turned. His heart seemed to tumble over at the sight of Calista looking so wan. If it were another woman, I would grab her and force her to listen to my explanation and everything would be straightened out in a second, he thought. But if it were another woman, he would not have lain awake all night cursing himself for causing her unhappiness. Nor would his pulse be racing and his body yearning so just from the memory of her. And come to think of it, he probably would not be so tempted to black the Squire's smug eye again just for the very act of sitting too close to her. Don't overwhelm her. Keep things light. She will come around in her own time, he reminded himself. So he nodded pleasantly but coolly. "Good morning, Mrs. Ashton. Miss Ashton. Squire Greystock."

It is as if we were strangers, Calista thought miserably.

"Heard about Rose Cottage!" the squire hissed in a loud whisper. "The news is all over town. Won't go into details, old fellow, ladies present and all, but I'll go odds endurance on horseback ain't your only skill. Heh-heh."

Hermione fidgeted uncomfortably, and Lady Lyttworth pokered up and shot the squire a warning glance over her shoulder. Stanhope noticed only the way Calista's already pale countenance blanched. He clenched his jaw against his longing to whisk her away from Greystock's coarse innuendo. "I had not planned——" he began, his distaste apparent.

"No use denying it, you sly dog!" The squire winked.

The conversation was interrupted as the Reverend Ashton came rushing in, out of breath, and took the pulpit. "Ahem. Good morning!" he began, giving Stanhope the opportunity to turn forward, effectively ending Greystock's offensive speculations.

"Welcome, parishioners. Honoured guests." Adolphus inclined his head toward the Lyttworth pew.

"I think you will find Adolphus's sermons quite out of the ordinary in their inspiration, my lord," Lady Lyttworth assured Stanhope with confidence.

"This morning's sermon," the reverend intoned, "is entitled *He Who Covets the Decanter of His Better Shall Be Forever Destined by the Lord to Drink an Inferior Vintage: or, A Lesson in Two Parts for the Commoner on Accepting One's Station.*"

"I just *knew* it would be one of his best this morning," she whispered with satisfaction. "What a shame Ossie, Neville, Squibby, and Elmo are still abed! I'm certain they will be quite cast down to hear what they have missed."

Adolphus was even more tedious than usual. Ordinarily, Calista chafed at the sermon, but this morning she couldn't seem to pay attention. Her eyes were riveted by Stanhope's back, covered in perfectly fitted blue superfine, and his even breathing. Next to her, Hermione fidgeted, distracting her further. If only I could get warm, she thought, shivering and wrapping her arms around herself in an effort to chase away the cold that seemed to emanate from the very core of her being.

Finally Adolphus wound up his sermon. "And so, if the Lord were to descend upon Deepdene, I, as his messenger here on earth, am here to tell you that He would say, 'Tenants! Farmers! Workers! Commonfolk! Accept what has been brought unto you here on earth as the blessings of a Just and Bountiful Lord who knew what He was about when He filled your cup. Drink your tankard of ale in humble thanks, and aspire not to your social superior's glass of tawny 'eighty-four. And in heaven you shall see your reward: perhaps a sweet sherry, albeit nonvintage, with the Angels. Rejoice in your good fortune!' "

"*Truly* inspirational, as usual," applauded Lady Lyttworth, wiping a tear. "I have not regretted his appointment one single Sunday. I am positively *moved* this way every week. Last month I was nearly overcome by his sermon in which he called for the repeal of the Peel Act—he said that it was the Lord, in His all-knowing beneficence, who graced the serving classes with betters to keep them employed round the clock to occupy their hours with work instead of the vices native to them. Why, when he said, 'Thank the Lord! Thank your betters! Thank the fourteen-hour workday! For they keep you from sin,' I don't mind telling you, I wept! Surely he has the character and compassion to rise to lofty heights within the hierarchy of the Church! But we can tell him so at nuncheon, as they will dine with us at Moreford Park. Where," she added coyly, "we will be celebrating some happy news!"

The Baron Lyttworth let out a gentle snore.

"Doncha think his point would have been better taken if he'd said an 'eighty-seven? Who'd covet an 'eighty-four?" Squire Greystock demanded of Calista, who sat dumbly. How was it possible to find a man despicable and yet want him so much?

she wondered, looking at the way Stanhope's dark hair just brushed his collar. She envisioned her hands twined in the silkiness of it as he kissed her senseless. She would be warm again. And *his* hands would be—enough! she told herself sternly, trying very hard to forget the places his hands had been just a few days before.

"Now on to village business," Adolphus announced, rubbing his hands briskly.

"I hope this won't take long," grumbled the squire. "I'm a bit peckish. Must've finally digested that breakfast. Hope Gladys puts out a good spread—been known to be just a tad cheeseparing about the food."

"Are there any announcements?" Adolphus asked the congregation.

There were a few. Some pigs for sale. Two births. A christening next week. A death. Solicitations of help for the spring fête. Calista couldn't get Stanhope's hands out of her mind. Against her will, she remembered them as he had unbuttoned her nightgown. There was no question that he knew what he was about, but despite his practiced manner, his hands had been shaking ever so slightly, and he had uttered husky endearments as he had kissed her mouth, her hair, and the skin he was rapidly baring. She had thought for a few brief moments that it was possible to die of happiness. And longing. She had never imagined such fire or such sweetness could exist. Why, she wondered, had he stopped? At least then I would have had him once, she thought, horrified at the wild direction her thoughts were taking. And in church, no less!

And then Adolphus cleared his throat. "And, um, finally, *I* have an item of business. One that gives me great, er, great, ah, *joy.* I wish to, ahem, announce the . . . ah, the first of the banns for the, uh, the *marriage* of my sister, Miss Calista Ashton, and my good friend, Everard Greystock!"

Thirty-four

Calista was vaguely aware of a sudden buzz of hushed conversation. This is my punishment for having blasphemous thoughts in church, she thought wildly, feeling in that brief moment that nothing was real, as if she were falling through time and space. She had the fanciful thought that were she to reach out and steady herself on Stanhope's shoulder, it would somehow stop her fall. But, of course, she couldn't. It wouldn't. She was enveloped in a white, dizzying fog. This cannot be happening, she thought.

But it was.

"For goodness' sake, Calista, smile," Hermione hissed, grabbing her arm.

The squire snaked a sweaty and proprietorial arm about her shoulders. Adolphus banged on the pulpit to quiet the babble. "I will post the banns for the next three Sundays," he announced. "And, of course, barring objections to the union"—he paused and chuckled weakly to show how unlikely he considered that possibility—"the ceremony will be held on fifteenth May. On that date, Squire Greystock has been so kind as to invite the entire congregation to join our families for the wedding breakfast."

"In a hurry, but not for the reason you think, you old leaky rattle," the squire bellowed to a hunting crony several rows over. "Paying the nanny and nursemaids a demmed fortune. Why shell out good blunt when a wife will do for free? Eh, what? Plan to turn 'em all off as soon as possible."

"It gives Mrs. Ashton and myself great pleasure to welcome such a fine gentleman to our little family as a brother," added Adolphus as an afterthought.

"Gel needs a bit of work," Greystock announced loudly to another acquaintance. "S'truth. Bit of a rough diamond, but all she needs is a firm hand"—he winked—"and a few babies to take her mind off all that bookish nonsense! I'll have her sorted out in a trice."

I must put a stop to this, Calista thought. I must stand and say that there has been a misunderstanding. But suddenly everyone was converging on her. Congratulating her. Offering genuine, if dubious, felicitations.

Stanhope stood, waiting for Calista to say there had been a mistake. He for one was not at all certain that he could get through even one Sunday of banns without voicing violent objections. Or killing the squire. You will never be happy without me, Calista. He can never give you fulfillment of body and soul, and I am not at all certain I can live without you, he wanted to yell. But instead, he forced a smile and a small bow, while he waited for her to dispute her brother's words, and said in polite tones, "Squire Greystock. Miss Ashton. My felicitations to you both."

He doesn't care a rap about me, Calista thought. He can't even meet my eye, he is so relieved to be shot of me. There was no question of this marriage ever coming about, but she would die before she would let Stanhope know that she would pine for him forever. So she shaped her mouth into an upward turn. "Thank you, sir," she forced herself to say.

A wave of nausea washed over Stanhope. She had *agreed* to this? He knew that Calista had been uncertain of his devotion and that she was badly hurt by what she believed to be his perfidious actions, but he had assumed that there would be time to explain the misunderstanding once the situation had cooled down. But how, *how,* no matter what she believed of him, could she have agreed to *this?* The thought made him physically ill.

"Heh-heh. Gel's not of your caliber, of course, Stanhope," chortled Greystock. "But the older, plainer ones can be a deal easier to handle. Don't expect so much, y'know. If a fellow's away hunting for a long spell or has a few diversions on the side, they don't kick up nearly as much of a fuss as do those diamonds of yours."

It was as if everything went red before Stanhope's eyes. For the first time in his life, every trace of reason fled. And he heard the words before he realized they were his own. "The thing of it is, that actually, I've an objection. I am sorry to say, sir, that Miss Ashton cannot possibly marry you."

At the squire's insulting words, it had felt to Calista as if her old spirit had reentered her body. She had been about to put a stop to this disastrous farce without further delay, when Stanhope had spoken. *"What?"* she gasped, wheeling around to face him. "How *could* you?"

At the same moment the squire, who had gone purple, gasped, "Beg pardon?"

Although there was still an audible buzz of excited chatter in the church, the little group around the Ashtons' pew had gone quite silent. Stanhope's voice sounded unnaturally loud to his own ears. He took a deep, steadying breath. "I am afraid I have compromised her," he said, being careful to avoid Calista's eyes.

For years afterward some people stuck doggedly to the conviction that it was Lady Lyttworth's shriek that cracked the stained glass window next to her pew. Others held to the opinion that Billy Trent had a lucky hit with his slingshot later that afternoon. Both schools of thought, however, agreed that no sooner had those words left Stanhope's mouth and the echo of the scream died away than the entire church had fallen silent. And that while Calista herself was the only one with wits enough to wave a vinaigrette under Hermione Ashton's senseless nose, the Dowager Lady Dabley had broken the hush by bellowing at her cringing granddaughter, "Well, of course he's compromised her. Any chit with a twopenny of sense would let *him* make love to her. Just look at 'im. And he's rich too. If you hadn't been so busy cowering behind the ferns, my gel, maybe you could have been the lucky one!"

The Reverend Ashton had ignored this outburst and turned to Stanhope. "Far be it for such a humble man as myself, with no claim to your rank, to question the words of such an exalted personage as yourself, my lord," he had begun, not forgetting, even under the circumstances to toady, "but surely there is some mistake."

"There is no mistake, Reverend."

"What exactly are you saying, my lord?" Adolphus had inquired.

"I am saying, Reverend Ashton," Stanhope had replied in a perfectly level voice, "that I have compromised your sister and would be honoured if you would give your consent to our marriage."

And then Calista had risen from her ministrations to her sister-in-law and stamped her foot and said in a calm voice, "I've heard enough. This is all utter foolishness. Every last word of it. And I shall not marry either of you, under any circumstances. Not," she had added in heartfelt accents, "if my very life depended upon it!"

And then the recently revived Hermione had promptly fainted again.

Thirty-five

The conversation, it was agreed, would be better continued in more private surroundings, so the participants adjourned to Moreford Park. The party that assembled in Lady Lyttworth's drawing room a short time later was less the festive nuncheon she had envisioned than a council of war. The champagne—not the best for this occasion, naturally—remained firmly ensconced on ice, and the players scattered grimly about the room on chairs instead of gathering gaily at the table. Calista, feeling like a prisoner, had been firmly placed on a sofa between Hermione and Adolphus, where she sat in silence, her brief resurgence of spirit apparently over.

"How on earth do you expect us to believe that *you* could have compromised Calista Ashton, my lord?" asked Lady Lyttworth, who was clearly leading the proceedings, her disbelief writ on her face.

"We have been alone together, La—er, Cousin Gladys," he replied evenly.

"That would be compromise!" crowed the Reverend Ashton, scarce able to believe his good fortune.

"Nonsense!" exclaimed their hostess, her relief apparent. "We do not abide by such strict rules of propriety in the country. I realize that there is a different protocol in London, but here it is not socially unacceptable for an unattached female to ride out with a gentleman. The ladies here generally ride without grooms and are frequently unchaperoned. Especially," she added with a dismissive wave, "when the female is of Calista's advanced years. There can be no obligation in that quarter, my lord."

"You misunderstand me, madam," replied Stanhope, still assiduously avoiding Calista's eye. He would pay for this day's madness, but it would be worth it to keep her away from Greystock's vile hands. He had waited for her to rise to her own defense, but she had failed to do so, and her uncharacteristic passivity alarmed him. Aside from her brief flare of spirit back in the church, she had been unnervingly silent. "We have exchanged . . . intimacies." It hardly seemed a fitting word to describe the sweetness and fire that had passed between the two of them. In fact, as a description it seemed curiously unsatisfactory, so he went on. "That is, I have taken advantage of her, ah, trusting nature to make love to Miss Ashton." That sounded slightly better, but judging from their expressions, his audience disagreed.

"Leave the room, Sofie," Lady Lyttworth commanded without withdrawing her eyes from Stanhope.

Sofie knew that her odds of ever bearing witness to such excitement again were slender indeed. Even losing the prize matrimonial catch of the decade could hardly dampen her enthusiasm for the drama being enacted before her. It was not as if her heart were engaged. In fact, truth to be told, she found Stanhope, with his quick wit and good looks that almost eclipsed her own, a trifle intimidating. And of late he had seemed preoccupied, forgetting to compliment several new gowns and failing even to mention when she had changed her hairstyle from à la Venus to ringlets all around her forehead crowned by a topknot! Lord Gresham——now, there was a handsome gentleman who was not in the least intimidating——had noticed immediately, paying fulsome compliments. No, it was altogether too excellent a scene to miss. So when her mama had said *Stop woolgathering and remove yourself this instant, Sofie!*, she stomped her little foot and said, *Under no circumstances!*

To this, her mama replied in tones so awesome that Squire Greystock began to rise in obedience. "Get out. This is not for your ears!"

Recognizing when her mama would not be budged, Sofie reluctantly made for the door with every intention of pressing her ear immediately to the other side. Plans that were thwarted by the fact that Ossie, Squibby, Neville, and Elmo almost fell upon her the moment she emerged, engaged as they were in that very activity.

"Can't hear a blasted thing through that door," Ossie complained.

"What's going on in there?" Elmo demanded.

"D'you mean you don't know?" smirked Sofie, thrilled to have the upper hand over her brother for once.

"We would hardly be asking a peagoose like you if we already knew, would we?" replied Elmo.

"If certain people bothered rising in time for church . . ."

"Stow it, Sofie, and spill the beans, or I'll hang you by your heels from the apple tree as I was used to when we were children. See if I don't!"

Not certain whether her brother truly meant his threat, but unwilling to find out, Sofie tumbled out the tale. "Adolphus read the banns for Calista's marriage to Squire Greystock in church and then Lord Stanhope stood and announced that *he* would wed her as he had compromised her and Mama screamed and Hermione fainted and the Dowager Lady Dabley was shockingly indiscreet and the squire turned purple and then we all came back here and now Mama's in a terrible taking and has *banished* me from the room." Her lips trembled. "And now I shall miss all the rest and you have *threatened* me! Was anyone ever served such an ill turn before?"

But the four gentlemen were not paying the least heed to her.

"Stanhope is to wed Miss Ashton?" gasped Squibby, throwing himself to the floor and clutching his head.

"I should be more careful if I were you," advised Neville. "You shall crease your clothing, throwing yourself about that way."

"Shut up, Neville! Don't you realize what this means?" moaned Squibby. "We laid bets that Ossie would win her, and now *Stanhope is going to marry her!* I'm going to lose a bundle!"

"Well, *I*," said Neville, buffing his perfect fingernails with a small chamois cloth, "stand to *make* a bundle."

"What?" squawked Ossie.

"I bet against," Neville replied. "Couldn't see you bringing yourself to the sticking point somehow. I was willing to bet that you'd court her, but then, when old Skeffingham raised the ante to the banns being read—"

"The banns being read?" asked Ossie in a terrible voice. "Who said anything about that?"

Squibby, flat on the floor, eyes closed, asked Neville, "D'you realize what you've done, you imbecile?"

"Don't worry. I won't take your blunt, old man. In fact, I'd thought to generously share my winnings."

"Are you mad?" Squibby glared at him. "Knowing all the time that you had laid a bet *against* Oswald's success, you still accompanied us here. And then, to top it off, you plan to share your winnings?! You numskull! Everyone will think we've rigged the bet and Ossie's thrown it. We'll be outcasts!"

Going quite pale, Neville reached for the banister and sat heavily on the bottom step. "I—I hadn't thought of that," he choked.

"You bet *against me?"* Ossie squeaked. "You are the veriest worm I have ever known! And I *never* said anything about the banns being read—"

"Wagers? What wagers?" asked Sofie, looking from one to the other. "Mama will pitch a fit if she thinks you've been gambling, Elmo!"

"Go away, Sofie. This is not for your ears," said Elmo.

"I shall tell her if you continue to mistreat me!" Sofie threatened.

"I have not forgotten exactly how high up from that apple tree to hang you," countered Elmo.

"Well!" Sofie glared at her brother. "Fine. I shall go out into the garden and seek solace in my watercolours. But I shan't forget how shabbily I've been treated at your hands, Elmo," she warned her brother. "And when I've made a brilliant match, I shall give you the *cut direct* and you shall no doubt be shunned by all the best people." And with her nose in the air, she swept out to have a footman assemble her easel in the rose garden. Which is exactly where Peter Gresham found her when he came to call.

"And that is what must be done, Oswald," Squibby, who had risen from the floor and was pacing the hallway, proclaimed.

"You can't mean that!"

"He's right, m'fraid," agreed Neville with a sigh. "There's no other answer."

"A gentleman can't appear to welsh on his bets," Elmo was quick to add.

"But I never said I'd *wed* the chit," Ossie objected.

"Well, yes, but that was before Neville here made such a mull of things," Squibby pointed out.

Neville shuddered and the beginnings of a sob rose in his throat. "We'd be *ostracized,* Ossie. Just think, White's would most likely strike us from the membership lists! And the best tailors would refuse our commissions!"

Ossie was aghast. "D'you think that could happen?"

"Indubitably," Squibby assured him. "Remember Sumner Waldorf? Couldn't get a decent waistcoat made in London to save his life after he threw that bet!"

Neville slumped against the step. "I recall. He never had a waistcoat in the first stare of fashion again."

"But suppose she *wants* to marry Stanhope?" Ossie objected. "Not that I can see it m'self, but all females seem to."

"And his boots were just *awful* after that," wailed Neville.

"It does not matter what she wants, Ossie. You must do your duty." Squibby's voice was sharp.

"Very well," Ossie said on a sigh. "Never let it be said that I didn't know where my duty lay!"

"It'll all come about," Squibby said comfortingly. "You won't have to see her above once or twice a year."

Thirty-six

" 'Tis apparent I've nurtured a viper in my bosom," Lady Lyttworth was wailing as the four young men trooped into the drawing room.

"I am deeply sorry if my actions have caused you any distress," Stanhope replied, sounding as apologetic as he was able.

"I was speaking of Calista!"

"Now, Gladys," began the Baron Lyttworth, who had been awakened from his comfortable doze in his chair by the window by his wife's wail, "you are overwrought—"

But his wife was far past soothing. "Shut up, George," she shrieked. "You knew he was a guest in my house," she accused shrilly, jabbing her finger at Calista, who sat mute and stony-faced on the sofa, "that he had come here to propose to my daughter! And still you, you *seduced* him!"

"First off, Miss Ashton did not seduce me, and second, I came here to purchase a horse," Stanhope pointed out in a reasonable voice.

"Stubble the horse," howled Lady Lyttworth crudely. "Why *you* thought you were coming here is entirely beside the point! We all know that men will entertain themselves where they can by consorting with women of low morals when the opportunity comes their way!" At this, her husband flushed a guilty red. "But for Calista to take advantage of that weakness is quite beyond anything! And as for the fact that you are too much a gentleman to admit that is what happened—don't you see? That is what she was counting on!"

"Ahem." Squire Greystock cleared his throat. "Come to think of it, I've compromised the gel myself. Long as she's not in an *interesting condition,* don't see why I shouldn't marry her any-way—for a reduced settlement, of course," he added with a quick look at Adolphus. "Still work out to be a demmed sight cheaper than that staff I employ. Not passing off one of your by-blows as my own though, Stanhope. A man's got to have standards, y'know."

"That's extremely handsome of you, Everard," said Lady Lyttworth approvingly.

Before Stanhope could open his mouth to object, the newly arrived Ossie, who had been trying to be as invisible as possible, piped up from the corner, "Er, actually, fellows, think I should be the one to get shackled to her." He sighed, his curls and his shirt points looking decidedly wilted. The room went silent as everyone turned to look at him. He smiled nervously and shrugged. "Compromised her too."

There was a collective gasp.

"How 'bout we compare stories and whoever compromised her first gets her?" suggested the squire. "With me it was at the Stanleys' Venetian breakfast. Good food. Demmed fine spread Elleanor Stanley always puts on. Anyway, I kissed her in the—"

"That," said Stanhope softly but in a way that silenced the squire instantly, "is absolutely enough—"

"No, Stanhope," Calista interrupted him, rising from the sofa and speaking for the first time since they left the church. "How dare you! Any of you!" she spat out through white lips. "I have sat here and listened to all of you discuss me as though I were a piece of property! Chattel!" Her fury was apparent behind each shaking word, and Stanhope relaxed a little. She might be mad with rage, but at least she was no longer so terrifyingly apathetic. "And you, Adolphus! Hermione! You sold me! And now you just sit there and let them talk about me as if I were a lightskirt because you are so afraid to speak up to anyone with wealth or influence. You've been toadying so long it's be-come part of your natures. And don't bother to deny it."

She turned. "And as for this business of compromising me!

What utter and complete nonsense! It is a backward and out-moded idea. Why, in a progressive and forward-thinking society as we purport to be, women should be free and equal and as able to decide their own future as men! Why should *I* be ruined by *your* disgusting slobberings and gropings? Goodness knows, from my perspective it's all of *you* who should be considered not fit for marriage! You *sicken* me, and I'd not marry any of you if it were the only way to save myself from a *lifetime* of scrubbing floors, which, thankfully, I don't think I shall be re-duced to. But if I am, I shall do it *gratefully* if it means I shall not have to consort with the likes of you!"

God, I love this woman, thought Stanhope, lost in admiration even though he knew he was included in her condemnation.

"You"—Calista pointed a finger toward Squire Greystock, knowing she was going too far and not caring—*I just might have to leave town after this, but it will be worth it,* she thought—"are an odious, disgusting, clutch-fisted lecher! And *you*"—she turned toward Ossie—"are the most ridiculous frib-ble it has ever been my misfortune to meet! And you, Stanhope," she said, still looking at Ossie, feeling all the fire drain out of her as her voice broke. "You are by far the worst of all—" And suddenly she was overcome by pure misery and she stopped, unable to go on, as tears began to roll down her cheeks, and she slumped back on the sofa.

"That is enough of this ridiculous display, missy!" snapped Lady Lyttworth, collecting herself. "*We* shall decide what is to be done with you. You have put yourself beyond the pale this time. In fact, I'd be shocked if Everard is still willing to have you, after all. And you owe an apology to our distinguished visitor, his lordship, not to mention—"

But Stanhope had stood and was crossing the room to where Calista sat. "Calista," he murmured, sinking to his knees in front of her. Ignoring the shocked expressions all around him, he spoke as though they were the only people in the room. "I'm so sorry. I didn't understand. Please look at me, love."

Lady Lyttworth gasped. Calista shook her head, refusing, but her anger had dissipated, leaving her curiously drained in its wake.

"I've gone about this all wrong," he said to the top of her head as she gazed down at the floor. "I thought, you see, that you'd *agreed* to marry him after all, because Annie told me that you'd heard about Amanda coming to my bed the other night and decided I was playing you false. I knew you didn't love him, and I just couldn't bear the thought of you married to someone who wouldn't adore and treasure you with all their being, so I tried to force you into a position where you'd have to marry me instead. I should never have told anyone that I'd compromised you—I know I promised that that could stay between us, and it should have. What I should have said was please, please, marry me because I love you to distraction and can never be happy otherwise, and neither, I think, will you."

She still refused to look at him, so he went on, heedless of their shocked audience. "I am your future, darling, as you are mine. Please believe me," he begged, his voice intimate, "that Amanda is nothing to me and I did not arrange a rendezvous with her. It was a misunderstanding, but she knows now that I want only you, and has gone back to London. I swear on all that is dear to me that I've not even thought of another woman since the day I met you."

"But you purchased Rose Cottage for her!" accused Calista, sounding less certain of herself.

To her surprise, she saw out of the corner of her eye that he smiled. "No, sweetheart," he said, possessing himself gently of her hand. "I purchased Rose Cottage for *you*. My solicitor should be calling shortly with the deed."

In her shock she looked straight into his eyes, which she had warned herself against. Eyes that seemed time and time again able to make her forget herself, so she looked away. "For me? Why?"

His hand was exerting a most comforting pressure on hers. "After you sent me away, I knew you were still uncertain about me, but I was afraid that your brother had the leverage to force you into a position where you had to accept one of us simply because you had no place else to go for the six months until you came into your inheritance—which I knew about from Lady Enright."

"Now, see here—" blustered Adolphus.

But Stanhope was not about to be diverted. "So I thought if I gave you Rose Cottage, you would at least have the option of refusing us both, should you so choose. I had intended, of course," he said with a smile, "to court you slowly and let you discover for yourself what a truly wonderful fellow I am. I assumed we had time, until this morning, and then I couldn't see straight. The last thing I wanted to do was force you into a marriage you can't like. I'm so very sorry."

"You did that for me?" she asked wonderingly.

His nod was rueful. "But was ever a gesture so misconstrued?"

"I would never have accepted it."

"I had planned to extract a promise of payment in due time."

"Oh, Stanhope," Calista breathed, tears of a different kind beginning.

"Tristan."

"Tristan."

"Wait just a moment—" blustered the squire.

"Do something, Adolphus," commanded Lady Lyttworth. "This situation cannot be satisfactory!"

"Er, yes. Absolutely right, my lady," said Adolphus, turning to look at the couple, who appeared to be rapidly becoming oblivious to everyone else. "Will there be a settlement, my lord?" he queried in a timid tone. "After all, Greystock had offered . . ." He trailed away as he became aware of the look in Stanhope's eyes. "Er, of course, there's no need to work out the details right now," he amended hastily.

"That is not what I meant when I told you to do something, you ninnyhammer," snapped Lady Lyttworth.

"Will you wear my ring, Calista?" Stanhope, who was still on his knees before her, asked as he pulled the signet ring off his finger once again. "Could you possibly marry me?"

Calista smiled down at him, but before she had a chance to reply, there came a knock on the door and all heads turned as if of one accord.

"There is a *personage* here, my lady," said Enders, the butler.

"I have said you are not at home to callers, but she is most insistent."

"Get out of my way, man. You are wasting my time," came a stentorian voice from the hallway, and Ossie wilted further as the Dowager Viscountess of Elston burst in.

"My lady," said Lady Lyttworth, rising quickly at the sight of such an exalted visitor, then sinking into a curtsy. "Welcome—"

"Be quiet," ordered the dowager in an extremely rude fashion, leaving her hostess staring. "All right, where is the wagered chit?" she demanded. "Where is Calista Ashton?"

Thirty-seven

Ossie, quailing in the face of his mama's fury, pointed mutely at Calista, who still sat on the sofa between Adolphus and Hermione with Stanhope on his knees before her.

"Well, well," said the dowager, eyeing the scene, her displeasure apparent. "Whatever can you be about, Stanhope? I'll warn you now that I've had you checked out, my girl. Thoroughly, you can be sure. You are not, I confess, what we had been hoping for," she said, furrowing her brow beneath her red and silver turban. "But your birth and connexions are unexceptionable, so I suppose you'll have to do now that you've been wagered into the family."

"How could I have forgotten? You *wagered* on me!" Calista recalled, looking at Stanhope in horror, as reality intruded. "Like a . . . a *horse!*"

He passed a hand over his brow but had the presence of mind to recapture hers before she could escape from him. "No!" he all but yelped. "This chapter, I think, is my cousin's to explain," he said, gladly passing on the responsibility. "Ossie."

"See that you do, son," thundered his mother, sinking into a chair and crossing her arms over her massive chest. "I find I am excessively interested in your explanation myself!"

Looking positively bedraggled, Ossie sighed deeply and made a clean breast of things. He had fully prepared himself once again to bear the brunt of Miss Ashton's fearsome rage—really, she was almost as bad as his mama! Thank goodness, he reflected, that he had escaped the parson's mousetrap with her!—but to his surprise she seemed to have forgotten his very existence and was again smiling down at Stanhope with that misty look.

"I have heard enough, Oswald," said the dowager, advancing on her son, "to realize that this is not at all what I had in mind when I ordered you from town to court a suitable female. This, in fact, is exactly the type of rackety affair I had banished you on account of. Since it appears you won't be marrying Miss Ashton after all, and since I think you can safely consider yourself persona non grata, for the moment, both in my books and at your clubs—considering how many people probably lost their blunt on you—I think that this is the perfect opportunity to tell you that your aunt Ottile has fractured her foot and requires someone to assist her recuperation and to escort her around Bath for the next several months. I shall immediately volunteer you."

At Ossie's gasp of horror and Neville's crack of laughter at his friend's plight, the dowager turned her attention to Ossie's cronies. "Perhaps it would interest the two of you," she said dangerously, "to learn that I have consulted with *your* mamas and they are *both* of the opinion that you should join your friend. A nice spell in Bath should do you all good!" Satisfied with their cowed expressions, she once again made herself comfortable to observe the rest of the scene.

"Lady Earla," said Lady Lyttworth, attempting to salvage something of the situation, "I do so hope you will stop with us for a few days. I think you will find us quite a congenial little society."

"I doubt that highly," the dowager snapped. "And you can be sure I've no intention of staying a moment longer than necessary. Never could abide the country! No, as soon as I find out what my nephew is doing in that ridiculous position before the wagered chit—as last I heard he was going to leg shackle himself to the little Prescott slut, shocking, I tell you!—I shall quit this loathsome burg."

Calista was still gazing at Stanhope, heedless of the conversation around them, and he was doing likewise. "Do you mean you actually came here to *save* me?"

He nodded.

"But you didn't even know me," she breathed.

He inclined his head modestly. "I told you that you would no doubt think me a capital fellow if you gave me a chance."

"No doubt," she replied, recalling herself enough to make her tone dry.

"No good deed was ever more amply rewarded, my love," he whispered, raising her fingers to his lips, "but you may spend the rest of our lives thanking me, all the same."

She attempted to ignore the heat that the merest brush of his lips left in its wake. "I am not sure—"

"That you will know how to do it properly? Don't concern yourself, as together I am sure we can think of ways," he said in a way that caused her to blush.

"That is all very well," she said, drawing back slightly. "But my reading and my work—I am not ready to give that up, you know."

"I know, love," he replied, his eyes turning serious. "Nor would I expect you to. Reform to your heart's content. The more radical, the better. We will be known as the wildly eccentric Earl and Countess of Stanhope. I will even build a house in this blasted town should you desire, although I must draw the line at Rose Cottage. Far too damp. And by the way, I think you will be quite pleasantly surprised by how progressive conditions are on my estates, although I shall value your advice greatly. As it is, we go to great lengths with schooling and our efforts to help people find suitable employment that will raise their station in life. My mother takes quite an interest. She is, in fact, great cronies with Sydney Smith." He paused to enjoy Calista's astonishment.

"She is?"

He nodded.

"I can hardly wait to meet your mother, Stanhope." Really, the man was full of surprises.

"Tristan."

"Tristan."

He smiled at her. "Good. I know she will adore you, my love. So much so, in fact, that I think I must keep you to myself for a while if you don't mind too much." He ran a gentle finger along her lips, careless of their audience. "That is why I must insist," he said with a grin, "on a long, long honeymoon."

"I suppose I've no objection," Calista said in a voice that made him wish they were truly alone.

"Excellent," he said, taking the opportunity to slide the ring onto her finger. "We are, for once, in agreement."

"No, I will show myself in, Enders," came yet another voice at the door, and it was again thrown open. This time to reveal Lady Enright with the beleaguered-looking butler standing behind her.

"It's all right, Enders," sighed Lady Lyttworth, and he took himself off, closing the door behind him.

"It is *not* all right, Gladys! There is something you all must know!" announced Lady Enright in her most dramatic accents. *"He,"* she said, pointing at Stanhope, "compromised Miss Ashton. In a bedchamber! *Under my roof!"*

"Thank you for that intelligence, Roberta," commented Lady Lyttworth dryly. "But you, as usual, are too late."

"Hello, Roberta," said the dowager viscountess.

"Earla!" replied Lady Enright, noticing her. "Whatever are you doing here?"

"Please, do not ask."

"Actually, you may wish us happy, Lady Enright. Calista has just consented to become my wife," said Stanhope, rising and pulling his beloved with him.

"Oh, you dear children," she exclaimed, embracing Calista and regally accepting Stanhope's salute on the cheek. "I'm so happy for you that I can almost forgive you for taking all the wind out of my sails! I heard from Alice that Adolphus announced the banns, and you can be sure I hurried over as fast— where are you going?" she asked as Stanhope placed his arm firmly about Calista's waist.

"I am going," replied Stanhope, still holding on to Calista as he dropped another fond kiss onto Lady Enright's cheek, "outside. Where I plan to kiss my fiancée in peace. Preferably for a very long time. Really, far too much of this courtship has been conducted in public for my taste!"

"I really must object," said Adolphus, rising.

"I will have my man of business contact you in the morning," said Stanhope without looking back.

"Well, in that case—" Adolphus settled back against the cushions.

"Hey, Stanhope, er, my lord!" Squire Greystock called out. Stanhope paused, hand on the door.

"What about me? This business shall cost me a pretty penny what with all the staff I shall have to keep on now!"

"I so enjoyed thrashing you the first time, Greystock," Stanhope replied in a conversational tone, "that I can only assume I'd enjoy it doubly this time. And," he added pointedly, "as this time I'd be defending the name of my future wife—"

"No need for that!" the squire yelped before he could finish.

"Goodness, I love a happy ending," sniffed Lady Enright, dabbing at her eyes with a handkerchief. "Just imagine, our Calista! A countess!" she exclaimed, enjoying the way Lady Lyttworth's face paled.

"Imagine!" echoed Hermione smugly. "And poor Sofie, still unwed!"

"At least *I* can take solace in the knowledge that *Sofie* has not behaved like a wanton, Hermione," sniffed Lady Lyttworth, crossing to the floor-to-ceiling windows that looked out on the rose garden, where her daughter was being soundly kissed by Lord Peter Gresham. Her scream this time was loud enough to rouse the baron.

Thirty-eight

"Calista," Stanhope murmured huskily, lifting his head. Dissatisfied with his action, Calista twined her fingers into his thick hair and pulled his lips back to hers to continue their sweet exploration. He moaned softly as she molded her slender body against him, and the blood seemed to surge through his veins. With a sigh, he disengaged his mouth once again and put her a slight distance away from him. Unable to bear complete withdrawal, he took her hand and ran his finger gently up and down her wrist, sending delightful shivers through her body, while he caught his breath. "You keep distracting me," he complained.

She looked up at him, her mouth so inviting, and her eyes so languid, he had to fight to keep himself under control. "My apologies, Stanhope," she said with patently false meekness.

"Tristan," he murmured.

"Tristan," she replied. And Stanhope was so overcome by the way it sounded on her lips, he could not help but resume kissing her for a long while.

"I daresay it is *you* distracting *me*," Calista accused some time later. "It will be very difficult," she said as severely as she was able, "to have a conversation when we are alone together if we are so easily distracted."

"Conversation, you know, Your Ladyship, is greatly overrated," he said on a smile, and she gasped in horror.

"I cannot possibly be a countess," she gasped. "I had forgotten about that. It is part of my political principals, you know.

I do not believe in the use of titles. Even 'my lord' is difficult for me to choke out."

He grinned in return. "Calista, for all I care, you may have every servant in my employ—*our* employ—from the under-grooms to the butler address you by your first name as long as you marry me," he murmured against her throat.

"Well, I have, you know, learned quite a bit about fashion at your cousin's hands," she said pertly. "Although perhaps not enough to be a truly *grand* countess, mind you. I am extremely *au courant* on cravats, however."

He laughed delightedly. "Excellent. You can remove mine every night," he said, his voice husky. "Let us talk about the wedding though." She looked up at him, finally secure in his love, and her look made his heart turn over. "Things seem to get out of our control so very quickly that I think we should do the thing as soon as possible."

"That is fine with me," she replied.

He frowned slightly. "You do not care for a grand wedding, love, in St. George's? Because if you do—"

"No, Tristan, I do not." She looked at him in wonder that she had ever thought life without him could be enough. "Do I seem like the grand wedding type?"

"No. It is yet another one of the reasons I love you," he admitted with a smile. "Then I've another proposal. Much more to my liking." At her nod, he continued, looking at her in a way that made her flush with the awareness of him. "We are going back to my rooms at the Horse and Castle, where I shall very slowly remove every shred of clothing we have on"—he paused and ran his hands down her arms with a hungry look that almost made her knees buckle—"and begin those lessons I promised in baser appetites. By morning you will be so thoroughly com-promised that there will be no question of you marrying anyone else. Ever. And if anyone asks where we are going," he muttered darkly, "I shall tell them just that! And then—" He cupped her face and kissed her deeply.

She shivered in delighted anticipation. "And then?"

"We shall have Adolphus marry us in the morning, which, under the circumstances, I should think he'd be falling over to do, and invite the whole damned town to a bang-up wedding breakfast at the Horse and Castle. I have a special license—several, in fact, one of which has been entrusted to someone else for safekeeping. So no matter how many you tear up, there will still be one left."

For reply she laughed and kissed him. *"Thoroughly* compromised as I will be, I doubt even I would dare," she teased.

"You do not mind being compromised tonight and married tomorrow?" he asked, suddenly anxious lest he was rushing her.

"I can think of few things I'd like more," she replied, stretching up to kiss him in a way that delightfully confirmed her words.

He took a deep, shuddering breath. "Then what," he asked, against her lips, "are we waiting for, Miss Ashton?"

ABOUT THE AUTHOR

Jessica Benson lives with her family in New York. She is currently working on her next Zebra Regency romance, which will be published in February 2001. Jessica loves to hear from readers, and you may write to her c/o Zebra Books. Please include a self-addressed stamped envelope if you wish a response.

BOOK YOUR PLACE ON OUR WEBSITE AND MAKE THE READING CONNECTION!

We've created a customized website just for our very special readers, where you can get the inside scoop on everything that's going on with Zebra, Pinnacle and Kensington books.

When you come online, you'll have the exciting opportunity to:

- View covers of upcoming books
- Read sample chapters
- Learn about our future publishing schedule (listed by publication month *and author*)
- Find out when your favorite authors will be visiting a city near you
- Search for and order backlist books from our online catalog
- Check out author bios and background information
- Send e-mail to your favorite authors
- Meet the Kensington staff online
- Join us in weekly chats with authors, readers and other guests
- Get writing guidelines
- AND MUCH MORE!

**Visit our website at
http://www.zebrabooks.com**